For my mom and dad. I miss you. I feel as if my anchor and my tiller have died. I hope, despite the distance between us, I make you proud.

PROLOGUE

THURSDAY
Seth

"I'm going to wash my hands," Seth said to his father as he scooted off the diner's red vinyl seats. "Order me the biggest hamburger they've got."

To his surprise, his father didn't object, he just nodded his head and asked Seth's mom and sisters, "What looks good to you? Order anything you like."

Seth turned his back on his family as his sisters echoed his own thoughts.

"What's up with the Mr. Nice act, Dad?"

"Yeah. Where's the 'flesh' lecture?"

Though his back was to her, Seth knew his sister just finger-quoted the word *flesh* by the emphasis she'd placed on the word, and he agreed. His father was what military brats like himself called a "hardball", basically hardheaded. His failure to reprimand them with the typical admonition to only eat meat *'in time of famine'* could not go unacknowledged by the Johnson children. He'd fully expected his father to take him by the arm, barring his escape to the bathroom, and raise an eyebrow at him, forcing Seth to reveal his *real* order, the BBQ salad with onion rings instead of chicken.

But the stars had aligned, and Seth would soon bite into his first American hamburger.

Oh, there were hamburgers in the other places he'd lived, but according to those who knew, Americans did the burger best. Just like ta'miya was best in Egypt.

Unfortunately, you couldn't just walk the streets of Cairo any longer and pick up some ta'miya, unless you were anxious to get knifed. Another reason to be glad he and his family had left.

Things were still ticking along here in the good ol' US of A. It was like Americans didn't even know there was a war heading their way. The thought sobered Seth and knotted his stomach. They'd been in emergency mode for weeks, not stopping their flight for anything, and now this; a detour to Missouri, of all places!

Seth's thigh rammed into the corner of a table he failed to maneuver around, and the pain pulled his thoughts out of their spiral. His watering eyes attempted to focus, as he limped toward the food prep area and bathrooms. Rubbing at the bruised leg, he noticed a man with sculpted black hair and a suitcoat gesticulating to a line-cook. He caught Seth's eye because he looked odd back there in the hot, greasy area in his nice clothes and sunglasses. The rich man looked at Seth and lifted his sunglasses off his nose to tuck them in a pocket just as Seth found the out-of-sight hallway leading to the lavatory.

Pushing open the door labeled 'Gents', Seth gingerly stepped between bits of toilet paper littering the tile floor. Annoyed at the forced gymnastics, he was still impressed by the fluffy mess. This little restaurant in the middle of Nowhere, Missouri had loads of paper products and smelled like nondescript fruit. Pretty much the most heavenly public bathroom he'd seen since his father was stationed in London, four years ago.

Cairo loos were total holes in the ground, literally, and the Greyhound bus they'd just left behind wasn't much better. But it was the cargo ship that brought them from Egypt to America that was the worst. It was so nauseating, in fact, that Seth had barfed in those toilets as much as anything else, so he felt grateful for this one—with its freshly painted walls and automatic hand dryer.

GUARDIANS OF THE GARDEN

THERESA POCOCK

Immortal Works LLC
1505 Glenrose Drive
Salt Lake City, Utah 84104
Tel: (385) 202-0116

© 2020 Theresa Pocock
www.theresapocock.com
www.cleanlit.com

Cover Art by Ashley Literski
http://strangedevotion.wixsite.com/strangedesigns

ISBN 978-1-953491-01-5 (Paperback)
ASIN B08HMJDQ6X (Kindle Edition)

It occurred to him that gratitude for a bathroom was a bit strange, but he couldn't help it.

Smiling, Seth moved to the pristine white sink. He slid the silver dial to the side and let the cold water run over his hands and lower arms. It felt rather wonderful, all cold and soft, and he watched as the water turned brown on contact with his hands, scattering little speckles of diluted mud.

Though they'd been walking on paved roads since the bus dropped them off, the wind—or 'the scourge of Missouri' as he was beginning to think of it—constantly blew dust and dirt up in little twisters. The grime caked his every crevice. He seriously considered stripping down and shoving as much of himself into the small sink as he could, but decided against it just as the door to the bathroom creaked open.

The sound brought Seth's glance around. A tall, bald man in military pants and a tight t-shirt pushed through the wooden door and clomped through the toilet paper with his standard issue military clodhoppers, effectively gathering the mess up.

Following right behind the large bloke was the slicked-back looking gent from the kitchen in his tailored suitcoat and loafers.

After living in the dangerous demographics of Cairo for four-plus years, warning bells went off at the sight of this rich man and his bodyguard.

He would have to forgo the fancy hand dryer and opt for the quickness of a paper towel. Grabbing one, he used it as he moved around the two men. But Mr. Rich-guy greeted him.

"Hey there, you're Seth, right? Seth Jones?"

His loud voice using Seth's first name threw him off and got his heart racing. "Nope, sorry, you got the wrong kid."

"Oh, that's right. Ezekiel, that pinafich, changed your last name. What was it again?" Seth stopped his cautious progress toward the door. "Johnson. That kind of sounds like Jones doesn't it? Jones' son. Your daddy has always been too smart for his own good, but he's never been accused of being creative."

Seth moved in a more determined manner now. He had no idea what this all meant, but he knew he wanted out of it. However, the big guy blocked his way.

The young guy continued speaking, "Hey, kid, don't flip out on me. I'm Jeremiah Jones. I'm your dad's cousin, remember?"

They all paused, letting this new information sink in. Thankfully too; it stopped Seth from kneeing the bodyguard in the nuts before running for his life.

Jeremiah said disarmingly, "I contacted you like six months ago about the pocket watch. You said you'd never heard of me. You told me your dad claimed all your relatives were dead."

Seth blinked at the man, not understanding how this could be happening. This man was Jeremiah Jones? His father's cousin. Seth's cousin once removed.

Blinking, Seth recalled when he'd found the golden pocket watch in his dad's underwear drawer with the inscription *'Jones to the bitter end. Your true brother, WJ'*. He'd put the watch on the web, hoping to discover a long-lost family member, or at least a clue about whose watch it was.

With no roots, no relatives, no one to connect him to on this planet, Seth felt lost. Even in his immediate family, things were hard. Abigail and Lillian had one another, and the fact that they were twins deepened their bond. They tolerated him but they didn't need him.

His parents both had big lives, careers. His dad's job moving them around all the time exacerbated the issue of Seth finding a best friend, or any real friend for that matter. Sometimes Seth looked around himself and realized that in his seventeen years of life, he had yet to truly connect with another human.

Seth narrowed his eyes, examining his cousin skeptically. This Jeremiah guy did look like his dad; with his native American skin tones, thick dark hair and large, clear, brown eyes. He recalled his conversation with this man. He'd called about the watch. Claiming it was his cousin's and asking where Seth got it, and a conversation about his extended family commenced.

The words, *this is my cousin*, pinballed around in Seth's head. Finally, he shook that idea out in the form of, "How in the world did you find me?" He gestured to their surroundings. The once posh washroom felt awkward now.

"That is a crazy story. I'll tell you some time. But look at you. You are the spitting image of your dad." Jeremiah held out his arms as if he wanted a hug.

"Jeremiah in the flesh. I can't believe this." Seth said, tentatively moving toward the taller man who took him by the shoulders and gazed at him before clapping him in a friendly man-hug, with lots of back-slapping and awkward laughing.

When Seth pulled away, he thought of something. His father knew about the watch and Jeremiah. He wasn't sure how, but once it had blown up and was out in the open, their relationship never went back to the easy thing it was before. His father's serious betrayal resulted in constant, father focused, over-the-top hostility on Seth's part. Naturally the thought of Jeremiah—whom his father obviously would rather think of as nonexistent—being here with his highly trained, militant father in the next room was a recipe for drama and possible dismemberment.

Worried Seth asked, "You're still in one piece, so I assume you haven't seen my dad yet."

Jeremiah laughed nervously. "He's made it perfectly clear he'd rather I be feeding the fish in the great Missouri. So no, I don't want to chance it." He glanced over at his bodyguard.

Seth spared a single thought to acknowledge that the big bodyguard might be able to take down his dad, maybe.

His cousin continued, "Actually, I came here for you."

"You came all the way here just to see me? How did you even know I would be here? We left Cairo so suddenly, you know, with all the bombings and the gathering military...here in the States it's not as bad, but how could you possibly find me in all the chaos?" Seth clamped his lips shut to stop himself from rambling.

Jeremiah smiled indulgently and stated, "Simple. Money. Money can make lots of things happen. I knew you'd be an adult soon and thought maybe after you were out from under your father's thumb you might want to connect. So, I kept an eye on you. But it was all a waste because your father brought you right to my doorstep. I own this diner. I live up the road at The Compound."

The back of Seth's neck clenched in a prickly sensation. This man cared enough about Seth and the lies his father had forced on him that he used expensive resources to keep tabs on him. Now, Seth's throat clenched; he blinked excessively and shook his head to clear his watery vision.

"I can see you are a Jones in your heart. We, none of us, like to be separated from our people."

Seth nodded, still trying to contain his overwhelming emotions.

"That lie, the 'everybody's dead' lie, it did a number on ya, hey? I know kid. I know. These things are hard, and we can never understand how or why they happen. But hey, you're here now."

Seth nodded as he looked at his relative. And just like that, Seth felt, down to his toenails, a connection to...something. The world. Life. Blood. He wasn't sure. It was an odd yet welcome feeling.

"Do you think dad brought us here to meet you?" Seth asked hopefully.

"I'm certain he did not, Seth. Your father wants nothing to do with us. Though none of us knows why."

Confused by the comment he looked down at the linoleum floor. Before too many moments had passed Seth felt another emotion building in his gut and pounding his heart. Anger. Anger at his father, his mother. Anger that he'd felt alone his whole life. Needlessly alone.

He'd had nothing. No one.

Until now.

He had to swallow it down, the wave of emotions. "Is he my relative too?" Seth chin-gestured at the big guy.

"Gerald?" Jeremiah's face scrunched up. "Uh, no. He's the help. But kid, there *are* a bunch of us. Just up the road there's a small colony, if you will, of Joneses and our hired help. Been there since the 1800s."

At this, that anger sitting in his gut that he thought he'd momentarily smothered, flared. His father was a total douchebag liar. He'd kept them all a secret. For what reason? That was the biggest unanswered question of all. He opened his mouth to find out the answer, but Jeremiah moved on.

"Unfortunately, knowing your father, I don't have very much time before he comes in here to check on what's taking you so long and catches me talking to you, but I have a lot to say. First, I know why your father is here, and I know where he is taking you. And kid, it's not a place you wanna be, believe me."

Surprised, Seth sputtered. "How? What do you mean..."

Jeremiah interrupted. "Kid, you gotta listen. This place, it's backward and strange. It's going to seem like Hicksville full of rainbows and butterflies but let me tell you the people there are eccentric and dangerous. In fact, there is one person in particular that is extremely dangerous."

"Dangerous, how?" Seth had little trust for his dad of late, but he did know one thing for certain, his father was fiercely protective. How could he be taking them to a dangerous place?

Jeremiah answered him. "I can't tell you everything, I've learned from experience that seeing is believing."

"Okay?" Seth said and tilted his head to the side, wondering where this man was going.

"So, I know we just met, but you just happen to be in a unique position to help us with a huge problem. And as a member of the Jones family, I'm hoping I can count on you."

Wary again, Seth leaned back. "You want me to help you with a dangerous person?"

"Yes, but not in the way you think." Jeremiah protested noticing Seth's obvious hesitation. He took Seth by the shoulder. "We just need eyes and ears in the place. You see what I'm getting at? We would never compromise you at all. Just watch and listen. See what you can find out."

"What exactly will I be listening for? And who is this dangerous person?" Seth asked, a little thrill racing up his spine.

"This dangerous person is a mystery and the only clue we have is that the person is probably your age. So, trust no one."

"My age? Seriously?"

"Yes."

"What does this person do that's dangerous?"

"Seth, please. I need to tell you more, and we are out of time. Once you get to Edenia, all will be clear. Just look for what's out of the ordinary and tell me about it...with this." He pulled out an old, thick, flip phone from his tailored slacks.

Seth took the phone.

"Now that phone might not work inside Edenia. We've fixed it so it won't break, but it might not work except in a certain place. The town is in a sort of dead zone. Keep it secret. Don't let them take it from you or I won't be able to help you. Call me, secretly, with that before you leave the diner. I'll tell you more then."

"Edenia?"

"Yes."

"Will I need, like, other gear?" Seth asked that thrill racing up his back again.

"No." He patted Seth again. "You won't, I'm sure of it, but just in case." He tapped the phone. "We have endless monetary resources. Seriously. If you come up with a plan and need something to pull it off, I am a phone call away."

"Okay, and the dangerous person?"

"We will talk about that later. Seth, this information is important to me, to us, we need to know anything and everything unusual that you see or hear. Okay?"

"Okay."

"Now, I understand that when someone does a job, they need to be paid. Right?"

Seth cocked his head to the side, not understanding this turn of the conversation.

"We are willing to pretty much give you whatever you want for it. Cash, a car, a house, college tuition, you name it." All Seth could think of was how none of that stuff would do him any good when war was coming, but Jeremiah went on. "But I have a feeling I know what you're going to ask for." Jeremiah got this pained look in his eye, this sadness knotting his forehead. "It's something you want bad, something your parents are ignoring right now, something that has to do with someone you love very much."

Confused, Seth considered. But then Jeremiah's words brought on a flash of understanding. Suddenly Seth knew what this detour was NOT about. It was not about his sister, Lillian. He could feel anger and sadness battering at his tear ducts and breath and heart. "Are they just going to let her die? They are, aren't they?" He whispered. "They are taking us to some tiny town with no specialist, no cancer treatment center, nothing. They are giving up."

Jeremiah nodded. "I know it's hard to believe." More shoulder patting. "I know." The man paused for a moment, before going on in a quiet, intense way. "She's my cousin too. But Seth, there is hope. What if I promise that I will do everything money can buy to help you with that problem? In fact, I can guarantee, if you get me what I need, not only will she get better, but your sister will live a long life. All you have to do is this one little thing for me."

Though he didn't understand how a promise like that could be possible, he grabbed the lifeline and held it fast. Words and tears of relief and hope poured out. "Yes, um, yes of course, I'm in. I just watch and report anything out of the ordinary to you?"

He nodded. "For now. Once you get in, I will tell you more about the dangerous person." He took Seth by the shoulder, "And hey, you're acting like part of the family already. Us Joneses, we stand by one another come rain or shine, come snow or drought, to the bitter end."

CHAPTER 1

Friday
Miriam

Miriam's mother white-knuckle gripped the golden braid that hung to her waist as she chided, "Please do not use contractions, Miriam, you know how it twists my ears into knots." She then turned back toward the sitting-room window and resumed glaring at nothing and everything.

Miriam's mouth snapped closed forcefully enough it moved her whole body and almost knocked her from the little hemming stool she stood atop. Once she gained her balance, she looked down at her aunt who was hemming her skirt just as the woman shook her head in a warning.

Miriam took her aunts advice and dismissed her mother's pedantry as a matter of course. Instead, Miriam chose to admire how the woman's voice rang out, each word crisp and clear, like a clock lived inside her head, forcing words to leave her lips with the even tick of the second-hand.

Gripping the unfinished skirt encircling her waist, she looked at the back of her mother's head. Miriam didn't understand what upset her so much. The woman acted like a caged animal, and it frightened Miriam.

Frustrated, she gripped her own straw-colored braid.

Her Aunt Sarah erupted into the tense silence. "Luanne, stop glaring out the window. You'll start a fire." When her mother's head didn't move, Aunt Sarah took it further. "Why the Master, in all his wisdom, blessed your Nature to be fire, I'll never understand. But if you burn down Jai's mama's house, I won't stop him from drowning you like a cat."

That did it. Not only was Aunt Sarah bossing her mother around, but she was using contractions, and threatening violence. *Heaven forbid.* Her mother turned narrowed, amber eyes toward her aunt. "There is much to fear Sarah. If you took something other than your needle and thread seriously, you would see the outside is coming here today! This one thing could wreck us all." Her mother's face was a white, quiet kind of angry, and there was enough venom in her words to spark a war. Aunt Sarah's head jerked to the side slightly as if she'd been slapped.

Then amber eyes met amber eyes.

Miriam had been singed a time or two by her fire-wielding, amber-eyed mother, but had never seen the matching ferocity in her aunt's eyes before. These sisters had obviously gotten into plenty of fire-laced disagreements.

Miriam's skin flushed as the air in the room warmed. She hated this.

With desperation pumping her heart, *her* Nature rose inside her. As if it could challenge these women. The sensation confused Miriam.

Unlike anyone else in Edenia, her Nature was a multifaceted gem, one she hadn't completely explored. Perhaps she did have something that could help. As soon as the idea formed, she knew the answer. She submitted to the power, the Nature inside her, and immediately cool tendrils of something—peace perhaps—wrapped around her, and she knew what she needed to do.

Her hands twitched.

Slowly she shifted her weight so that her leg bumped her aunts' needle hand. The small movement had dangerous consequences. Sarah's lethal amber eyes flashed up at her. The orbs looked like sloshing pots of molten gold, churning and boiling, about to turn lava red.

However, when the amber eyes met violet, Miriam guided the cool tendrils of power toward her aunt. They hovered and swirled around Sarah, seeking entrance. Her aunt allowed the peace and when she did, Miriam felt the power leave her fully.

Keeping her aunt's gaze, Miriam watched the older woman's irises settle and still.

Three heartbeats later her aunt's crystalline voice chimed mildly as she looked away from Miriam and down to her hands, "Very good, my dear. I didn't know you could do that. What an excellent trick." She glanced up.

Miriam smiled down at her aunt and felt her heart warm. It was always there, this confidence and trust.

Her mother was an entirely different subject, though. She was ready for a fight. When the woman turned her fiery gaze on Miriam, her eyes narrowed further. Her mother was barely able to keep the heat behind those amber orbs in check. As subtly as possible, Miriam reached out her Nature and touched her mother with the calming tendrils but there was no acceptance there. Her mother's face just went pale.

With bloodless lips she hissed, "Stop it. Stop it, Miriam. If I choose to be angry, it is wrong to take that away. You cannot take my freedom. You cannot."

Her mother's attitude and disgust hurt Miriam's heart. Yet another reason to loathe her particular Nature. It not only felt like exclusion, out there in public, but it also felt like rejection; a mother's rejection of a daughter.

"Oh, hush that crazy talk, Lu." Her aunt came to her rescue. "Don't be upset, Miriam does very well. She merely touched me with her Nature, she didn't force me to take it. You should be proud. And we are extremely blessed that the Master chose to give this particular Nature to a person who is guided by an unquenchable desire to obey." The needle in her aunt's hand moved again, and she pursed her lips and then flashed a wink up to Miriam. "Pity though, I see some consequences. Soon none of us will be able to have a decent fight without you interfering."

Miriam wanted to smile back and revel in this new facet to her Nature, a facet that had nothing to do with taking memories or compelling. Unfortunately, a part of her perfectly understood her mother's issue, and it soured everything. If things continued down their current road, controlling anyone's moods, actions, thoughts or Nature would be as easy for Miriam as it was for her mother to burn down a house.

Unlike her mother's Nature, which was practically as old as Natures themselves, Miriam's Nature was new and came with a whole slew of moral implications and quandaries. Most of which, Miriam was just at the beginning of figuring out.

Besides these little *helpful* comments from her mother, she was unhappily on her own to navigate that ship.

Mother opened her mouth, but Aunt Sarah wisely ran right over her, too. "Why are you so angry anyhow, Luanne?" Her aunt's hands stopped pinning the hem of the exquisite teal gossamer Miriam wore. Then she turned her own, equally perceptive, amber eyes toward Miriam's mother. Those eyes searched the window, and then the road beyond the yard. Finally, a knowing smile tightened her cherry lips. "This is about you-know-who, isn't it?"

Her mother's stiff-straight shoulders flinched, and one side curled in on her. She used it as an excuse to turn her body back toward the window and touched the glass as she gazed.

"For all that's good and holy, Luanne! He made his choice. You can't change that, no one can."

"Except he has. Think, Sarah. If your mind was not so muddled with daydreams and sewing patterns and contractions, you would be able to see that I do not care about his leaving, it is his coming back that scares me." She flung a hand toward the window and the Edenia road.

As the two sisters regarded one another knowingly, the past and the present of their relationship filled the small living room of her aunt's home. It was like, all of a sudden, Miriam wasn't there, which was hard because Miriam wanted to ask a million questions about a man who left Edenia—a thing she thought had never happened before—and was now coming back.

Her Aunt turned fully toward her mother, and in a soft voice said, "We knew a summons would come. It is the way of things." She paused, pressing the meaning of her statement into the silence. "Though it still surprises me that there are people willing to listen to the summons." Her hand unthinkingly brushed the hem of the teal material encircling Miriam's waist, her face stilling with the thought. "With all Garren told us, I just feel the world is going to hell in a handbasket. I know you hate that saying, but for once it is accurate, and I know you at least appreciate accuracy."

Her mother acknowledged the comment with a huff and a shoulder shrug.

"So..." she began, and her eyebrows rose in discovery, "so, we are calling our own home." Taking a deep, satisfying breath, she rubbed at her neck, "He is our own, Luanne, and if this world is coming to an end wouldn't you rather have Zeke here than out there?"

A shiver ran up Miriam's back. This was another topic Miriam wished she was privy to. What would an ending look like here in Edenia?

Silence reigned for several minutes as they all thought about Sarah's words.

Miriam noticed her aunt's face lift in discovery, as if something obvious occurred to her. The woman began to speak, but stopped and thought before beginning again just to stop once more. Finally, she raised her eyebrows at Miriam's mother and spat it out. "Surely *you've* put the past completely behind you?"

Miriam's mother rolled her eyes in response to this.

Her aunt paused yet again in her pinning and sewing. "So, if that history is all settled in the past, and if the Master and the council are willing to give him another chance," Aunt Sarah paused then went on, "don't you think you can too?" She used the same mild voice, the same concern-crinkled set to her eyes that she did when comforting Miriam. And in that moment Miriam's heart burst with love for the woman.

But Miriam knew her mother wouldn't listen or answer. It wasn't her way. Luanne Miller didn't explain her feelings until she was mad enough to yell them. They both saw the red in her mother's cheeks spread to her neck and knew there could be another fight on their hands. They held their breath, but the firestorm did not come.

Aunt Sarah turned back to Miriam to share a look full of understanding.

Miriam recalled two years ago when that understanding look was on *her* behalf. Miriam had just been taken by her Nature—a new, different Nature, a Nature invasive at its core—and she, in a town full of Guardians, instantly became a pariah.

Miriam had a brief flashback of Josie—her best friend at the time—lying on the floor, her black, kinky curls splayed over a face staring up, unblinking.

She trembled in earnest as she thought back.

Josie's family was different. Not as stringent as her own. They talked of personal things, uncomfortable things. So, when Josie began to tell her mother the story of how, days earlier, Miriam had started her monthly womanhood at school and needed to borrow some vitals from Josie, Miriam had completely flipped out.

She wished with all her heart that she'd never told Josie, had never gone to her friend for help.

In that moment, Miriam's Nature took her for the first time and her wish for erasing the whole incident came true. Literally.

It was a spiritual ripping of soul, gruesome and painful. A moment where Miriam saw, with perfect clarity and understanding, Josie, as she was on the inside. Miriam saw Josie's love for her mother and for Miriam. Her relief at not being the only girl with a monthly. Her confidence in her mother's acceptance and understanding of the girl's trials that day. Miriam saw it all.

Her Nature pulled the day out in backward order, sucking the memories and feelings and precious experience from Josie, minute by minute, hour by hour.

The scariest part was that Miriam didn't know how to stop the pulling.

By some miracle Miriam's Nature left her as quickly as it took her. With an intake of breath, all that used to be her beloved friend's recent memory moved into Miriam. Cut from her friend as surely as one cuts a blossom from a stem.

Josie hit the kitchen floor, almost as if Miriam had struck her. It was a relief when Miriam herself followed her friend into unconsciousness.

When Josie woke, she didn't know what had happened, but she was scared and trembling. The whole thing was exacerbated by Miriam waking up soon after, her eyes—blue from birth—now violet. No one had violet eyes. And Josie had lost her memory of the past day. It was gone, erased.

At least that was what everyone thought.

Miriam arose that day changed in more ways than just her eye color—everyone had *that* change when their Nature took them—she woke to find a bit of her best friend *inside* her.

She'd never told Josie that the memories were inside her, she'd never admitted that the memories had not floated off into the ether. That they were not wisps of air. She kept it to herself that memories were physical things and they could be taken. By her.

Even now, Miriam felt them swirling and floating inside her in a place she had no name for.

Sometimes Miriam felt like Josie knew. Like the way you can stumble across a letter and before even reading it, you recognize the handwriting. Or like when someone relives a memory out loud, and even though it is from their perspective you recognize it, because you were there too.

Miriam thought of that piece of Josie now and it rose inside her, flitting through the dozens of other pieces of soul she'd stolen over the last two years via her *Nature*. Josie's memory was different from all the rest. When she took it, it was full and clear. It was like watching, hearing, tasting and smelling a memory. The words known, the emotions understandable, the scenes and people real.

It made it hurt all the more. She pushed it down. Thankfully she couldn't experience it again now that it was inside her. She also pushed down the bile. And the shame.

Afterward, Miriam was seen as dangerous and was ostracized. Which now, two years later, Miriam saw as the hypocrisy it was. In a town of fire Natures that could burn you to a crisp in a moment, or earth Natures that could use the earth to swallow you up or any number of other potential horrors, it was Miriam that was a threat to everyone.

A freak among freaks. Tears gathered at the corners of her eyes. To stop them from submitting to gravity, she sniffed and turned her attention to her surroundings.

"I cannot protect everyone." Her mother was saying to Sarah. They had continued their conversation about the Zeke-man while Miriam was lost in her own thoughts. "Hirum has promised me he will make it clear that Ezekiel must keep his radical ideas to himself."

Ezekiel...

Miriam let the name roll around in her head. He was coming back? Which meant he'd left Edenia. No one left Edenia. Not permanently. Everyone went on sabbatical, in order to get a trade and to experience the world, but everyone came back.

Except this man. Miriam's heart leapt at the thought.

"I will at least protect Miriam, who already lusts for the outside with more fervor than is healthy or proper." Luanne stated uncaringly.

All the fuss surrounding this extravagant dress was just a bandage for Miriam, who was not going on sabbatical but getting married off. At sixteen. Miriam—because of her Nature—would not finish school, nor get a trade, and worst of all, she would not go on sabbatical.

"Speaking of which, have you narrowed the list of potential suitors for our beauty here? Last we spoke you were at five."

Miriam's hands trembled.

"Yes, we have." Her mother answered almost cheerfully. "We actually had Miriam help us get it down to three. Todd, Foster, Wazeen." Her mother answered and looked proud, as Miriam panicked on the inside.

Lately, the subject of boys had left the realm of gross and entered a complicated place in her brain. This place warranted further exploration, which made the upcoming betrothal inconvenient.

"Nice group. I vote for Todd. He is stalwart and smart and handsome. Miriam has always had feelings for him."

According to her parents, Miriam needed a babysitter. Someone to help her, to be her only friend—because she had no real friends now. What better way to gain a friend than to marry one? A stalwart young man would keep Miriam from making mistakes with her Nature. It would help normalize her. She knew her parents did this out of love, but she still hated it. Her gut clenched, and so did her teeth. Blood pumped through her veins in a million microscopic whirlpools.

Through the red haze of anger, Miriam looked down at her aunt who instantly recognized the expression for what it was. Panic. Toxic meltdown.

"Would you like me to tell you a story about the outside?" Sarah offered. Miriam welcomed the distraction.

"Sarah, you know it is best if we are silent on the subject of outside." Miriam's mother said with a pointedly antagonizing look in Miriam's direction, once again taking a choice from Miriam.

Her heart roared at her mother and her inflexibility. Right then, in that moment, as Aunt Sarah worked her needle, Miriam felt as if she could burst out in tears, and she looked at her mother's back with something other than love in her heart.

Sabbaticals were the absolute rite of passage in Edenia for several reasons, but most importantly; it was a time to choose, to figure out for certain if the life in Edenia was the life for you. Of course, the pressure to come back was intense, as evidenced by the fact that, though they were taught from infancy they could choose to be a Guardian or not, ALL chose to be one.

Those were the stats, one hundred percent.

The hope of that choice had become an obsession for Miriam.

However, a month ago her parents informed her that she, Miriam, would not get that choice. She was forced to accept life here. To be an Edenian. To be a Guardian.

She was forced to live with little pieces of other people's soul inside her. She was forced to use her Nature on their enemies and collect more soul slivers. She felt like a wraith as it was. Thin and claustrophobic in her own skin. And she could only imagine how that feeling would get bigger and heavier as she was forced to use her Nature for the good of Edenia.

Tangled up in the lack of choice was anger at how she would be robbed of any outside experiences.

Aunt Sarah was convinced that Miriam was born with an adventurous spirit and that it expressed itself as a wild hunger and thirst for things that were more complex than the simple life of Edenia. Her imagination dreamed of creating, forging new and beautiful things. Of feeling the ocean wind and seeing the whole history of life on planet Earth through remnants and ruins. Books were not good enough. Her hands ached to touch the places she'd read about. Her eyes longed to feast on the colors and majesty and variety of life.

She wanted to see it all, then choose for herself to either stay in the world or to leave the world and come back to Edenia, to Guardianship, to family. That was the deal. Everyone got to choose.

Except her.

Force. The word had a different meaning to her now than it had when she was a child and her mother had forced her to learn how to iron. It sure felt a lot more like prison bars.

She wiped her face knowing there would be tears there.

She didn't understand all that was happening here, but one thing was certain; the stats she'd been taught as a child were not completely accurate. One hundred percent of Edenians did not come back jumping for joy to take on the yoke of Guardianship. One person, a person her mother was watching out the window for at this very moment, a man named Ezekiel, had chosen the outside world over coming home to Edenia. With that one bit of information Miriam felt palpable relief. She wasn't alone. All her wishing to escape and never return was justified in one man. Then again maybe there were others. Edenians knew how to keep secrets, perhaps several Guardians had done the same.

She glanced at her mother's roving eyes and came full circle in her mind; it looked as if Edenia got them all in the end. Ezekiel had been summoned, and for reasons unknown, he had decided to obey.

CHAPTER 2

Peter

Sweat, barn-dust, and dirt clung to Peter's skin, proving he'd done his chores in a hurry. Under his homespun tunic, the coating mixed and dripped unpleasantly down his spine, making him simultaneously long for a breeze and empty hands. At present, the steaming pile of dung he cradled in his gloved hands stood between him and a good itch.

As Peter struggled to rub his back against an obliging tree, he considered this prank. Garren, his target, sat thirty feet away, in the middle of a half-harvested straw field, forking in pasta salad. The fluidity which his brother's water Nature granted him certainly would help with evading the poo, but Peter had the element of surprise which, he determined, trumped speed. At least in this circumstance.

Besides, even if Garren's water Nature took him fast enough to move out of the way, the poo would still have a chance of landing in the pasta.

Poo-pasta. Peter smiled at the alliteration. With effort he swallowed down his nervous jitters and silently sloughed off his mucking boots.

Looking down at his bare feet, his grin faded. He hoped his Nature would work today. Leaning out, he moved his russet-colored eyes north, and south, searching for witnesses. Orchards and barn looked empty for a rare moment.

Stepping from behind the tree and into the grass, and keeping his gloved hands as far away as possible from his nose, Peter called upon the part of him that remained dormant until it was needed. His Nature.

He was in luck. It worked—well, worked in the way Peter had gotten used to. Instantly, toes and soles were cloaked, gone, invisible as only earth Nature could do. Wistfully Peter considered the day his Nature would take his whole body. With that thought he took a silent step forward, his feet so pliant they didn't rustle a blade of grass.

These feet were the instruments of Garren's demise, no, his poomise, Peter thought with yet another grin.

Moving forward, Peter kept his target in view. Taking care to not make noise with the rest of his *noncompliant* body, he attempted to ignore the beauty of an Edenia harvest. Yet the smell of the almost autumn air was a bit too amazing for Peter to shut out. Thankfully he was downwind from the poop.

As Peter stepped from the cool green grass to the yellow spikes of previously harvested straw sticking out of the clotted ground—his feet merging to the new surface perfectly—he exhaled as silently as he could.

When he reached five feet from the target of his brother's back, Peter held his breath, his hands tingling. Three more steps, two, one— he reached out for Garren's collar and tipped his hands down.

Before the first clump tumbled, Garren swerved and in a blurring flash, streaked through the air and coalesced ten feet to the left of his picnic blanket. Dirt and clumps of straw were flung in the air by his escape, but Garren was already done moving before Peter noticed that.

He did notice his twenty-one-year-old brother was poo-free and crouched as if ready for attack.

The sound of the last few nuggets leaving Peter's gloves and hitting the ground brought their eyes down to the picnic blanket. The dung had fallen in fragrant little plops right into Garren's now rather scattered lunch.

"Poo-pasta," Peter said, and smiled a bit.

Then he looked over at his brother. He also was frozen in place, gaping at the brown lumps. Their eyes found one another's; Peter's russet, wide with chagrin and Garren's gray, rolling like the deepest, deadliest part of a wild river.

Peter's tenor came out of the corner of his mouth. "Well, that didn't go as planned."

Garren raised a challenging eyebrow before saying, "You'd better scream for Mama, you little turd."

That was all the warning Peter needed. Turning, he ran for all he was worth, though he knew with Garren's Nature upon him he would be lucky to get five feet. Still he yelled, "I'm gonna tell her you said..." before he could finish his threat he was face down, teeth full of dirt.

Garren was on him, but not painfully. He whispered singsong-like in Peter's ear. "How about you finish off my lunch, Petey? I'm suddenly full."

It was then that Peter considered the possible foolishness of taking on Garren. His eldest brother had an impressive set of skills. He could see that now. But he knew it was time to up his game, get a little meaner with his pranks. Since he couldn't use his Nature to protect Eden yet, he could at least come up with some really unpleasant Plan B's, and if he could sneak up on Garren, he could sneak up on a Jones.

Thankfully, it was soft blades of grass and not sharp straw spikes that made their way up his nose and into his mouth as he attempted to speak. "I give."

Garren put a bit more pressure on his neck, shoving his face that much farther down. "What was that?"

"I give, I give!" Peter muttered as loud as he could, his tongue tasting earth.

"That's right, you disgusting little mongrel." The pressure eased off Peter as his brother finished, "I should stuff that dung down your foul little gullet."

Peter coughed and spat, then spat again. When his mouth was

clear, he slowly stood, pulled off his soiled gloves and chucked them. Then he checked the part of him that hurt the worst, his knee.

Yep, it was bloody. Peter brushed himself off, and after a moment glanced carelessly up at Garren.

The man had a weird smiling grimace on his face.

"What?" Peter demanded and walked over to retrieve his boots. But his brother stayed silent, so Peter did what he did best; add insult to injury.

"You need to retake *Lingo and Slurs from the Twentieth Century,* Garren; 'foul little gullet'...are you a pirate? That's how you draw attention to yourself."

Garren's response was instant and a bit more venomous than necessary.

"It doesn't matter now, does it? My sabbatical is over. I'm stuck here from now until eternity. Besides, no one in Edenia notices how I speak."

"Except Mama."

"Huh?"

"No one but Mama cares what you say or how you say it, and I am so telling her about the turd thing."

Garren's face tightened with anger and he glared at Peter.

Garren had changed while in the outside. Peter had eavesdropped on conversations. He knew that it was scary out there. That things were happening. That the world was changing and becoming distinctly dangerous. He could see how the time had hardened his brother, and it was understandable but disheartening as well.

And this—thing—was happening more and more. Those few who were out, and those returning seemed scared. They came home damaged. No wonder Pa didn't want Gabe or Eve or Miriam to go on sabbatical. Peter agreed, he didn't want his siblings to see what Garren obviously had seen.

Still, it annoyed him a little how they were coming home all angry, like Edenia was a death sentence or something. Being a

Guardian was the best, most important job in all the world. He couldn't wait until he was fully a Guardian.

After a second, Garren huffed out a great burst of air, catching Peter's attention once more, and his anger had disintegrated. He hung his head and shook it. Feeling awkward, Peter went after his manure-smeared gloves. "Oh man, that was a fresh one," he commented, and beat the gloves together in hopes of dislodging the lingering bits. "Old Bull must have gotten into the berries."

When he looked back up, his brother smirked at him. All of a sudden, he was chuckling, looking more like himself than Peter had seen in weeks.

"You are a pesky little flea, you know that. But I'll be danged if you didn't almost get me that time."

The grin that erupted from Peter's mouth could have made a goat happy. "Really?"

"Oh, yeah." Garren pulled the collar of his shirt tight around the back of his neck and peeked nervously behind him. "Oooh," he shivered, "I'm gonna be watching my back for a month." His gray eyes squinted, "So gross, Pete. How do you come up with this stuff?"

"It's a gift." Peter replied without hesitation.

"I wouldn't call being paddled every day of your life, a gift. And speaking of tattling, Pa will give it to you good if I tell him about this."

"Yeah, he hates it when we waste food." Peter added with a sniff.

"Or use our Nature for stupid things." He took a step toward Peter, "You did use it, right? 'Cause I didn't hear a thing."

Peter nodded.

"And? Did it go any further up your leg than last time?"

"Nope, no change. And no overwhelming feeling of being taken either. Just the normal, slow dribble of power," Peter commented, disgusted, and looked at the ground.

Garren touched him on the shoulder.

"I don't know why it's not taking you like it should, but I do trust that there is a reason for it." Then his brother graciously changed the subject by laughing again. "Pa would be so mad." He paused and

Peter looked up at him. "Although, he might just hoot instead. I think you've worn them both down."

Peter went along with the subject change and rubbed his bottom where bruises from yesterday's paddling ached. "I don't know. This week he seems to have a new vigor about it. I think it's stress relief for him."

Again, his older brother snickered. "What is the council going to make of you, come sabbatical time?" Garren raked his hand through his sandy hair, messing it all up, his face back to sober consideration.

"Pa's not overly concerned that I'll live that long."

The comment pulled his brother back. "There is that."

Leaning down, Peter plucked the last blade of grass from his clothes, then his ears caught the sound of an unfamiliar, far away rumbling. Garren noticed it too. They both looked up. "Is it a Jones?" Peter asked. But Garren didn't respond, he only searched the sky behind Peter.

Then a glint of something shiny caught Peter's eye. Stepping to the side, he stared up at a man, in head-to-toe camo, hanging in mid-air from a sky-blue parachute. He glided silently downward toward the actual garden. Eden.

He was way too close. Peter's eyes flitted back and forth between the man and the short twenty feet that would land him directly within the thirty or so large trees that was the only part of Eden still on this physical plane. Peter felt the blood drain from his face.

A powerful gust of wind hit Peter's side and raced through the sky to tangle with the stranger's equipment. Throwing his body upside-down in a sort of crazy aerial cartwheel movement. It soundly snarled his legs, arms, and cords in a mess, but it also threw him fifty feet through the air. Looking around, Peter saw Sergio, a short man with very spiky hair—a wind Nature—standing a hundred yards off with a shovel in his hand. He must have heard the engine too and ran from the vegetable gardens. Thank goodness, or that Jones would have certainly landed inside the circle of ancient trees.

The stranger careened and struggled, but was now thankfully far to the left of Eden. However, he was also in mortal danger. And, Jones or no, the whole mission of the Guardians was to keep idiots like this Jones from getting killed by the power that surrounded the Garden and its Cherubim. Though, of course, they would never appreciate that.

Garren turned, and after a shocked second of taking in the scene, his gray eyes swam with the full ferocity of his water Nature. "Peter, run! Get Gale and Jai."

Then Garren moved, and it was like time stood still. He was just that fast; he was like a rushing river. The image of his brother blurred and in the space of a heartbeat Garren was two hundred paces away following underneath the crashing stranger who was coming down fast. Sergio whipped up the wind again and Peter watched as it pushed the stranger right into Garren's waiting grasp. The wind also fought against gravity to soften his landing. Peter could tell by the way the parachute fluttered. Garren quickly gathered the intruder's chute in one hand. He yanked it so hard that the scrabbling stranger knew running away was out of the question.

That reminded Peter that *his* feet should be moving. He decided he needed to gather up Miriam as well, for this stranger had seen too much.

CHAPTER 3

Miriam

Miriam watched her mother, Luanne Miller, retreat from the window with a hand at her neck and scarlet in her cheeks, a move uncharacteristic of the bold, strong-willed woman.

Miriam's thoughts were pulled out of their depressed state and into the present by the state of her mother.

Sarah stood up so quickly she knocked her little sewing stool over, "What is it? Joneses?" her aunt asked.

They both moved toward her mama as she spoke. "Master save us. He's here."

Stunned to stillness by this declaration, her aunt beat her to the window, squinted out toward the road and smirked, "That's Ezekiel alright. I would recognize that shiny black mane of hair anywhere."

Miriam found herself also at the pane of glass. Out on the street, kicking up dust, walked two men, a woman and two adolescent girls. All five wore their jet-black hair long. Their vibrant colored shirts, jeans and large backpacks stood out like a rainbow over a field of fresh-turned soil.

As Miriam took in the five travelers walking slowly toward her home, an uneasiness swirled in her stomach.

Aunt Sarah laughed happily and started toward the door but Miriam's mother grabbed her aunt's arm, "Do not even think it, Sarah."

Miriam's aunt's curly blonde bun bounced as she shook the grip off. "I have nothing against Zeke, Luanne. I will go out and greet him if it pleases me to do so." Her inflection had changed to haughty, along with her expression.

"Of course, you will," her mother said persuasively now. "However, Hirum has asked us to keep this quiet. I told you and Miriam of this in confidence. Truthfully, I could not help it. It has hampered my peace for weeks; but word must not spread. If you go to meet him, all will remember that you know him and questions will be asked." To her credit, Aunt Sarah thought for only a moment, then she nodded and stepped back to the window. "Thank you, Sarah. Hirum only wants to assess their disposition regarding the summons before any permanent arrangements are made."

"And it makes no sense to stir the kettle if they end up leaving again. There will be enough questions as it is," Sarah added, looking at Miriam with regret.

"Correct."

Strangers *did* come into Edenia. Some stumbled in unawares, but most had been summoned. Those who were summoned came as families, packs on their backs and confused determination in their eyes. Within a few days they were changed into Guardians, making them a part of Edenia. After that they would no sooner choose to leave than choose to stop breathing.

But this man had chosen it. Only a miracle of epic proportions could bring him back.

Miriam wondered what that miracle could be.

The family slowly drew closer. Miriam examined them as her stomach lurched in that odd way again. Her eyes found the face of the young man in the group. Tall and lanky, his black hair framed the light brown skin of his boyish face as his dark eyes flitted all around. Those eyes never glanced at her but she could see their almost panicked tightness.

Miriam got the impression that he was not at all happy to be here, he was frightened and angry and...determined.

Tearing her eyes from the handsome boy, she looked to the two girls at his side. They both looked to be around Peter's age, perhaps a bit older. One of them looked sad and was clinging to the other's arm. That one looked irate; more so than the boy. Brown skin flushed, shoulders tight, her hand protectively cradling her sister's hand. The girl looked up at her father, at Ezekiel, and her jaw clenched.

Miriam's eyes moved to Ezekiel. He was handsome. Tall and broad and manly, he had a cleft in his chin and a shadow where the day's growth of facial hair had darkened his already-brown skin. His straight hair hung to his shoulders. It, along with his eyes, glistened like a dark pond of still water. Ezekiel looked directly into the window and met Miriam's gaze. In spite of the stoniness of the man's face, and the set of his teeth, Miriam saw the weight of his sorrow and regret in his tight jaw and shoulders.

At some point, her mother and aunt had stepped back from the window, and as Miriam took her eyes off Ezekiel to look at his wife, Aunt Sarah said, "I guess we should finish the pinning. Jai will be around any minute looking for his lunch."

She glanced over at her aunt and nodded, but she stepped back from the window slowly, wanting to get a feel for the last member of the group. Ezekiel's wife was lovely. Bronzed skin and almond eyes, her long hair was a tangle of curls. She looked tense too, her hands gripped her backpack straps, and her eyes darted uncertainly.

This was a family full of beautiful people. Unhappy people, but beautiful, nonetheless. Miriam felt awed by their direct emotional transparency. With the way Edenia was managed and the secrets it had to keep, being emotionally forward was a luxury only experienced within the walls of each home.

Miriam turned and stepped onto the stool as her aunt instructed, but her stomach did not settle.

Silence reigned as her aunt's hands caressed the soft material and wove pins through it. Miriam looked down at her betrothal dress and her mind wished she could call upon her Nature to calm her own issues.

In what felt like the next moment, her aunt tapped her leg. "All done. Hop down and strip off the dress."

Miriam obeyed and stepped into her own camel-brown skirt. The last button of her pine green blouse was barely shoved through its hole when Uncle Jai opened the door.

His hat went on a hook and his hand pushed back his midnight hair. His merry, gray eyes acknowledged Miriam and her mother before he stepped toward his wife. "Where be my lunch, woman?" He forced his voice deep and caveman-like as he placed his hands dominatingly on Aunt Sarah's shoulders. But he was from Sri Lanka, giving his English an Indian accent, so the statement just sounded ridiculous, which, of course, was his purpose.

Miriam grinned at him but couldn't shake the tingle of fear that still lodged in her stomach.

Brushing his hands away like she would a buzzing bee, Sarah stood and kissed her husband's walnut cheek. "You have two hands, do you not?" She said this in perfect French and raised a playful eyebrow at him.

He looked down at his hands, shrugged and smiled. "Oh yes, I suppose I do."

Jai, his gray eyes twinkling, stepped to Miriam and gave her a one-armed hug. "Hey, sweet one, how goes the fitting?" Miriam's name meant bitter, so Jai always called her sweet.

Jai's happiness rubbed off on Miriam. She smiled genuinely. "It is the most beautiful material. I am grateful for that."

"I know, I helped your mother choose the color. It needed to be just right for your pale skin and hair." He touched her brow with love and compassion, for he knew all about Miriam's struggles with a forced marriage. He'd escaped one himself.

He added in the most ridiculous, over-the-top dramatics, "Besides, I cannot help myself, I simply love teal." He took her hand and twirled her in a circle. "You will be as beautiful as a Siroi when you marry the lump of a boy, may he strive to deserve you."

"Leave the poor girl alone," Her mother chided quietly.

"And I will take all the credit, for it was my idea to get teal." He bounced his eyebrows up and down and smiled spinning her again.

"Jai..." her mother lifted her own eyebrow at him.

Jai raised his hands in surrender, letting Miriam spin out. He headed toward the kitchen, but not before he gave Miriam a wink.

Aunt Sarah called, "I have apples, bread, and cheese cut."

"Thank you, dearest."

Her brother Peter whipped through the door. "Uncle Jai, is Uncle Jai home?" he yelled at their aunt. Jai moved into sight, bread to his mouth, and when her little brother saw him, he waved his hands frantically and shuffled back onto the porch. "Uncle Jai, Joneses, in the North field. Garren needs you. Gale's on the way too. Miriam?" he added.

Miriam watched as Jai's Nature took him in half a moment. Jai's irises spun, sloshed like a stormy, rain-filled pool and as fast as a leaf is swept away on the surface of a river, he was gone. A moment later, almost as if in suspended animation, the slice of bread, he'd been eating hit the floor.

Both mother and Aunt Sarah moved to the door. "How did they get in today?" Mother asked Peter as all four of them left the house behind.

"Parachute," Peter answered simply. "It was a close one too. If Sergio hadn't been there..."

Aunt Sarah pressed, "Peter are you sure?"

"I heard the plane in the distance. They must have been high enough, or maybe the man had a flying squirrel suit like the last one."

Miriam's mother exclaimed, "Is there no end to their ingenuity? You would think they would have worn themselves out by now."

"Really, you think they would learn." Peter declared.

But their mother squashed his smugness quickly. "*You* never learn. How can you expect differently from others?"

Peter kicked at the ground and muttered, "It will not matter what he saw, we have our secret weapon." He glared daggers at Miriam and Miriam knew what he meant by that glare.

Poor Peter and his defective Nature. Slowing, she sidled up to him. She wanted to comfort him, but didn't know how, so she walked next to him, pulling her Nature around her and mentally touching her brother with it. Perhaps the calm would help. Since it was a new trick, he would never know she did it.

A breeze licked her face, and she turned into it. Cold and sharp and fragrant. She closed her eyes for a moment and let the waves of air fling her hair all about and chill the tip of her nose. When she opened her eyes, she saw the direction the wind came from.

Her senses traveled past the river Eden and into the perfect circle of trees it encompassed and continued onward and inward to the only part of the Garden of Eden in this terrestrial plane. The breeze came from that small forest, rustling the leaves of the ancient trees of Adam as they stood reaching toward the sun, and moved over the shining river as it skipped and danced over its many rocks until it kissed her face.

Her feet moved as she pondered those primordial trees. How Father Adam and Mother Eve surely had touched many of them. What would they think of her and her desire for escape? Would they pity her or think she was scary, too?

It didn't take her family long to get to the north field, so she put her wandering thoughts away. Breathing deeply, she prepared herself for what she knew she would have to do.

One gesture from their mother told Peter and Miriam to stop at the grass line on the edge of the straw field. The women continued toward Garren, Gale, Jai, Sergio, Uncle Brian and the Jones man. But there were four other people. Three men and one woman. They were obviously outsiders; their clothes had that all-sizes-fit-no-one look to them. But they were bedraggled, unkempt, skinny.

"I thought you said it was one man?" Miriam asked looking questioningly at Peter. She could only take one person's memory at a time.

"When I left there was only one," he exclaimed excitedly and pointed at the Jones, who like his counterparts, was a warrior-like man. Still, he had on excessively strange clothes for a Jones; lots of straps, clips, pockets and buckles.

"What is happening here?" Miriam asked, looking at her mother.

All of a sudden, the woman in the depressed lot cried out, her voice loud enough for Miriam to hear. "We are just hungry. Please give us some food. You have so much." She gestured to the orchards, fields, and the large vegetable garden. "I have children."

The big uniformed man leaned away from the others with a look of contempt on his face.

"How do you know he is a Jones, Peter? Couldn't he be some random person?"

"I just assumed." His jaw jutted out, defensively.

"Well you know where assuming gets you." Miriam touched her brother's arm, "Did Garren show them his Nature?"

Peter's warm russet eyes met hers. He nodded. "I know at least the big one saw it."

Miriam took a deep breath. "He knows the rules and still he chose to show off. Keeping our exact Natures from the Joneses is one of the most important secrets we can keep." She lectured knowing full well Peter knew this fact as well as he knew his own face.

"It wasn't like that, Miriam." Peter pulled away from her and took a step to the side. His eyes, again, glaring daggers.

"I don't care what it was like. Now I will have to clean up his mess, and I hate doing that. I hate it." Her voice was cold.

"Miriam," her mother called, pointing at the large man. "We need you to take care of this one dear." She took a step forward, her heart pounding the breath out of her. Her mother added, "Peter, would you get a buggy and team ready?"

"Yes, mother. Bring it here?"

Mama nodded, "Thank you love." She turned to her brother. "Brian, will you go with Peter?"

Uncle Brian nodded.

When Miriam approached, she knew right away this man was a Jones, strangers didn't react like he was acting. Strangers didn't trust what they saw, and they just acted confused. This man knew. Sweat rolled down his face, he looked scared. "They've been talking. Saying weird things. No one can remember. They don't remember." The man had red hair and a large space between his two front teeth, and he spat through it as he spoke. "Is that what they want you to do to me?"

Miriam flinched at his words. The idea that Joneses could be talking about her sent a chill down her arms.

He pulled against the lines of his parachute which were snuggly held by Garren. It almost pulled her brother off his feet, but in an instant Jai and Gale were there to help. When he knew he wouldn't get free, he yanked at buckles and pockets looking for something all the while begging Miriam. "Don't do it. I won't tell anyone what I saw. I swear." His scared brown eyes glanced at Garren.

Miriam looked away from the big man, not frightened by his size or his countenance. Her family was near, and soon enough he would be in her power. She looked toward the others; how would they take care of those? "Mother these do not look like Joneses to me."

"They are not."

"Did they see anything they shouldn't?"

"Garren says no."

"I don't understand why they look so hungry."

"It is because the world is falling apart, Miriam. While we sit quietly and safely here, the country that harbors us hangs by a thread. The people are soft and spoiled and they do not know how to live off the land. They did not listen to the warnings."

Miriam felt very confused by this statement, for she felt that if the world outside was hanging by a thread, that had to effect Edenia. Her mother was just trying to scare her.

The grubby people bent their heads dejected, most of them. But one teenaged boy glowered at her mother's words. "A tornado took our home. We had supplies, but they're gone now."

Miriam watched her mother's face move from superiority to pity, and she knew her mother would take care of them; she was flawed, yes, but her mother was full to the brim with charity when she felt like someone deserved it and would appreciate it.

Smiling tightly, she turned to the Jones. "They are not with you?" She nodded toward the care-worn group.

"Of course not. Mr. Jones is a man of means. He is not suffering. And he will not quit no matter what. None of us will. Immortality at the world's end is priceless and worthy of the blood toll." His hand flung toward his chest and pulled something velcroed to his vest. Jai and Gale were there, and in an instant deftly pulled the man's hands behind his back.

"That is never going to happen." Jai hissed.

That's when she saw it, what he was grabbing for, his walkie-talkie. How could he forget that electronics did not work in Edenia? The wind Natures made sure of that. It was just foolishness. Gabe saw it too and removed it.

"Why do you have that?" She pointed at the device.

"Enough talk." Her mother stepped between them. "Miriam, do it."

Anger raced up Miriam's back and stung her cheeks.

Garren looked at Miriam. "Sorry Miri, I didn't—I did not think. He was so close."

"It has to be done, regardless." Miriam replied with a deep breath.

She looked at her mother, who nodded at her without a shred of hesitation. Or any of her earlier disgust. As she stepped even closer to the man, Jai took him to his knees. Her mother turned to her Uncle Brian. "Put these others in the cart with as much food as we can spare and take them to..." She left it hanging but pointed northeast toward the foothills.

Brian hustled the non-Joneses away, leaving Miriam free to do her job. As her Nature took her, she placed her hands on the sides of the huge, bucking man's head. Her power took him instantly, and he stilled.

She pulled.

His memories, in spirit form, spanned the distance between them, and once they touched her, the flood came. It was not visual, nor were there words; only feelings, impressions—tangible and understandable to Miriam when her Nature was on her. She dissected them, waiting for the telltale emotion of fear. That was usually the place to start pulling. Very soon she sensed it. She felt him experience the fear. Probably from seeing something unnatural, and the amazement that came with the revelation. That had to be Garren, showing off.

She inhaled and her breath pulled the memory away from him as if she were pulling taffy. Back and forth between them the sensations moved, in a tide that was unique to her and her gift.

As she moved down the timeline of his actions, she felt his strongest emotions in each moment. Backward she pulled, reaching. Soon she felt strong, excited emotions. Somehow, she knew this was him flying. She had never flown before, but feeling it through this stranger was elating. She breathed more deeply, pulled a little further at his feelings, forcing his mind back and back. Suddenly she felt a hot joy. Perhaps a flying leap.

He enjoyed the power of the sensations, while she enjoyed the pulling. This was delicious. It wrapped all around her like something new and exciting.

Her mother touched her arm. Miriam gasped, taking in the impressions suspended helplessly between them, sucking them in with her air. Two more quick lungs full of the substance which comprised the memory and emotion of a human's past was all it took. Now the memories were hers *and* his. They stretched between them like cheese cloth, inside of her but not yet cut off from him.

She braced herself. This part was uncomfortable.

Pulling her hands off him severed the link and the spirit. She felt an instant moment of loss, his loss, but the moment felt like hours. She learned—in this moment of theft—what it was like to not exist. To be an empty vessel. The shell of her soul only held together by moment upon moment of grief, of guilt. Tethered to this plane by moment upon moment of fear that she would fade from this physical existence and become a wraith among the memories she'd stolen.

A small fragment of specific guilt rose from the torrent. Her tired mind acknowledged it; she hoped this had not been the man's only flying experience, for he no longer had it to enjoy. Then her mind emptied, and as the darkness filled her vision, her body set her free from the mental agony as she collapsed into Garren's waiting arms.

CHAPTER 4

Seth

So, this was where his father grew up. He couldn't wrap his mind around the possibility of roots, his roots, here. They'd be deep, old, roots from the looks of things, and Seth hated his father all over again for keeping this a secret for so long.

Edenia looked fairly normal—if it were the beginning of the twentieth century and Wyatt Earp was still running the show. Still, he'd seen older villages in Europe and Egypt. Those places looked old for a reason, they were ancient, but they didn't act old. This place and these people were purposely backward. Concededly so, and it grated on Seth's nerves already.

The Edenites, or Edeners, or Edenians—he wasn't sure which they called themselves—named this circular town center 'the quad.' It was dotted with wooden benches, rock encircled fire pits, barrels with potted plants, and antique streetlights. Not a hint of cement, power poles, or blacktop to be seen.

Inside the big main building—First House or something primitive like that—most everything was in raw element form; wood, stone, brick. Okay brick was questionable as raw, but their jagged bricks totally looked the part, so in Seth's book they counted. The outside was the same. The cobbled circle was lined with huge, broad-leaved trees. The wall-like enclosure of greenery was broken at intervals by the dirt of several main roads. They jutted out like massive spokes of a wagon wheel to reveal more wooden structures right out of the old west. There was a certain charm to it. Sort of.

The point. This place was as backward as Jeremiah had hinted.

The meeting they'd just finished had not gone as he'd thought. He'd learned *absolutely nothing* of use. He'd hoped it would be a simple matter of getting the info required, dumping it, and collecting the cash. No. It wasn't. Of course, he shook his head at himself. If it were easy Jeremiah would have done it himself.

All-in-all, the adults in the room knew how to be cryptic, and Hirum showed how intimidating a bumpkin could be. Though the man had tan skin and dark hair like his father, Hirum's eyes were flaming blue. When he looked at Seth, it unnerved him. It could be that he was keyed up to begin with, but it felt like the man knew Seth's one and only reason for coming to this technologically forsaken place.

The most interesting tidbit of the whole five-hour ordeal though, was this; Seth had never seen his father defer to anyone, yet he did to Hirum. This rocked the universe where his dad was the captain and co-captain of all switchkickery and no one messed with him and lived to tell about it. Seth wondered if Hirum was the dangerous man he was supposed to watch for. He certainly fit the part. It was always the seemingly kind and gentle men that were the monsters.

His father, mother, and Hirum talked excessively about who would share corn, oats, apples and berries with them, and how it was Seth's job to work with the animals in 'North barn' after he attended his first day of school at 'North school'—having primitive jobs was one thing, but the primitive names were, again, just annoying.

A few things *were* strange, but certainly not the 'strange' Jeremiah would be interested in.

There *was* all this talk of a garden. Over and over again, the garden this, the garden that. With all their words there was little said that Seth understood. They talked *around* the garden. In fact, Hirum and his father needed to discuss this garden in more depth, and had left to hold a secret meeting. Seth breathed deeply, assuming that the secrets of the turnip were for sure to be expounded.

At this point Seth was pretty much bored to tears and unable to think, let alone make any guesses as to what untoward thing was going on here.

Seth watched his father's back as he left and felt a bit smug. *He wouldn't be living here long; he wouldn't be spending his last year of high school in the frontier. He hoped.*

There was a looming 'if' over all future plans. If *the world survives, I definitely don't want to finish out my senior year here in Edenia. If we don't all die from the airborne virus killing everyone in Asia, I'd like to get out of this podunk town and make a life for myself, be an adult, ya know?*

He yawned and reached into his pocket for his cell phone, only to feel the big fat old cell phone there. His heart plummeted. Would he ever play Battle Flatulence again?

The phone Jeremiah had given him had no internet access and came with strict orders—they'd discussed it all on Seth's second conversation they'd had before leaving for Edenia:

No turning it on unless he was outside of Edenia in a little shack Jeremiah had set up for him.

No calling anyone but Jeremiah.

No showing anyone the phone.

Break the rules and all deals were off.

Currently, he had nothing to report to Jeremiah except that he would be cleaning up horse poop daily for the foreseeable future.

Still, having a contraband phone and a secret mission made things bearable.

In the vein of hiding things, Seth wondered why his dad pretended like he didn't want to be here when he was around Hirum. He complained like it wasn't his choice to come.

As far as Seth knew, there wasn't a force on earth that could make Mr. CIA Negotiator, special ops, ambassador liaison Ezekiel Johnson do anything he didn't want to do. Seth's father was the force that forced all of *them* to come here. In the process of said forcing, he blatantly ignored all the reasons they'd left Cairo for America in the first place; i.e. war, sickness, cancer. His father had doggedly steered them southwest, away from Baltimore where they needed to be right now. Seth had heard him talk while they traveled. *'American healthcare is still hanging on, even in the midst of world war, and Lillian needed help yesterday. It is the only choice.'*

Then, despite how crucial every moment was, his parents seemed relieved to be wasting time in Edenia. At least their exchanges of worried looks all but stopped. As if with the last bend of the dirt road, they were here, on vacation or ignoring reality or something.

The seed of distrust Jeremiah had sown grew, and the questions multiplied.

Why, oh why, had his parents lied to them about moving to Baltimore, and then come here? Why make everyone think this move was about Lillian and then come here? Why were they acting like this? No help was available for literally miles. And as far as he understood, Lillian was already living on, if not borrowed time, then very limited time.

He couldn't understand, but he could be pissed, and he was.

This thought made Seth so angry with himself for believing them. He should have known. He just assumed they cared about Lillian, but obviously they didn't. How stupid of him. He was glad that he'd been offered a backup plan, and it would take care of everything.

That thought sustained him through the remainder of the waiting and refocused him on his task of getting information. Information that could save his sister's life.

CHAPTER 5

The crisp evening air felt of fall. Ripe orchards of fruit and bonfire smoke brought the smell of autumns past to his mind while the warmth of the last rays of sunshine, almost twilight, surrounded him. On the south side of First House, below a window, lived a large bush which offered great cover for Peter's clandestine habit of spying on the council members' meetings whenever anything of note occurred in Edenia.

Unfortunately, said bush felt a bit pokey to the behind, so for long spying sessions Peter had stowed a cushion between a drainpipe and the house.

After placing the cushion in the most convenient spot and settling himself astride it, he realized the new family and the council remained in the annex to their normal conference room. "Bugger!" he whispered. That meant he would not hear a thing if they stayed put.

Peter spent the light of twilight prying open the swollen and creaky wood-framed window before him. Once that job was completed, he proceeded to wedge in as much of his head as would fit inside.

He hoped his efforts reaped a reward. If not, Edenia was a sad place indeed. Contraband information always lifted his spirit when his pranks failed to do so. Plus, it was always best to have a bit of warning if at all possible when a spanking was inevitable. Since technically it was his fault Garren had shown a Jones his Nature, Peter wanted to get a handle on his father's mood. If he was feeling good, that offense should not provoke a whipping, but if his father were already upset by his day, then it surely would. His father seemed upset often of late.

Providence shone on him, and once his head was rammed in the window, he could make out a conversation. However, after an hour of listening to uninteresting instructions like *'This is your house, these are your chores, this is how Edenia works...'* Peter was bored out of his skull. The only interesting time was when his father asked them to hand their electronic devices over. That part was always funny. Outsiders didn't know how to live without their phones.

As per his custom in the moments of the tedium necessary for all good reconnaissance missions, Peter sat back on his cushion and allowed his mind to wander to the most important topic in his life, his defective Nature.

Instantly, he felt anger and hopelessness wrap around his mind. From the time his mother told him his name meant 'stone' Peter knew, he just *knew*, he would one day have earth Nature and since then all he thought about was being a Guardian.

When puberty began and all the typical early signs came but no Nature burst out of his primed body, his frustration formed. Soon, he felt so wound-up inside with anticipation, he just knew he would erupt. Still nothing. People talked, parents worried, and Peter felt like a mutant.

Then, finally one day he felt it, his Nature. He felt it building, but instead of exploding out of him, turning him from a regular kid into a Guardian in a single second, Peter's Nature turned his big toe into a Guardian. And he didn't even know it had happened. Of all the rotten luck, it was Miriam who noticed his toe was missing—or invisible. From then on, it trickled upward, touching only his toes, then his feet, then on to his calves and there it remained.

Still, he *did* have earth Nature—as he knew he would—and it was by far the coolest Nature there was. He'd once seen his mother light his Uncle Brian, also of the earth, on fire. It seemed like an oddly *practiced* situation, as if his mother used her Nature in this manner all the time. Perhaps in adolescence? Uncle Brian had pulled his Nature to him in time, but since his clothes were not impervious to fire, they burned, leaving him naked right in the middle of town. The cool thing was that as they burned, the outline of a human shape encased in flame formed. But this fire man didn't run around in search of water. He just stood there, solid and unperturbed by the surrounding blaze. He was a *man of fire* just walking home to get some new clothes. It was amazing.

The point: fire can't hurt stone. He would be that stone one day.

Then there was fighting off the Joneses. Though they never technically fought, *fought* (like with the intent to kill) per se, the Edenians outwitted and outmaneuvered the Joneses daily.

Scenarios of Peter's participation in this mostly non-violent war played in his mind, and a grin lit his face.

Suddenly, someone opened the door to the conference room and closed it. Voices jolted Peter out of his daydreams.

"The garden doesn't need to be guarded, Hirum. Period. The Master can take care of his own business like he has for six thousand years. Or are you saying the power and might of the cherubim is inadequate?" This deep, accented voice was one that Peter didn't recognize.

Peter recognized the next voice as his father's. "When you went in, did you see him? I never have seen anyone. I have walked right up to the tree and touched it without repercussion. That is what I'm trying to tell you."

"Stop, just stop. I've heard this all before." The louder, unfamiliar voice cut in. "We've gone the rounds, Hirum. You think you need to keep people away from the entrance to the Garden itself. I know, I know. Your egocentricity astounds us all. Can't you see it's all one and the same? If a few people get their heads whacked off, they will learn to leave the tree alone. Problem solved."

For some reason Peter's father's voice went in and out, making it unintelligible.

But he did hear the man's reply to whatever his father said. "You and all the people here are just messing with his methods and you might be fine accepting the obvious consequences for that, but I'm finished with it. I have no desire to be a freak again." His voice was condescending.

Peter leaned in more closely, contorting himself to do so. *Freak...again?*

"Your words betray you, Zeke." His father's voice was passionate, but controlled. "If you believe all you have told me today, I am confused why you are here. I don't know why you left, I don't know why you stayed gone, and I don't know why you've returned. One would think I don't know you at all."

After a short silence, the strange accent responded, but he started with a preemptive sigh, all the fire gone from his voice. "The outside world is going to hell right now. Perhaps there is safety here, I don't know." Another sigh. "I might as well tell you; the cargo ship we took out of Alexandria could be one of the last sanctioned vessels heading for the U.S." A pause. "I cannot begin to explain all the ways the world has exploded. There are bombings daily outside Cairo, and I hate to say these words out loud, but just as we left, there was talk of things turning nuclear. It is beyond, anything..." he petered out but then started up again, "and it will only get worse. Another World War is coming. The economy here in the U.S. is on the edge of collapse, and we have threats from all the communist countries, threats from the Middle East, of course, and the list goes on and on." The man his father called Zeke paused again and then scoffed, "I know you're out of the loop here but someday this is all going to affect even Edenia." He seemed to struggle to find the words, then Zeke whispered reflectively, "Again, I just can't believe that I am saying this out loud, but I'm afraid this is the end, Hirum. My position in the government offered my family some protection, but the CIA has started recalling assets and agents, and that's when I knew I had to do something. Everyone feels what is coming next."

There was a long break this time.

His father prodded softly. "And?"

Some shuffling sounds and a sniff. "And about a year ago, I began receiving the summonses. They haven't let up. So..."

"So..." His father waited. But Zeke didn't answer. Then his father laughed. "That never made a difference to you before. Now, after all this time, you're obeying? Come, now, you don't expect me to believe that, do you? Why else, Zeke? The real reason."

Frustration touched the stranger's voice now, "I live inside my head, Hirum. Believe me, I know what I did twenty years ago. But here's the thing you can't get a handle on; I don't regret it." He said the last words slow, with emphasis.

"I can see that, and yet I am still confused. Are you just trying to get away from the summons? Trying to save your own hide because the world is exploding? What, Zeke, what? Do you just expect the Master to leave you alone because you came here? I don't believe you are so foolish. Spill it. I can see as plain as day that you have other reasons for coming here."

The man spoke between clenched teeth. "I just want to know why. Why has he summoned me? I left his service. I left this place. I turned my back on this life. I need to know the reason why, at this particular time, with the world falling apart, he has called me back. Hirum, his 'why', his timing, it is extremely important to me and to my family to understand."

There were boot clomps and floorboards creaking and suddenly his father's voice was very clear and close. "You want to know why he still cares about you? Why he would call you back here, out of harm's way when you've rebelled so strongly at his help in the past?" There was understanding in his father's voice. And love.

His father continued in that same heartfelt tone. "We all knew the Master had plans for you before you left. However, you chose a different path..." Peter heard a chair scrape and then footsteps stomping. "Please wait, Zeke. Stop. You wanted an answer. Well, this is all I have." There was another silence before his father went on. "I know you felt awkward about your Nature before, but you are a man now, and you are needed to perform a task. You have something special and now is the time to use it. Right now, when the world is in trouble, when things need to change, you have the power to change them. He has called you back to complete your mission." His father's voice held warmth, comfort, and confidence. "Listen, I know you have your secrets, Ezekiel. Things you either won't or can't share. I have secrets too, we all do. So, keep them. I won't pressure you to share anymore, none of us will." He sighed. "Only stay," he pled. "Your challenges will be different this time, yes, but I am here, and we are no longer fighting over childish things. We need you. The Master needs you. No one can do what you can."

"Wait. Are you telling me no one else has been cursed the way I was?" There was deep confusion in the question.

"It was not a curse..."

"Stop!" the voice yelled. There was an uncomfortable pause. Then a whispered, "Just answer the question."

His father's tone was dejected. "No. You are the only one with the Nature to see the future. To be a prophet among us. You yourself said, it's the end of days. What other time in all the history of the world would that Nature be more useful? We need you."

The man made a hissing sound before speaking. "I thought for certain..." The scraping sound of chair legs against old wood planks came next and the ominous tone of this conversation, curled Peter's toes. What would this obviously volatile man do next?

"Well, there you have it. Once again, this place will turn me into a freak, but this time my family, my children will have the pleasure of watching," the accented voice remarked bitterly. Then he laughed in an almost maniacal way. It took a long time for the man to speak again. When he did, there was regret in his voice. "Sorry for raising my voice." A sigh followed.

"It's understandable. I take it you thought someone would take your place."

"I'm a freak, Hirum."

"No, Ezekiel. You are a leader."

"I'm not! I don't want to be! I don't want to put my family

through all that goes with that. I don't want them to go through some sort of revolting change themselves. I don't want them to feel like freaks, too."

"Hey, I don't like your word, but how can you feel that way here? It makes no sense; you must see that."

The man ignored the very good point his father was making. *Not having a Nature was the only thing that made you a freak in Edenia, well, unless you were Miriam. Or him.* This realization, combined with the outside news this stranger brought, clenched Peter's gut.

"Plus, everyone here is going to hate us. I'm the only deserter. For myself, I couldn't care less. I made the choice to leave, with all its repercussions. But Jenna, Seth, Abby and Lilly, they will pay for that choice."

"We are not like that, my brother. You know we are not."

"Don't call me that!" the man yelled. "At one time we might have been brothers of the heart, but we are not of the same blood." Someone cleared their throat. The tension in the room filtered out through the window and bunched Peter's shoulders. Confused by the conversation and the emotions, Peter leaned in.

"I have no understanding of what has happened to you, but I do know one thing. You are my only brother, Ezekiel, no matter what runs through your veins. I am tied to you, by hours of play as a child. By sharing secrets. By sharing first loves. By work and by loyalty. I have always loved you no matter where life has led you or changed you. I love you with a love that does not tarnish with time or distance. I always have, I always will, brother." The room fell silent once more.

Peter realized his heart beat rapidly. Ezekiel. That name scared him, the memory of overhearing a conversation about this man came back to him. It was the name of the only person to leave Edenia on sabbatical and never come back. This was a little secret Peter knew that no one else his age did. Was this *that* Ezekiel? *Stupid,* thought Peter, *of course it was.* Peter's realization made the conversation he'd just overheard actually make sense. He was real. And he was Peter's...uncle? Or his adopted uncle.

His father's tone was pleading when he spoke again, pulling Peter out of his thoughts. "I know that you disagree with our reasons for being here, but you are here. You came. You have your own reasons and I will not judge you for them. How could I? So...can we just look past all the unresolved issues and work this out day by day? Trial by trial? I am happy to have you here. I will put my pain aside so we can heal anew. Perhaps you can too."

"Lucky for you, you had a shoulder to cry on, and someone to share your pain with." There was enough angst in this comment that Peter felt the hair on his neck rise.

After yet another awkward silence, Peter's father replied in his official First Elder voice, his business voice. "I am so sorry about that, but it is behind us now. We both made choices, and I think you would not change yours if you could. So, I refuse to fight with you any more about it." Immediately, his voice changed again to a soft sincere, timbre. "I really am so happy to see you again."

"I am happy to see you, too." The words were grudging. But then a mumbled aside was issued and Peter felt the mood change. "But mostly I'm glad because I know for a fact that I could kick your butt. No contest, no competition. You see these? This is the best the U.S. special forces, and some rather high-quality steroids, can get you, and I got it, baby."

"Dream on. You are still like a tiny little kitten compared to me."

"I think this competition might just need to happen."

"You're on, any time, any place."

"Nice."

What in the world? Was his father truly participating in this male bravado?

There was some manly-sounding patting going on before his father stated, "Ezekiel, you are needed here. So, I hope you and your family will find a way to be happy. Accommodations-wise, do you want to stay at Aunt Blanche's old house?"

"Um, If I remember, is that the house right next to where Luanne grew up?"

It sounded like the men were leaving the room. Peter's whole body cramped from holding still for so long. He bent over to rub out the sorest appendage, his foot.

It seemed the stranger would stay, because that is what his father wanted. Peter looked forward to gathering more intel on the man and his family. Knowing that nothing as insignificant as his trouble with Garren would be discussed in the face of all this info, he slid from behind the bush.

His feet didn't have long to walk before they reached Edenia's square. It was filled with people. However, Uncle Jai and Aunt Sarah happened to arrive just as Peter did. He caught Jai's eye and his uncle waved him over.

Maybe he could talk to Jai about the crazy stuff he'd just heard. Perhaps, another time. Now, it was show time. It gave him a thrill to know he knew something no one else did. He was excited to watch the surprised faces when his father announced that his long-lost brother, Ezekiel, had returned.

CHAPTER 6

Miriam sat in the music and firelight, basking in the energy around her. Somehow, everything on the outside of her felt excited. Her insides though...

The quad looked spectacular. Small lights and lanterns lit. Garlands of popcorn and dried wild berries strung with care. Jolly music and laughter seeping into every foot and heart.

Miriam's feet itched to dance with Josie and the other girls though she wasn't sure she would be welcome. How could best friendships dissolve so quickly? Almost as if she knew Miriam was thinking about her, Josie looked her way, her bright blue eyes blinking dramatically behind midnight lashes and eyelids. Josie's skin was so dark in the pitch of the night that her eyes almost seemed to be floating. Their connection did not last, and Josie didn't smile as she only looked away.

Miriam watched, her heart aching with the loss of her friends, and her stomach bubbling and roiling because of the newcomers.

Looking to First House where Ezekiel's family would emerge any moment, she thought of the man who had returned. The words *deserter* and *oath breaker* repeated inside her, over and over. Her mind flipping them from good to bad with each repetition. She'd learned that Ezekiel simply did not return from his sabbatical.

A little niggling feeling began in the back of her mind. It wiggled and squirmed until she allowed it forward. Would she have come back to Edenia? Would she choose this life? She shoved the mental answer, probably not, back into the depths of her heart.

Her gut twisted, and she put a hand over the offending organ.

She was a total mess. But clearer on several material points than ever. More self-aware than before.

Ezekiel returning scared her because it tempted her to follow the deserter side of herself. He made it feel possible. He made it seem forgivable. Her whole body seemed to well up. She felt positively green. One thing she was certain of, she needed to think about something else because people were eyeballing her in that are-you-going-to-vomit way.

She determined to pull herself together, to get herself under control.

Miriam sat on a log bench, under a streetlamp, just close enough to the fire that she wasn't cold. She swept her hair out of her lap and it piled nicely on the sanded and varnished bench where she arranged the curls she had painstakingly added to the ends of her hair for this occasion. This was a job she could do with exactness and it calmed her and pleased her to see the lovely little blonde circles.

She didn't even notice when the doors to First House opened. She did notice, though, when the music stopped and the voices quieted.

First among equals on the council, her papa stood on the oversized veranda—where he gave all of his speeches—with his hands held up.

Papa couldn't use his wind Nature to carry his voice like he normally would when addressing a crowd because it was important to keep Natures as secret as possible from any new people.

From experience, Edenians knew the transition went much better with as little warning as possible.

"Good evening. I'm glad to see everyone having a wonderful time." Papa took Ezekiel by the shoulder, patted it good-naturedly and cleared his throat. "I would like to introduce you all to my baby brother, Ezekiel Miller."

The fire felt hot to Miriam's widened eyes. The one man who left Edenia, the man that made her dreams of leaving this place a possibility, was her uncle?

Her father continued, "Zeke has been living as a Johnson on the outside and seems to prefer that surname, for now. So, this is the Johnson family: Jenna, Zeke's wife. And Seth, Abigail and Lillian, their children."

Miriam looked around. All eyes were on the new family—her relatives—and some of those eyes, those of the older generation, were filled with distrust and anger. This man knew what was here, and he'd left it all for worldly living. Dislike and distrust seemed unavoidable.

But her Pa spoke again, and his finish was pointed. "I hope we will all make him and his family welcome." After the almost-threat he went on with a pleasant curl to his lips. "Henry, if you please."

Henry's bow arm pulled at his fiddle strings once more, starting the music back up.

Papa took Zeke by the arm and pulled him toward where Miriam sat. The Johnson family followed closely behind, looking uncomfortable.

From all sides of her, familiar figures converged through the crowd, knowing where their father and Uncle Zeke were headed. Uncle Zeke was honey, they were the bees. Before her papa stood before her, she was surrounded by eight buzzing siblings.

"Ezekiel, Jenna, these are my children, well most of them." Papa said as he spread his hand out to the swarm huddling into Miriam.

Uncle Zeke and his son were even more handsome close up.

Jenna's dark eyes went wide, and she choked out, "All of these?"

Luanne Miller had again outdone everyone else. Ten children in one family was unheard of in Edenia.

"Well Luanne, my wife, is at home with Dorothea, our youngest. She's three and the poor dear is grouchy, she missed her nap."

Not exactly true, Dot barely needed a nap anymore, and she

wanted to come just as badly as the next person. Miriam's mother was the one that was grouchy and unwilling to come.

"Anyhow, this is my eldest, Hannah, and her husband Nate. They have two rug rats I call grandchildren running about somewhere." Miriam's fair and willowy sister stepped forward and shook hands with the Johnsons.

Pa turned. "Garren, my eldest son." More hand shaking. "And Esther and Gabe come next."

But then things got interesting; pa pulled Eve out of the crowd. Seth's face, which Miriam tried not to watch too closely, rearranged with unabashed interest. His huge dark eyes lit up, and a smile turned up the sides of his thin, angular lips.

Sure, Eve was exquisite. Her tiny boned body, golden hair thick with waves, huge eyes and full lips, made every boy in Edenia sigh. But Eve's hair wasn't the only thing that was thick. Eve didn't get anything, bless her heart. Well, except how to heal, but that was her Nature. Plus, she talked about herself incessantly, the poor little narcissist.

Miriam shook her head but then papa's big finger pointed at her.

"This is our Miriam." As eyes were directed at her, she met them one by one. However, she saved Seth for last and when their eyes met, nothing happened. She was a bit blown away by how handsome his face was, but if she was expecting to have some reaction to him, it didn't happen, and that greatly relieved her.

Jenna spoke, "Wow, Miriam, what unique eyes you have." Jenna's voice was clear but had that same strange accent her husband had.

Miriam turned and smiled at the lovely woman. But before she could respond to the complement, Peter, who was standing right beside her, answered using his playful voice, "The better to *see* you with my dear." He sang the word 'see' and tapped his fingertips together conspiratorially.

He was showing off, of course, and at Miriam's expense, which made it all the more fun. For him.

The twin girls, Abigail and Lillian laughed flirtatiously at Peter and he looked over at them like he didn't understand how to take their response. He was a bright kid. It wouldn't take him too long to figure out this new crowd and play them like an accordion.

Papa laughed too. "Yes, Miriam is special." She hated when father called her special, because it always prompted Peter to retaliate. Peter was convinced Miriam was a mutation, or an alien or some strange hybrid accident.

"Extra-Specterrestrial." Peter added with over exuberant joy.

Of course. So tonight, she was of alien variety.

All the kids, including her siblings, laughed or giggled. That play on words never ceased to make the whole world laugh.

"Peter," Papa warned.

Peter gallantly took Miriam's hand with downcast eyes, "Sorry, dearest sister. You know I am only jealous of your dazzling beauty and dizzying intellect."

"Yes, her lovely eyes are only matched by her principled mind. We in the Miller family admire both qualities," her father offered.

Just to hammer home his point, Peter added, "Miriam here will not even tell *us* her IQ scores. She fears wounding our fragile pride."

Seth's eyes met Miriam's again, but only for the briefest of moments before turning toward her younger brother. "You guys take IQ tests around here?" His strangely accented voice started out confident and aggressive, but as he finished those dark eyes darted around uncertainly. "I thought you had like a 'separation from the world' rule or something." He added quotes with his fingers.

Zeke sighed, "Seth, if you'd listened at all this afternoon you would understand everything you need to know."

Seth lowered his voice. "Sorry dad, it just felt like the only facts worth listening to were the terms of this banishment. Go live with some religious zealots, check. No Xbox, no TV, no cell phones, no girls, no going out or having fun, check. No hospitals or doctors, check." He said this last with over-exaggerated harshness. "I guess I just wasn't aware that we were *allowed* to take IQ tests." He gestured animatedly as he spoke, and the veins protruding from his neck showed Miriam the struggle it was for him to keep his voice low.

Once the tirade was over, Seth's light-brown cheeks flushed. He stalked out of the circle knocking his father's shoulder hard.

Jenna immediately took the defensive. "Zeke and I weren't able to tell the kids what we were doing or where we were going before we got here today. And I'm afraid the meeting we just had didn't answer some of their vital questions. This is all a bit of a shock." Her eyes followed her son's back. "Seth wasn't happy to move away from London to Cairo, and moving again..." She looked around the simple, clean quad and then up at her husband. "This is going to take some getting used to."

Something didn't feel sincere about Jenna's comment. Like her excuse wasn't at all what the problem was. Also, the list Seth made seemed strange. And Jenna conveniently left out why Seth included hospitals and doctors.

On top of papa's reassurances that 'all was fine', Esther asked in her nosey way. "You lived in Cairo? How amazing. I would love to hear all about that." Though she was an adult woman, she glanced at papa as if for permission.

Miriam almost said 'me too, I want to hear about Cairo' but saw the look and the little shake of the head her father gave her.

He said to her sister, "That's fine Esther." Then to Ezekiel, "Esther feels a bit deprived. Her sabbatical took her to Michigan to learn languages."

Jenna asked Esther something in Arabic and her lime green eyes flashed as she answered excitedly in the same language. Then Esther took Jenna's arm and led her out of the firelight.

Miriam felt her bottom lip tremble, but she bit into it and turned her face away. Halting the tears on the outside did not get rid of the emotions that formed them. All of this—every part of it, hurt. The separation from friends, expectations, the teasing from family, the 'oh look you're different,' the concern for Esther's so-called deprivation and callousness for her own. Just the total lack of understanding...it all ate at Miriam's heart.

She had to just get away from everyone.

She stumbled away from the firelight.

CHAPTER 7

Seth

A little part of him didn't feel right about the whole familial situation here and how everyone fit in with the Joneses. Hirum; his uncle also? How was that even possible? The leader of the Edenians was his uncle and the leader of the Joneses was his uncle. How did this all fit together? He would have to figure it out. Along with the million other things he had to figure out about this place. Why, why was this place the way it was?

He imagined some long-ago dispute, the kind you see in English history where two brothers have different ideas about how the kingdom should be run so they split and build two kingdoms that end up fighting for hundreds of years.

Whatever the reason for the history here, one thing was certain; his father's deceit was rich and full and thorough.

Wanting to distract himself, Seth wished to see that gorgeous Eve girl again. He looked around at the crowd surrounding him in the lamp-lit quad. All the girls in their odd skirts and blouses and the boys in their eccentric trousers or homemade looking jeans, button-ups, and work boots.

He felt the absence of something, and it took him the good part of an hour to figure out what: body modification. He'd grown accustomed to tattoos, piercings, augmentations and off-color hair, but seeing all these cleanly groomed males and females with perfectly natural long hair and natural nails and skin was refreshing.

But, also strange. This voluntary void of forced individuality felt alien.

Something else brought him to this comparison; their eyes. Even in the soft lighting Seth could distinguish every person's eye color, their irises were so bright and unnaturally colorful and uniquely out of place with their skin and hair. The way it drew him in felt odd.

He shook his head.

These people were something out of a Stranger Things episode. Any moment the unnaturally vibrant blues and greens and browns of their eyes would change to a glowing red. Then all the red-eyed demons would converge upon him and cut out his spleen.

Seth shivered and rubbed at his arms as a few monsters—or cousins—approached. As if he wished her here, Eve also came. And wow, his first impression was accurate. She was seriously gorgeous. Almost stunning.

Seth wasn't too picky. As long as the girl looked good walking away and had a nice set of lips that could curl into alluring expressions, he was happy.

But Eve was overkill. Super long blonde hair, bright greenish-blue eyes, not too skinny. She was soft but tall, with long legs. Though the only reason he noticed her in this way at all was because he couldn't think of her as his cousin.

Honestly, he didn't feel any connection to these people, not like he did his family, or Jeremiah even. The alien idea that this was his family curled his toes. As much as Seth longed for connection, for family, finding out that your long-lost relatives were this...he shivered yet again.

If there'd ever been a link to anyone, a picture, a pushy aunt that invaded their life biannually. An occasional visit to the yokels in Missouri...But there wasn't. Seth saw himself and his family as people with no roots. His father and mother were only-children of dead people who were only-children of dead people.

At least that's what he'd been told, his Whole. Entire. Life.

He saw his lying sack of a father sitting with that weird girl, another one of his supposed cousins. He watched her wide, violet eyes flash over to him. They were so strange and yet kind of amazing, and they totally derailed his internal angry tirade. He wondered if anyone else in this place had bright violet eyes. Was that even a real eye color? They were so bright that from thirty feet away he could tell every time she blinked.

Several minutes later he realized he was still staring at the girl, his cousin. He just couldn't look away from her freakishly long white/blonde hair and those eyes.

A friendly, "How's the shoulder bro?" was shouted at him over the talking and music and he jumped and looked at the bloke in front of him. Seth remembered this boy's face from the familial intros. He was another so-called cousin.

He rubbed at his joint. It actually still hurt from when he had jarred into his father. The man was like stone. Seth looked into the muddy brownish-green eyes of the older boy and shrugged noncommittally.

He went on, "Your dad seems...intense."

"Yeah, so does yours. Maybe being a jack-wagon is in our blood." Seth said with a sardonic smile. He turned to look back over at his dad, wanting the anger that shook his hands to take over again.

What a liar.

Out of nowhere, Eve stepped in front of him taking his breath and anger away with one smile. She said, "Gabe, don't tease our new cousin." She took Seth's arm and looped her arm through his.

Seth looked down at her arm resting on his while his cousin, Gabe, said, "Actually no, I didn't mean anything by it. You alright, dude?"

This kid was trying too hard. When his parents tried to talk "teenager" it sounded strange on them too. "Yeah dude, I'm fine." He emphasized 'dude' in the same awkward way Gabe had.

Eve pulled him away from her siblings. "Don't mind him. He's just trying to sound like you. Can I walk you around, introduce you to some people?"

"Do you have to?"

Eve laughed as if he'd told her a joke. He was absolutely serious. Still, Eve walked him all around the quad. She introduced him to several of her friends, soon to be his classmates. One boy he met was named Gregory. He eyed Eve's arm on Seth's with objection.

When Eve hinted that she was thirsty halfway through a conversation, it was Gregory who jumped to get her a drink.

"So, what's up with Greg? Is he, like, your boyfriend? You do date here, right?"

"Well, I guess in a way he is." She said absently.

Seth leaned over so he could catch Eve's wandering eyes. "Either he is or isn't." She blushed a little and he let go of her arm. "Hey, I'm just your cousin. It doesn't matter to me who you're dating unless he's a dick."

Eve jumped a little and covered her mouth with both hands. "What?"

She started laughing. "You said..." she laughed nervously and turned away blushing.

Seth realized his mistake, again. "You can't call someone a dick around here?"

Eve covered her ears and turned back toward him. She was still tittering, but she shook her head 'no'.

Seth bit his lip. "Sorry."

She swung her head from side to side, but she took her hands off her ears.

Seth returned to the subject. "So, he's your boyfriend."

Turning back toward him she answered. "I'm betrothed to him." She said it nonchalantly and picked at nothing on her skirt.

"What? You're like...seventeen. How can you be betrothed? Who even calls it that anymore?"

Eve rushed out an answer. "We don't go around betrothing everybody. It just needed to happen with me."

"Why?" Seth asked, getting a little impatient.

Eve sighed. "Because..." She hesitated and blushed again, "...

many of the boys wanted to *court* me. It was causing a problem. So, my parents and I chose one. Problem solved."

Seth looked around at all the teenage boys hovering nearby; their bright eyes flickered to Eve incessantly, and he snickered. "I don't think it *solved* anything."

Eve's eyes flowed around their small area, and then she giggled. Gregory returned, and he actually brought a drink for Seth too, which was class-act of him.

"So," Seth said after a thank you and a swig of the water. "Can we leave the quad or is that against the rules?"

Gregory looked at Eve and said, "We could show you around." He emphasized the *we*.

"Great. Let's go."

Eve and Gregory both held lanterns up high. After walking down the main street and seeing some rather tidy but crude shops, they made their way around to show Seth the infamous *garden*.

Spread sporadically through the fenced in, cultivated area, there were a few small utility sheds with electric spotlights on them. It was just a regular garden with lots of green stuff in it.

"Is that a fence?" Seth asked squinting into the dark.

"It's more like a wall, but yes, it surrounds the entire outer perimeter of our farmlands and protects them." Greg answered.

"Protects them from what?" Seth scoffed. "Bunnies nibbling the lettuce?"

"The outside, of course." Eve picked up an abandoned shovel from the mammoth vegetable garden floor they stumbled through. Gregory took it from her. He seemed helpful and Seth couldn't help like his protective sidekick persona.

Eve on the other hand, well, the longer Seth talked with her, the more he was sure that not all her screws were tight up top. She had moments of lucidity but mostly she giggled a lot.

Gregory tried making conversation. "I assumed you'd be different. That you'd know something about Eden."

"You mean Edenia?" Seth asked.

"Yes, that's what I meant." Gregory answered quickly and tried a little too hard to look convincing.

"Okay?" Seth said with a rising crescendo to his voice and promptly tripped over the uneven ground. He decided to pay more attention to where he was walking. "Anyhow, it seems my dad thought there was no reason to tell us about you or Edenia."

His mind flittered on an idea. How many relatives did he have in this little town? And why didn't Jeremiah and the Joneses live here?

Something suddenly bugged him about their walk. It seemed they'd been going forever, in a curved path. But straight to his left, through a rather small knot of trees, was the quad. Picturing what they'd done in his mind he attempted to figure out why they'd gone the way they had. Walking from the quad around the river and dam area, they next came to town and the main road, which reminded him of an old western ghost town with all its boxy, false fronted, porch hung stores and shops. All the while the river stayed at his left. Then there were the dirt roads, which jutted out from the main street like spokes of a wagon wheel. Filling those streets were squat, painted, wooden homes. But that only took up the south and east...of a circle. Yes, Edenia was a circle, and they'd gone halfway around. If he was right, then that group of trees was the center. The community garden and fence took up the entire northern portion. Eve said the grain fields were next and the orchards and stables last.

Seth looked to his left, "Does all of Edenia encircle that bunch of trees?"

Eve glanced toward the grove and then looked at Gregory.

He answered. "Yep."

"So, why didn't we just walk through it to get to here? That would have been so much faster."

"We don't walk through the garden." Eve's voice held a bit of shock and almost reverence.

Seth was confused, "Uh, what are we doing now?" He knew his tone was a bit condescending, but she was so weird.

"Oh," She laughed. "It's fine to walk through this garden, just not that one." She nodded to the trees.

Seth's face scrunched. "So, you have another garden?" This one fine to be in, that one not fine. His memory called up several of these conversations/arguments from this afternoon, but two minutes ago he assumed they were talking about this vegetable garden and why it would need protecting? But now, to be more confusing, there was another garden? "Why in the name of all that is sane would you need another garden?"

"It's not really a vegetable garden." Gregory stated haltingly.

"I can see that. It just looks like a bunch of trees. What do you grow there?" There was a pregnant pause and Seth wondered if his tone had been too harsh. So, he back tracked because he could feel the tension building and knew this was something he needed to pursue. "Sorry, it's been a long day. Please, explain this garden thing to me because I feel like you're speaking French."

Seth's boots hit a hard-packed dirt road. He hadn't even realized they were walking again, but the field was now covered in grain stubble.

Some part of his last few thoughts sparked the infant of an idea. When Seth snuck off to call Jeremiah after their first encounter, but before they'd gotten to Edenia, his cousin still wouldn't tell him much about what he was supposed to find here. He said he couldn't, only that Seth would know it when he saw it or heard about it. Jeremiah sort of mentioned that they might be protecting something, but he gave no other details.

For some reason, he felt very close to uncovering whatever secrets were here.

Seth wasn't watching where he was going and nearly ran headlong into a tree branch. It was a relatively small thing, trunk only as big around as a basketball but the great arching arms that feathered out were covered in dark leaves.

"Maybe you should be holding the light. It would definitely help you see what's right in front of you." Eve suggested with a merry smile.

Seth took her lantern. Then, seeing a bit more clearly, he looked up at the branches and saw big red heart-shaped apples.

Right then, Seth had a weird déjà vu moment.

When you moved around as much as the Johnson family did, you pared down your earthly possessions to two categories: essentials and important keepsakes. One of Ezekiel Johnson's keepsakes was a rather large painting he had taken with him everywhere for as long as Seth could remember. Even on this emergency trip, traveling on a cargo ship, his father had taken special care with the painting. It came to his mind now, for it reminded him of his current position. A man looking up into the branches of an apple tree just like this one. He felt like he was that man for a strange moment.

But as he recalled the other details of the painting, it pulled him out of his strange déjà vu. In the painting the man was naked, and he was with a naked woman, a snake and three weird glowing angels. One of the angels had a huge sword. As a kid he always liked that angel best and had many conversations with his dad about that angel.

"Seth?" Gregory asked, pulling him out of his reverie.

Seth backed up and glanced at the boy, but did not speak. A thought had started and he couldn't shake it. He looked over at the little grove of trees, which he could still see outlined by the dark sky and the lights of the quad beyond. That was the garden, not a garden, *the* garden. The way it looked to him, these people literally built their lives around it, they made it the center of everything. They would barely talk about it. Greg and Eve were uncomfortable with him bringing it up. So, it was a secret. He was looking for a secret. They lived a self-inflicted minimalist life, away from the world for no other reason, he gathered, than to keep themselves busy. Unless they were hiding something. He was looking for something hidden.

He recalled again this afternoon, his father's talk of the garden and a tree. His mind's eye saw the tree in the painting his father was obsessed with. The title of that painting was: CHERUBIM EXPEL ADAM AND EVE.

The garden.

Then there was the blaring truth that this town was called Eden or Edenia. He looked up at the apple again, then down at Eve.

It sounded so crazy, but it fit; and if there was information worth a butt-load of money, it would be this.

Jeremiah said he would know it when he saw it.

Seth's voice was a whisper when he finally spoke. "You crazy people think that, that," he gestured toward the grouping of trees, "is the Garden of Eden, don't you?"

CHAPTER 8

Peter

"What are we going to do, father?" Eve asked, worried. "I am sorry, I did not mean to do it."

"Shush Eve, it is not your fault. Seth is his father's son. Whether Ezekiel did it on purpose or not, he spoke about Eden around his children, you cannot just keep your entire childhood a secret. It was already in the back of Seth's mind."

"Should I pretend like he did not figure it out? What would that even look like? *I do not know what garden of Eden you are referring to, Seth?*" Eve said with a stilted, stupid inflection. "I do not think I can do that."

Peter's mother began, "Not exactly, Eve, for that would not be truthful. All we can do is not talk of it again." Peter could almost feel the gaze of steel his mother was leveling at Eve. "Do not give him more. Keep your mouth closed from now on. Change the subject."

"I get it, mother," Eve stated tersely.

"Good. Well then, go to bed."

There was silence for a moment, then Eve asked, "Can we just have Miriam take it from him?"

"No." His father answered, "I do not think that is the correct course. I think we let this play out. Why else would this happen, if not to fulfill the Master's plan in some way? He went to all the trouble of calling them home. This might be the catalyst that sends them down the path of fate."

"I think you are right, father." She moved into the hallway, and Peter stilled his breath. "Alright, goodnight."

After Eve entered her room, Peter slipped into his bed. He pulled the covers up and allowed his mind to wonder at how, without any help, Seth—of all people—have figured it out. Seth seemed like a sad little gutter snipe to Peter, mopey and unable to accept his lot in life, none too bright, and prone to emotional outbursts.

The only way Seth could figure out the secret was if someone had told him. The Joneses popped into his mind and the thought sent Peter into Guardian mode. He felt his Nature pull at him, tentatively. Like it was shy. It just would not burst forth. Peter pulled one foot out from under the bed covers, and sure enough, it melted out of the blankets like butter, not a sound. His Nature had taken him, well taken his feet.

He looked down, the cracked bedroom door provided just enough light to see that, where his feet should be, where he could feel them existing, there was nothing.

He did not understand this, this weird thing with his Nature. His father's words rang back in his ears. *Why else would this happen if not to fulfill the Master's plan in some way?*

Why else indeed?

And when Peter accepted that, he allowed himself to feel something new, and feel he did. It was excitement and dread and relief all rolled together. It was exultation like what he felt right before a prank.

It spread to include more than himself. Peter felt something building. Something big. Something everywhere. He knew he was part of it. He knew his Nature was part of it. It was life-changing, and he felt it. He knew it was coming.

CHAPTER 9

"Are you completely daft?" Seth punctuated each word, and it took every ounce of his self-control to not just swear at the man. "Tell me right now what is going on here and why we are living with these crazy people, or I swear I am taking Lilly and Abby and we are out of here."

His father raised an eyebrow at him, his face almost amused as he sat in an ancient rocking chair that took up an entire corner of their new living room.

Unblinking, the showdown started. Seth knew exactly what his father was thinking. *There was no way Seth could take anything that Ezekiel Johnson didn't want him to take.*

Seth blinked first, like he always did, and ran a hand through his hair. With confusion coloring everything from his voice to his face, Seth asked, "Do they really believe this is the Garden of Eden?" He paused before continuing, "Do you believe that?"

As always, when his father was caught off guard, there was no *physical* sign of it. His eyes did not deviate, his face did not twitch, his throat did not swallow; he only sat there with a half-smile on his face. Finally, he spoke, and it was that which betrayed him. "So, you conned it out of someone, did ya?" He tapped a finger on the armrest of the chair. "I had my money on Abigail. I guess I owe your mother fifty dollars."

"Don't worry dad, I'm sure the bank down the dirt road in Wyatt Earpsville will give you some monopoly money to pay her off."

His father laughed. That always melted away Seth's anger because he rarely made his father laugh.

Going with it, almost hungry for it, Seth scolded, "Anyway, where's the love? You bet on Abby?" Real disappointment touched his voice.

He got a second laugh, but when the smiles were over Seth realized he'd been conned. Conned right out of a good threat and an honest-to-goodness reason to be mad at his father.

Refocusing, he tightened his voice. "Seriously, dad." Seth sat on a sofa right out of *Amish Living* magazine. The wood spindles hurt his back, so he leaned forward. "What is going on here?"

"First, let's talk about your behavior earlier tonight."

Seth knew this was coming. "Sorry. That Hirum guy, with all his ten million kids, and all his ten million rules..."

"*Uncle* Hirum, Seth. Show some respect, he is pretty much in charge around here. And don't blame your anger on others. You choose how you act." He stared Seth down until Seth nodded. "Apology accepted. Now, we are all tired, it's been a long day, and you're going to have even a longer day tomorrow. We are meeting your grandparents. They've invited us over for lunch." Seth's mind hiccupped over the thought of grandparents, real-live grandparents. "So, let's sleep on this and then we can get up tomorrow and *all* of us can sit down and talk about what's going on here."

Seth was so not done with this conversation, but his father had that look in his eyes.

All he could say was, "Yeah. 'k." His father cleared his throat and Seth amended his lack of respect, "I mean, yes sir."

But Seth didn't go to bed once his father headed upstairs; he went down the hall to Abby's and Lilly's room. First, he would talk to them about their night, in an attempt to glean info. Then, depending on how they responded, it might be time to share the insanity. They would hear it all tomorrow anyhow.

He could hear the twins talking, so Seth knocked twice and waited, then he cracked open the door. A big window let in some moonlight and it sparkled between the twin beds that flanked the door. The girls' room was very small, just like his. He flicked on the light when he saw that both girls were sitting up in their beds. There was a small desk and a chair on one side, and a standing wardrobe on the other just like in his room.

Through clenched teeth and squinting eyes, Abigail asked him, "What in hell's name are we doing here Seth?" She mouthed the word hell instead of saying it out loud. To her, swear words only counted if you actually spoke them. One of the small ways she rebelled.

Abigail stood, moved to Lillian's bed and took her hand, "There are way more important things we should be doing."

Both of them looked at Lillian, who said, "Maybe they wanted me to meet my family before..."

"No Abby's right. Grandparents or no we have way more important things to be doing right now." Seth interjected.

Lilly didn't get angry very often, but when she did, tears rushed out like from a spigot. She wiped at her face, "Do you think they've just given up?"

Abby burst in. "Of course they haven't."

Seth went to her. He sat on the bed and wrapped his arms around her. "If they have, know that I haven't." he put heat in the declaration.

She pulled away from him, her dark eyes piercing. "What do you mean?"

He pulled away further and after a heavy moment of silence got up to pace around the room. "I mean, I have a plan, and it's legit."

He had both girl's full attention now.

"Seth, what plan? What are you talking about?" Abby demanded.

Seth hesitated. "I can't tell you everything. But I can tell you this. If you want to help, keep your eyes and ears open. If you see or hear anything strange, you tell me. Small stuff, or off the charts unbelievable supernatural stuff. Got it? Like anything at all."

"Seth, we have real issues here, and no time for your conspiracy theories," Abby said.

At the same time Lilly said, "Supernatural, Seth! Are you making fun of me because I believe in aliens?"

Abby rolled her eyes at Lilly. "You do not believe in aliens Lilly. Geez." Then she turned her snark on him. "Seth, you're not making any sense. , this whole town is alien. I could report to you all day long on how idiotic this place is. And, how in the name of all that's good and holy could something weird here help Lillian?"

Lilly's bottom lip went into her mouth and she chewed. She knew something.

Ignoring Abby's question, Seth jumped on it. "What are you thinking Lilly?"

"I don't know, it's probably nothing. And it seems totally insane. But it just struck me as so weird."

"What?" Seth insisted, "If you thought about it, then it's not nothing. And insane is just what we're looking for here."

"Okay," she paused again, "so after you got your macho on with dad and shoved him out of the way, mom asked about that girl, the one with the amazing eyes..."

She looked over at Abby who supplied, "Miriam."

"Yes, Miriam, well, mom asked about her eyes. Then her brother Peter made some joke about them being extra-terrestrial or something."

She stopped and looked at him.

"Yeah?" He asked confused.

"Well, what if they're aliens? Or she's an alien."

Seth burst out laughing.

"What? There were a whole lot of awkward vibes going on about that comment." Lilly defended.

"You laughing does not inspire honesty, oh mighty commander." Abby said as she picked at a fingernail.

Seth continued to laugh.

"Seriously. Look around Seth, this place is worse than Mars," Lilly whined.

"Makes sense to me," Abby added and then narrowed her eyes at him when this brought on a whole new bout of laughter.

"Okay, if you're so dang smart what have you come up with? And I reiterate, how can anything weird here help Lillian?" Her voice held the tone of impatient disdain he so frequently got directed at him.

At her words, Seth stopped laughing right away. He hadn't allowed himself to think about what happened just a short hour ago. But his father had practically confirmed the craziness. He cleared his throat and wiped his eyes. "I have found out one thing that will help with my plan." He looked at the girls who stared eagerly, "These crazy people think they are hiding the Garden of Eden." He said it slow so it would sink in. "Like the actual biblical garden. That was what all the serious talk about a garden was today."

"What?" Lillian exclaimed.

As Abigail said, "You're full of crap." and she went back to her nails.

"I just asked dad about it and he pretty much confirmed it."

There were instant rebuttals from the girls.

"Why would they need to hide it? Isn't there supposed to be some kind of sworded ram thingy protecting it?" Lilly insisted.

"He *said* the people of Edenia are hiding the Garden of Eden?" Abby questioned.

"He did his distraction, evasive measures thing."

The girls shared a look that said they understood. 'Classic dad'.

He sat on the bed. "He's making us have a *meeting* tomorrow morning to discuss it."

The girls jointly rolled their eyes.

Abby said, "I'm not speaking to dad."

Lilly was quiet for a moment but then admitted, "In theory, neither am I, but if he will divulge the secrets of why we are here—I might just have to make an exception."

Seth got up and headed for the door. "Still, whatever he says, remember your mission. Anything weird, tell me, okay?"

"Are you going to laugh like a maniac if we do?" Abby asked snarkily.

"Maybe, but even the littlest thing could get us what we all want. And what is that again?"

"Outta here." The girls said in unison.

"I still want to know what these things have in common, Seth, and how they connect to Lillian. I'm not letting this go," Abby insisted.

Seth slowly shut the door. "Just do it, Abigail." Seth answered and walked down the hall wondering if he should have told them everything.

CHAPTER 10

Saturday

Seth

Every chair in their new house was uncomfortable. Seth's father sat across from him in the same rocking chair as last night, his dark hair pulled back in a ponytail, his dark eyes tight with concern. Seth watched the slow tipping of his feet as he gently rocked.

"So..." Seth started.

Abigail burst in, "Daddy what is going on here? One day I am sitting in a scary but adequate private school in Cairo, with my iPhone, my girlfriends and a hot boyfriend, and the next, I'm sentenced to do the rest of my natural time on this earth in a rundown old western movie set."

"With crazy people." Lillian added.

"With crazy people." Abby repeated with a nod toward Lilly. Then, as she remembered her twin, her face instantly turned bright red. Her embarrassment made her add quickly, "And what about Lilly, daddy?" She asked as if she knew that it should have been her first objection, but the other comment burst free from her with a violence that ignored cognition. "What about Lilly?" She asked again, but slow and oh so scary.

His mother burst in before Abby went postal, "Cairo was dangerous, and getting more so by the second. The stress was not good for any of us, especially Lillian. You know your father's position afforded him special information, so we were going to leave Cairo any way."

Seth glared at Abby. "Seriously?" He looked back at his mother. "This isn't about moving, and you know it. Moving is like breathing for us, it's part of life. You are purposely ignoring the real problem here! You lied to us and now Lilly will suffer. You expect us to just not fight for her? And why here of all places? Why Edenia?"

Abby added solemnly, "Didn't the doctors say she could die, like, tomorrow if she didn't get treatment, chemo or whatever? Lilly can't get the care she needs here."

Seth chimed in again a bit more in control of his passions. "I think we all would like some answers. No more evasion. Coming here with negative info and no guarantees about Lilly—well, it's just wrong."

His mother stood and went over to his father's side. She took his hand. She had tears in her eyes, "We made the decision to come here, together, and it was mostly because of Lillian's tumors that we've gone about things how we have."

Both the girls started yelling objections, and that was when his father held up a hand.

"Girls, please, stop."

Once they quieted, he continued, "I don't think I could explain to you how incredibly difficult coming here has been for me and your mother. This has been..." he took in a huge lungful of air, "...the hardest thing I have ever done in my life. Having to humble myself. Having to face my past. Choices I made when I was young. The person I was when I lived here before. I hate to admit this, but things were very complicated, and the way I handled them..." he left that for a moment before continuing. "I left deep scars here. I don't want any of that to taint...the reason we are here. I don't want to set you all up for failure."

Their mother looked at Lilly. "Baby, we love you so much. But I need you to know. After talking it through with Doctor Allijed, we are convinced that the only thing that will do you any good is being here in this strange, eccentric little town."

"I've always felt you were keeping something from me. Are you telling me I'm not going to get better? Are you saying you're just trying to keep me comfortable until..." she couldn't finish.

His mother went to Lilly her face full of pinched helplessness. "Do you trust us, baby?" She asked as she enfolded Lilly in her arms. Tears rushed down her cheeks. "Though everything isn't crystal clear right at this moment, can you believe that we have a good reason for what we are doing?"

"Lilly, can you have faith in us?" His father asked from across the room. "Can all of you have faith in us?"

Lilly pulled back from their mom and bit her lip in an attempt to squash the sob that lay waiting. Finally, she nodded and buried her face in their mother's shoulder.

Seth watched his father look to Abigail. She purposely turned her face away from him and stuck her chin out as she let her own tears shamelessly fall to her lap. His father stared for a while, true grief lining his face.

And that was when Seth realized whatever his father had bought into, he was in it, heart and soul. There was no way he could be trusted. The man was crazy with grief and he was making crazy decisions.

And considering all the lies of late...

A lump formed in Seth's throat and he felt a stinging sensation in his heart. This was up to him now. Lilly's life was in his hands.

Abby looked over at him, her eyes angry, her face red and puffy, and he knew she was on his side. Good. Abby made him insane, but there was no one else he would rather have working with him on this.

He looked back at his father's pain-filled face and knew he had to be tactless. If he didn't steer this conversation in the right direction and get some real answers, no one would get what they wanted.

And now that he was certain this was Lilly's only chance, he took a deep breath and spit out, "Do these people really believe they live outside the Garden of Eden? That they are hiding it?"

Shocked silence filled the room. His father looked briefly at his mother then slowly answered, "Yes, they are *guarding* the Garden of Eden."

Blood rushed to Seth's face; his heart raced. If he played this right, he and his sisters could be out of here tonight. "Guarding it?" Seth pressed. Hadn't Eve used the same word?

But his question was overthrown by Abby, who jumped on this ridiculous statement to vent some of her anger. "What in the name..." she looked around the room as if mental patients surrounded her. "Are we seriously having this discussion?" She shook her head vigorously and blinked her eyes. "No, no, my parents did not just say something insane."

"Abby, it was you who were all 'aliens make sense to me' last night, right? Is this that big of a stretch from there?" Seth reminded her, but knowing the only reason he'd even been willing to consider it was because he'd had a heads-up from Jeremiah. And honestly it didn't matter what he believed or didn't believe, all that mattered was that the man with the medical care money believed it and wanted to know more.

"So, you believe this madness too?" She accused condescendingly. She looked around at the people she trusted and loved. "All of you?"

After a deep breath, and a few uncharacteristic twitches, his father answered. "The Garden of Eden is in fact located here, in the center of the town. I have personally been inside." He quickly glanced at Seth's mother before turning eyes blazing with defiance back in their direction. Those eyes dared anyone in the room to challenge his statement.

Seth's brain short-circuited. Even Abby was still.

After a very quiet moment where this idea of the garden became very real, Seth gave into logic and spluttered, "But that's...it's impossible! It's crazy talk. You're mental." He stood and paced. Everyone was mental, even Jeremiah.

Abby spluttered and gestured in agreement, her eyes wide, head bobbing, as if he'd taken the words right out of her mouth. But then she flipped on a dime and glared. "Of course, now that it's out of the horse's mouth he's on my side."

Seth ignored her, mostly.

"No, Seth, Abigail, we're not crazy. And once you have been here a short time, you will see that."

"A short time? That doesn't sound ominous or anything."

There was a pause where all the Johnson children looked at one another, their brains working furiously, considering this statement. It did indeed seem ominous. It also seemed uncharacteristic of their father.

"What exactly does that mean." Lillian asked.

As Abby asked, "Like how long?"

Their father shrugged. "I don't want to put parameters such as time on your understanding it."

And the hair on the back of Seth's neck rose, the way it did when he felt like he was getting worked over by the CIA part of his father. This statement was a jab, but also a lead.

"Try." Seth demanded hoping to back his father into a corner.

"I don't know exactly Seth, but let's say ten days."

Their mother jumped in. "Or seven."

Instantly there was panic. Seth backed away, toward the door feeling anxious and a bit suffocated. He knew it. "What happens in seven days?"

Abby burst in, "They're not going to take us in that place, are they?"

Lillian started crying again, "Why would they do that? Why would you do that? You can't make us go!"

His mother pulled Lilly to her again, "Shush love, no one is going to make you do anything."

"Well that's not really true, now is it? You made us come here, didn't you?" Abby added as she stood and moved back toward Seth.

"Stop this Abigail." Their father said in his business voice. "Let's just take this one day at a time. I promise all of you, that if you go along with this for..." He looked over at their mother, "...let's say seven days, not only will we all get what we want, but we will have a really long, very interesting conversation and you will understand everything."

"Yes, girls, Seth, just give it a chance here, please." There was real desperation in his mother's voice.

Lilly, who'd been silent a while, looked between their father and mother and asked, "Just seven days?" He couldn't believe it. She was falling for their scam. Of course, it would be her. She still trusted them. But they just admitted to lying and tricking their own children.

He almost said as much, but Lilly went on. "We play nice for a few days and you will tell us everything you haven't?"

Their mother nodded.

"I think I have seven days in me. I actually feel pretty good considering a black mass of dead tissue is eating my brain." She smiled. "But if this doesn't work out how you think, you take me to the doctor, right? Or am I going to die here, in the Garden of Eden or something? Is that the plan?" She shrugged, "I guess there are worse places to die."

Seth's father leaned forward in his chair and nodded, "Just trust me, baby. Would I ever let anything happen to you if I could help it?"

Seth ignored all the niceties. The truth was his father brought Lilly here to die when there were medical treatments that could really and truly save her. Edenia and whatever idiocy was here, that was his father's plan. Doctors were his.

His father went on, "But we mean full immersion. This is key. You must eat the food, wear the clothes, go to school, do your work. You make friends and everything, alright?"

Their mom added, "All as if Lilly's life depended on it, or if not Lilly's, yours."

"And as if you were never going to leave this place again. As if you love it here." Their dad clarified.

"So full-on brainwashing, complete and utter conforming? And you swear to me right now on the graves of your dead parents..." She paused, the words sinking in. "Oh my gosh, Dad. You don't have dead parents." Her hands flared and went into her hair. She rose and started to pace. Then her jaw tightened, and she looked at Seth. He saw fire in her eyes and knew she knew what they were dealing with. Turning to their parents, she smoothed her face and asked, "Just a week of full immersion, and it will help Lilly?"

Their parents nodded.

She was acting now; Seth could see it. He knew her well enough to see where her loyalties lay. "Wear the clothes, huh? I don't think that should suck too badly. I can't believe how cute their dresses are, for homespun, that is...I wonder how they do it?" Abby shook her head as if she needed to come back to the present. "You swear that you're not going to make us drink some red Kool-Aid at the end or something?"

Their mother huffed, "Abigail Elaine Johnson, how dare you say something so cruel?"

"But she's right!" Seth burst in. "You're asking a lot. What will happen after a week? Just tell us."

"Have we ever given you reason to distrust that we had your best interest at heart?" She asked.

Seth almost screamed out, YES! But the words were stripped from his mouth with Lillian backing down. "Okay, I will pretend to play nice if you promise nothing bad will happen." And Abby nodded her assent, but she shot Seth a look reconfirming she didn't mean a word of what she was saying.

His father spoke up, "You have my oath." But Seth, as much as he had once respected his father, as much as he wanted to believe, did not feel relief. His gut churned.

"Truly we are hoping for something not short of a miracle." His mother added, but Seth stopped listening. There was no way he would agree to this.

Then his father uncharacteristically cleared his throat. It got Seth's attention. "There is one more catch," His father said. "We need to keep Lillian's condition to ourselves."

"Why?" Abby asked.

Their father blinked and shifted his feet. "That stuff in the past that I mentioned, well it means people around here don't trust me and that could affect everything." His father's face was contrite as he said this, and then, quick as a flash, it turned hard and serious. "I will not let that happen. So, if people ask you about me or why we are here. Say nothing. Play dumb."

"We are dumb daddy." Lillian squeaked.

"I think that's the point Lil," Abby said. "They don't want *anyone* to know *anything*."

"Typical." Seth blurted out. He couldn't help it.

His father sighed. "I promise it will all make sense soon enough. Just keep your own counsel and everything will work out. Got it?"

"Yes." His mother added. "We must be our natural, normal selves. We need to go through the motions and the process. Okay?"

The girls nodded. Abby annoyed, Lillian determined.

Seth shook his head in disgust. So, his father had a *history* of screwing people over, lying to them, manipulating them. Big surprise, he was the same man that screwed things up back in the day. Lying to Seth about his whole ancestral history was par for the course. Regardless, it was not something you could just forgive and forget in one day.

This all just proved his point. In spite of the sincerity he'd seen in both his parents' faces, he knew firsthand how their lies affected people. Even now they were caught in a terrible web of his father's making.

He couldn't trust them, and he couldn't trust their promises, not when a life was at risk.

This was up to him. That fact settled in his soul.

So when his parents turned to him to ask for his trust, he shook his head and marched out the front door. It was his turn to be the hero. He would save Lilly. To heck with his father, and his plans, and his so-called *oath*.

THE CHAPEL—OR what he assumed was a chapel—was the only whitewashed building in town, and it caught Seth's eye. His feet moved toward the structure before his mind knew what his heart needed. Hirum had explained that Edenians were not religious, not in an obvious way. They did not go to church. Their lives were their church. They did not talk about God, though they knew a lot about God. They were kind of their own keepers. So, this *chapel* intrigued Seth even in his distracted and distressed state.

The door didn't squeak but was exceptionally heavy. After opening it, his eyes were instantly attracted to the huge latticed partition running down the center of the open hall. Seth plopped down onto the first wooden bench he met. The partition was elaborately carved, but unadorned. It took him several minutes of stunned silence to reconcile himself with the truth of its detail. It was masterful.

Blinking, he gazed around the plain room. No crosses, no statuettes, just light-colored walls, huge light fixtures, and the partition. No pulpit, but there was a slightly raised stage-like area.

Halfway down the room a woman sat, head bowed, rocking back and forth. Her very serious supplication reminded him of the trouble in his own heart. He had pitted himself against his father, essentially calling him out. He knew his reason was worthy, but he didn't know if he himself was worthy, or in all honesty, capable.

And then there was Lillian. Grasping—or attempting to grasp—the enormity of that responsibility overwhelmed him.

The door slammed and a man in a black coat entered. He gave Seth a surprised look as his head whipped back and forth between the two sides of the room. Then he thumbed at Seth, directing him over to the other side of the partition.

Because he'd lived in a Muslim dominated country for the last few years, it only took a moment to discern the man's meaning. They separated the men from the women too, by a latticed partition usually on an upper floor.

Stiffly, he got up and moved to the other side of the room. There, he noticed several men reading, and some humbly hunched over.

He hadn't come to pray, if that is what these people were doing, that wasn't his thing. Sure, he did it with his family at meals and stuff because his mother had religious traditions, but there never had been a time in his life where he needed God enough to pray. Except that one time when a bomb had hit the neighborhood next to his school, or that time he found out his sister had brain cancer, oh, and there was the time he found out his father had been lying to him his entire life about who he was in this world. Okay so he prayed, just not religiously, and none of those prayers felt real. They were out of desperation, which from what he understood, did not count.

In his mind, real prayer would come on a perfectly calm day. Like, when you didn't need it. Of course, his mother told him God wanted to hear from him whenever, but his mother believed a lot of things Seth didn't.

Scooting to the far inside of the bench, he leaned against the tight wood lacing of the partition. Peering through one of the small holes, he could sort of make out the shape of the woman on the other side of the room, but the thickness of the wood made it hard. It was like looking through a straw.

The genders were separated just as thoroughly as if there were a wall down the center of the room.

Folding his arms, he closed his eyes and thought. Not about his responsibility, but about this place itself. His mind skipped from his father and mother to the people here. They all believed they lived outside the Garden of Eden. That they were *guarding* it. Guarding it from what?

His father believing this blew him away.

Seth recalled all he knew about the garden. How it was supposed to be a paradise, with animals and plants. How the Tree of Knowledge of Good and Evil was there, and how Adam and Eve had eaten from that tree and gotten in trouble with God.

He thought about what happened after they ate. How God tossed them out on their own to work by the *sweat of their brow* or whatever. It was then that he remembered the other tree, the Tree of Life. Seth thought hard to remember what he knew about that tree from the bible. It, too, was in his father's painting in the background as a sparkling speck of light and willow branches. Didn't God say to Adam and Eve if they ate of that tree, they would live forever or something? He always chalked that up to some kind of symbolic mumbo-jumbo but...

...but, what if that were a literal warning?

Seth doubted it. Why in this world ruled by scientific laws would there be a tree that made you live forever? That kind of thing was reserved for fantasy. Wish fulfillment at its finest. People like Hitler, people obsessed with power, people convinced they themselves were saviors to their fellow humans, those were the people that believed in the holy grail. From his knowledge, in the end, that belief led to a lifelong obsession that was never satisfied.

This interested him, though, and it was exactly the kind of thing that would interest Jeremiah. He wished he had a bible so he could read the account and figure it out.

He *was* in a chapel.

Though these people didn't claim to be religious, they might have a bible here. Looking around, he pulled a book from a cubby in the pew in front of him. He flipped its hard cover open. The pages were covered with lines of music. He shoved it back and moved to the next book. He pulled out a book with some sort of oriental lettering on it. The next book he recognized as Farsi. He reached to the next pew and saw a big one. He pulled it out and looked. It had a golden embossed animal of some sort on the front. He flipped it open. It was a bible. Turning through the first few pages he searched. It took him several minutes, but finally, in chapter three, he found it.

Softly he read, *"And the Lord God said, behold the man is become as one of us to know good and evil and now lest he put forth his hand and take also of the tree of life and eat and live forever:"*

There it was. If they ate of the tree they would live forever. Maybe it explained more. His eyes went to the words again, scanning. Blah blah blah...

"...live forever in their sins." that didn't sound good. Like a pandora's box. He kept looking.

"So, he drove out the man; and he placed at the east of the garden of Eden Cherubims and a flaming sword which turned every way to keep the way of the tree of life."

Keeping his finger in the place he absentmindedly closed the cover, an idea forming in his mind. He looked down at the book with amazement but didn't have time to complete whatever seed was starting to grow because the golden animal on the cover of the bible caught his attention again. It had four heads, each with a different face: one of a man, one of a lion, one of a cow, and one of an eagle or bird of some sort. It also had four wings, cow feet, and under its wings, hands of a man, one of which held a sword.

"Wow." Seth whispered, intent on the embossing.

"It is beautiful isn't it?" A high, quiet voice asked him. Startled, Seth dropped the book and when he bent to grab it up again, he smacked his head, hard, on the pew in front of him.

"Ouch," he hissed and abraded the sore spot with the hand not picking up the bible.

Thankfully, no giggles came from the other side of the partition.

"Are you alright?" the rather concerned sounding voice asked.

Seth glanced over at the stranger. His vision blurry from the tears in his eyes, he managed to make out spots of yellow and blue. The lattice wood wasn't helping.

She asked again, "Are you alright? Should I fetch someone, your mother, or Doctor Harrison?" She started to stand.

"No, no, no. I'm not a toddler." He reached out toward her and got the carved wood instead. "I'm fine. It's nothing, a head bonk. Although it was served with a slice of wounded pride." Then he thought aloud, "You have a doctor here? What kind of doctor?"

"Um the typical kind I suppose, except he doesn't have any fancy equipment. I don't think a hematoma, even one the size of yours, requires a doctor though." She sighed. "Still, you should get some ice on that." She added also touching the partition as she tried to maneuver her gaze around the lacing of the wood.

"Who needs the doctor when you're here?" Seth asked wiping at the tears in his eyes and blinking. Wow, his head hurt.

"Oh," She said and turned away. "I'm sorry."

Seth realized his directness. Quickly he added. "I'm not trying to be..." He stopped and pulled his hands away from his face and glanced at the blonde streak of hair. "Thank you, for your...concern."

She turned a bit back, her face down. He looked through the screen of wood and tried to make her out. But with his watery eyes the only details were her light blonde hair and her blue dress.

"Okay." She said quietly.

"So..." Seth started rubbing at his head again. "...what brings you here?" After hurting her feelings, he didn't know what else to say. He hoped he didn't have brain damage.

"This is a place for quiet reflection. Did you not know this?" She whispered and again turned away from him, a gesture that told him to shut up. The gesture, the divider, and her whispering made him wonder if they weren't *allowed* to have a conversation here.

He responded anyway, in a whisper of course. "Oh, yeah, I guess it is." She would not turn toward him, and her hair did a right proper job of shielding her face from him. "So, is that why you're here? Don't get enough religion here in Edenia? But, wait, I thought you guys didn't believe in any religion, 'your life is your religion' or something."

She sighed, again, a great big weary one this time though. She, very purposely to his way of thinking, kept her face away from him. "Must you be so...offensive?"

This silenced him. He did have a way of putting his foot in his mouth. Especially when it was time to be extra careful. *Not all talents are appreciated.* He turned a little in his seat and rubbed his head again, while looking at the bible. How was he going to get what he needed if he upset everyone he met?

The girl surprised him by speaking to him again. "If you must know, I suppose I am troubled." Her whisper was businesslike, and it had an annoyed hastiness to it.

Seth smirked, "Tell me about it. Are you new here too?" The second the words were out of his mouth he knew they were ridiculous, and they betrayed too much of what was bugging him.

This girl was spot on; he needed to guard his tongue better.

"No." She said with venom, but he quickly realized it wasn't directed at him. "I will *never* be new to any place, ever. Can you imagine never going anywhere, never experiencing anything new? Do not answer that because there is no way you can understand, you came from out there." She sniffed and flicked her hair, but she went on so quickly that Seth barely had time to notice how long and blonde and fragrant that hair was. "There is one thing I have seen every night in my dreams, and that was me, living on the outside. And that, I suppose, is the point of my trouble. My heart was set and now it hurts." She sniffed again, making Seth wonder if she was crying.

For some reason, he found the mixture of her venom and her tears appealing. This girl wasn't a pushover, or a robot, or a maniacal do-gooder like everyone else he'd met in Edenia. She had a brain in her head. And she was dissatisfied, an emotion he could connect with, big time. Still, he didn't know what to say, so he latched on to the first thought he had and rambled. "I have this recurring dream too. So, I'm in a huge city..." He shifted in his seat, realizing how personal this conversation just turned. He'd never told anyone about this dream.

She sniffed again and turned her face a bit toward him. "Yes?"

He supposed it was too late to turn back now, so he barreled onward. "...but the buildings, they're not really buildings, they're like...people, but they look like buildings, but with faces. Yeah, weird I know. So, all the building/people are touching each other like, their arms and legs act sort of like bridges between them, connecting them, ya know? Then, in the middle of this city there's my family and me, only there's this great empty space around us. None of the arms connect to us. We just stand there, a small clump, and nothing ties us to anything. We are alone. We are different. And then they all look at us, the other buildings I mean. And I can't explain why, but I just know they are thinking we're abnormal. They pity us and hate us." Seth paused and shifted his unfocused eyes to the partition. "I have no idea why I just told you that. Probably because you mentioned dreams."

"I don't think so; this dream seems to mean something to you. In fact, I think you know the answer to this, you're just not acknowledging it."

He turned questioning eyes toward her.

She continued. "I heard that your father lied to you your whole life. Telling you that you had no family, nothing to connect you to the world and to the past. You felt different because if there is one thing everyone has, it is family. Good or bad, we all have them. It is weighing on your heart now because you suddenly have more family than you can deal with. Not only that, but as Ezekiel's son you are an important part of a community here in Edenia. You went from having no family to having a thousand family members. Basically, your dearest wish has come true. You have bridges now. You are connected. But..." she stopped.

Her words were blowing his mind, but he didn't want her to stop. "Go on."

"I do not know if I should."

This intrigued him even more, "Please."

She paused for a full minute and then added slowly, "But, I get the sense that family—gained this way—does not seem like a blessing, perhaps it seems more like a millstone around your neck. Perhaps you do not really want it if it comes dressed in homespun and dragging the odd traditions of Edenia behind it. Maybe in not too long a time you will be the one pointing and pitying and thinking we are the abnormal ones."

These words took him by surprise and cut him to his core. He had two current situations to contrast here. How easy it was to accept Jeremiah and how turned off he was by Hirum.

She was right.

Further, he hadn't known consciously what that dream meant, only how it made him feel, but now he understood it. This stranger helped him understand something he'd struggled with for years, perhaps his whole life.

He felt so overwhelmed. It was difficult for him to comprehend. And then on top of that, the shame her words brought him. He was doing that, absolutely. Being all judgy. Pointing at the Edenians and considering their way of life abnormal. Crazy or not, they probably had a reason for doing what they did.

Making sure eternal life didn't get passed around to the whole world, if a real job, would be a rather important one. He looked down at the creature on the front of the bible. God put a cherubim in the garden to guard it. The bible said so. So, why are these people here?

It all seemed confusing. Maybe if he understood that one thing he would be able to look past the oddness here and consider this an adventure. Or at least he might be able to connect with someone here.

He wanted to ask these weighty questions of this girl who had in a short time endeared herself to him with these tactfully spoken truth bombs. He wondered if she was a relative, but before he asked, she spoke again.

Her voice and tone softened in a subtle but attractive way so that he forgot his question. "I cannot imagine how hard all this is for you."

Forgetting the dream, he considered the last forty-eight hours and wondered at the violent swirl of emotions inside him. Without meaning to, and in spite of his recent decision of keeping things to himself, he opened his mouth. "It's just..." He grunted, "There were things...really, important things happening in our lives back home." After a little pause and a grimace at the irony of it all he continued. "You know, we were packing up anyway." He paused but not in a way that prompted a response. "Yeah, we were moving to Baltimore."

He breathed out heavily. "So, there we were, getting ready to hop on a boat, with just a few personal items in a bag. But then my dad takes the wrong terminal on the American side. *What are you doing? I ask him. Oh nothing, I just need us to make one stop first.* Okay, your timing sucks dad, but no problem. And the next thing I know, a bus is dumping us off in the middle of nowhere, a thousand miles away from our supposed new home and we walk into this place. Which so far hasn't been the end of the world, generally speaking. But in one particular way, it seems like the end of the world to me." he paused again and then found himself chuckling. "In an 'I-don't-want-to-face-reality' way it actually feels kind of like we're on a very weird vacation. Of course, I haven't started cleaning up animal poop yet so...yeah. That's my job here, FYI." His smirk lingered and before he knew it, he revealed one of his deepest angers. "Did you know that my dad didn't just tell us we had no relatives, he told us all his relatives were dead? How sick is that?" With this admission, the dream came back to his mind. He understood it so much better now, thanks to this random girl. But he also saw that the dream could change if he would allow it to.

There was a long pause from her as he thought and seethed. But then the girl asked, in a quiet, very confused voice, "So to get on a boat, you hop?"

Seth turned toward the girl, instantly bemused. What was she on about? Boats? He'd just bared his soul. Her voice was so serious and mystified, her question so ridiculous, so innocent that, in that moment, it just struck Seth exactly right, and he busted up. His loud laugh disturbed the entire room, but he kept it up until his anger and helplessness seemed to lessen, as if with each breath it seeped out of him...as if warm fingers of mirth pulled it out of him and loosed it like a kite in the wind.

Maybe a minute later he lifted his head from his crouched position, where he had been attempting to at least quiet his laughter, to find that the girl had gone.

He looked around the chapel but saw no one now. Confused by

why she'd gone, he still felt grateful to the mysterious girl and couldn't help smiling to himself. He felt better. At least for now. How bizarre was that? Also, it felt good to laugh. There'd been little of that going on in his life of late. The girl made it so easy for him to verbally vomit what was inside him, and letting all that out helped. Weird.

Even weirder was the way his heart felt. Like he felt connected. It could have been because he opened up, but it also could be just her. If there were a few more people like her in Edenia mixed in among his relatives, he might be willing to stay even if they were all crazy. He wanted to thank her right now. He stood to do just that.

He'd looked for as long as he dared but never saw the girl. He felt the loss, too, because his grandparents were weird.

Seth could not understand why the idea of grandparents meant so much to him. The dream of having a deep and profound connection to wise, lemonade drinking, white haired, smiling old people; to somehow have a tether of blood and genetics to stories and people long gone, was something he'd needed from the first moment he discovered he was the only kid without it.

So, to say that his expectations going in were high was an understatement. But he felt no magical connection to the elderly people sitting before him, nor any deep roots sprouting just by talking to them. In fact, they were a little stand-offish. Sure, they greeted him and his family with hugs. Sure, they smelled like old people, and sure, they looked and walked and talked like porch-sitting lemonade drinkers but there just was no connection, not like he'd had with the girl in the chapel or with Jeremiah, and the lack crushed a part of Seth's soul.

At the 'this-is-too-excruciating' point, his grandfather asked the kids and the women to all sit in the living room while he spoke with Seth's father alone.

His grandmother brought out water and meatless sandwiches for everyone and sat asking polite questions. She had bright green eyes that were the same extra-large oval as one of his cousin's; he couldn't remember her name. It was a unique trait, and it occurred to him that perhaps one day one of his children could have his grandmother's eyes. That thought warmed him for a moment. He also could see his Uncle Hirum in her face, in her chin and nose. She used her hands when she spoke the way that Eve did, and a glimmer of happiness flickered in his heart.

Seth looked at his sisters, hoping to see his happiness mirrored in their faces. There was no such happiness. Something caught his eye. It was the small dimple in Lillian's chin when she smiled. None of the Johnsons knew where she got that dimple. Seth looked back at his grandmother and couldn't help but catalog and compare her to his sister. The opposition of features was overwhelming.

Objectively speaking, the people before him looked nothing alike: lights vs. darks, thins vs. fulls, longs vs. shorts, round vs. almond.

Seth felt his flicker of joy disintegrate.

There was not a single resemblance between the Johnson twins and the woman before him.

When the old woman turned to him and started to ask another pointless question, Seth couldn't take it anymore. He quickly rose from his chair and asked to be excused as he rushed from the little living room. He fled out the door, across the porch and down into the street.

He'd been faking it. He felt nothing for any of them, and sitting around wasting time while Lillian suffered was just unbearable. After the family meeting first thing that morning, she'd gotten a horrible headache and stayed in bed until right before it was time for them to meet their grandparents. Those headaches were her life and it would only get worse. Small motor function loss was next, loss of purposeful speech, then loss of motion and speech completely, then her vital organs wouldn't receive the stimulus they needed.

He felt like he was suffocating.

Once he'd escaped, he started running. After an indeterminable time, his lungs ached and burned, and instead of feeling like he couldn't get enough breath he finally felt like he was breathing. At that point, his mind cleared, and it didn't take any thought to know what he needed to do or where he needed to go.

His feet took him toward the bridge that spanned the Eden River which led into the small circle of trees called the garden.

He saw his destination from a way off, it curved in a lovely arch over the water and was ornately carved. With the sound of the water and the backdrop of lush trees, this bridge made an ideal setting. As he jogged toward it, he glanced at the small wooded area beyond and wondered how he would know which one was the tree of life. Would it sparkle or glow or be massive and ancient looking?

He slowed to a walk as he wondered at the trees, trying to see what he could from his side of the river. He hadn't noticed the watery haze gathering on the ground. Within a matter of moments, the mist and fog were so thick around him he couldn't see but a few steps in front of him. By the time he'd gotten to the bridge his feet were parting a thick mist with each step; so much so he couldn't see where to step on to the bridge. The way it gathered so quick and the way it was so thick, it felt supernatural.

He looked up. The sun stood bright in the sky. Still, this eerie fog rose off the ground now, and rose until his whole body was enveloped. This forced him to grapple for the railing of the bridge.

He knew where he was going, though, and regardless of how freaky the fog was, he told himself it wouldn't stop him from his task. He continued onward, albeit at a much slower pace.

It took him quite a while, but he made it to the middle of the bridge. The wooden planks were slick with water, and the curvature of the bridge was steep, so Seth held tight to the railing. A half-dozen steps passed, then he brought his foot forward, his body at an angle. His arms pulled at the railing when a sequence of events took place.

His foot hit a solid object of some sort, perhaps an uneven plank or something, but the sudden loss of forward momentum caused him to stumble. Combined with the decline and the wet wood, he couldn't find any footing. Before he understood what was happening, his hand let go of the top railing, as his legs and feet slipped under the high guard rail and over the edge of the bridge boards. At the last second, he caught a lower railing and held on as best he could in the wet conditions.

When his mind caught up with his circumstances, he found he was dangling precariously over the fast-moving river.

Seth felt adrenaline pumping through him, but as he attempted to pull himself up, it felt as if something held him down. Though he was no stranger to pulling his body weight up, he could not make any headway. His arms strained. His hand slipped. Just before he gave in, he looked down at the mist-covered water. It wasn't too far to drop down, but he knew that the water moved swiftly. Still, he was a decent swimmer.

Before he could decide anything, the rail his fingertips held on to shifted with a screeching sound and his left hand was pushed off the edge. Now he dangled by one hand and he could only hold it a few seconds before he slipped. He splashed into the water and was swept away with the current.

Seth gasped as his head rose out of the frigid water. He attempted to swim, but it did him no good. The river carried him quickly along its own path. Coughing and swallowing water he attempted to stay at the surface. The rushing river brought him out of the fog and he could see up ahead there was the dam and spinning water wheel. He did not want to tangle with that, but before he could use the rest of his measly power to make a move toward the bank, it felt as if a wild current in the water carried him to the exact spot on the bank he desired. Then a force seemed to shove him out of the water.

Seth slipped and scrambled and splashed and made a ruckus of getting up the bank. Instantly, he shivered as he moved, tripping over the rocks and gnarled roots underfoot. He felt, rather than saw, someone behind him and when he turned, a large man stood next to him. He also was wet and seemed to have the back of Seth's shirt in hand, though he hadn't noticed it before now.

To his left he heard, "Ho there." and caught sight of someone jogging down the bank toward them.

Confused, Seth looked up at the man and chattered, "What's happening?"

"I just fished you out of the river. How in the blue blazes did you get in there?" The man had misty gray eyes so clear and bright, like water lapping on a shore of black pupil. Wait, was it the cold or were the eyes actually lapping? Seth shook the wet hair from his face and looked again. It was just his imagination.

The running man arrived with his face pink from the wind and the chill, his brown hair wild and his eyes incredibly bright blue. "Oh, good, Benjamin. You have him."

"Yes, tell me what is happening, Nate. This boy just about drowned himself."

The man named Nate was familiar to him; he was certainly a relative. "I was passing by the bridge when I saw him go over."

"I see." Benjamin said slowly.

"He's freezing. Let's get him home."

"Let us, indeed."

Benjamin and Nate practically carried Seth halfway to his house as he shivered and chattered with cold. By the time they deposited him at his door he could say, "Thank you. I got it." His mind enough with him to be embarrassed about having to be babied.

He stumbled to his room, stripped and huddled in his bed. His exhausted body shivered its way into a fitful sleep where there were restless dreams of drowning and nightmares of Lillian's death.

CHAPTER 11

The story went that when Peter Miller was five (after a rather nasty episode involving a throw-rug, a pair of socks, a warm apple pie, and a flight for life) he'd named the front screen door Butch. To this day Peter feared getting another chunk bitten out of him by Butch and this fear affected him every time he used the thing.

Butch's spring slammed shut with a deafening whap and nearly munched his leg as he exited his home, but not even that could get him down today. Taking the steps down to the yard two at a time, he whistled a happy little ditty and cut across the lawn.

Friday night after Ezekiel—his adopted uncle—was reintroduced to the town, Peter met his new "cousins", Abigail and Lillian. The highly attractive pair just happened to be his age, which worked out well for Peter because they wanted to know all the gossip about their classmates, and Peter, being at the center of everything worth gossiping about, had dished with exuberance about his latest exploits. Of course, he had to leave out all the parts where Natures were involved, making the stories sound more like child's play. Still the girls laughed.

As the night progressed and Peter learned more of the twins, he found that they were peas in his figurative pod. Thankfully, too, because Peter felt pretty lonely in that pod.

Peter appreciated that these girls were just what he imagined outsiders should be. They were beguiling and comical and interesting. Not anxious and submissive, like so many of the other new families that walked up the Edenia road.

Come to think, it had been two years since the last outsiders (the Oliver family) came as the summons required. They had two boys the same ages as Peter and Miriam. The eldest brother was a bit mentally challenged. (Not literally, but he was head over heels in love with Miriam. Enough said.) Bruce Oliver was in Peter's class and they had some fun times, but Peter felt like he had to force things with him. It felt like he couldn't be himself or else he would bring Bruce down, or something. In fact, he felt that way about almost everyone.

But now, the girls were here.

Sure, they were a bit snobby, but they laughed at everything he said, so naturally there was a kinship there. He got the feeling they were cut from the same devious cloth as himself, and if things worked out the way he planned, he'd have two very appealing sidekicks. He felt hope like a tiny little seedling being planted in his soul.

Then there were other things to be considered.

He couldn't decide which of the two he liked more. Lillian was most definitely prettiest. Peter thought of the jeans she'd been wearing and felt his face go hot. A hurly-burly of sensations started in his stomach. This had been happening a lot lately, especially when he thought about girls, and it was annoying but perfectly normal according to papa, but annoying, nonetheless. As the sensations spread, he knew he had to do something about it or there could be ramifications, so he followed his father's instructions and slapped himself across the face. Hard.

Grunting, he rubbed at his cheek as he walked through his sister Hannah's yard and on to his Uncle Martin's. "Ouch." He said aloud. When he looked up, he noticed his nosey uncle on the porch swing. The man worried more about Peter's dysfunctional Nature than Peter himself did. Peter wondered if he'd seen the whole slapping business. Embarrassed and uninterested in talking with his uncle he quickened his pace.

"How goes it, Pete?" Came the familiar voice.

Whenever his uncle asked this question, Peter knew what he meant: *has anything changed with your Nature?*

Unconsciously, he answered that question instead of the proffered one. "Nope." Peter said a bit more chipper than he should be on the subject.

His uncle's brow became knotted, but it didn't stop him from saying what he wanted. "I've been thinking, maybe if you spent more time in your books and obeying your parents, you'd have less time to use your wit like a degenerate. Then perhaps things would go as they should...with your Nature, I mean. What do you think?"

Peter's feet stopped moving.

He had never considered linking his dysfunctional Nature to his behavior. It just didn't work like that, did it? His mind spun into a million facets of how he possibly had sabotaged himself. Images of terrified relatives and friends running from his pranks, delirious chickens unable to lay eggs, upset cows mooing...and manure. Manure in everything from sock drawers to pasta salad filled his mind.

What had he done?

Horrible guilt—a feeling he'd rarely entertained—bubbled up in his gut, and he couldn't shove it back down.

He glared at his uncle and, without answering the man, stomped toward school. What was he going to do? Would he have to give up all his fun and become a goody-two-shoes in order to have his Nature take him fully?

He felt himself gag a little at this thought, but calmed the reflex. Mama had served grits and eggs this morning and there was no way he wanted to experience that twice.

Within a minute that sensation cleared, and Peter could think. He knew, down to his toes, that falling in line was exactly what he would do if it were necessary. He wanted to be a Guardian every moment his whole life long. Who could ask for a better job, or calling?

From what he'd read, the outside world fantasized with every line of literature that they were as cool as Edenians. He was like a superhero, or he would be. Just being born here made him unique. He didn't have to do a dang thing to earn it.

However, with that kind of privilege came responsibility and seclusion. Peter knew in less than a second that none of that mattered. Only being a Guardian mattered.

Bring it on, Peter thought as he tromped up the steps to North School. He would do anything necessary to be a Guardian, even change his whole personality if that was required.

In that moment he felt something, a kind of knowledge, overtake his mind. It filled him completely and distinctly and without any misunderstanding. His dysfunctional Nature had nothing to do with his extracurricular activities. The thought of timing imprinted on his mind. This was about having it happen at the right moment.

As he reached for the handle and pulled, the sun shimmered off the shiny metal, blinding him. Peter closed his eyes for a moment, and as he did, the familiar panorama from his dream popped before his mind again. It was scene after scene of perfectly timed pranks. For the second time in the matter of moments he felt the thick reassurance of this message. It reaffirmed the idea of timing. It reaffirmed that he was worthy. It reaffirmed that the Master was in control.

Relief tumbled through his belly. It shamed him that he'd doubted.

He thought about the neat experience as he walked through the hallway and he wondered if the Master had just touched his mind. The clarity of the thoughts made him think it was Him.

Peter walked quickly down the busy hall. He pulled open the door to his first class, *Western Mannerisms.* Sitting at his desk, he felt comforted by his usual group of classmates sitting in a semicircle. Turning, he noticed his sister.

"So good of you to join us, Peter." Esther, his sister and teacher, commented in her snooty way. "Why in Heaven is your cheek all red? Did mother already get after you today?"

Trena laughed. She would, she was such a brown nose.

"No, Esther. In fact, I was just slapping myself. Ya know, practice for later today when you bore me into a sleepy haze."

Everyone laughed then, even some kids in the adjacent semicircles.

Esther's face went so pink Peter thought the color might spread to her pale cornmeal-colored hair. Pink might be an improvement. She shoved the short waves out of her face, but she did not respond.

She knows better, Peter thought smugly.

Instead she demanded, "Sortez vos livres." She might be deficient as a human, but Esther's French was impeccable. At least by Peter's standard. Peter reached down obediently for his workbook and fumbled around a bit under his seat.

Plopping down the sought-after book, he pulled the brown-paper-covered flap open. This was not his French workbook; it was contraband; a Superman comic book. Garren would kill him if he noticed this book missing from his stash of forbidden outside imports.

Esther's eyes fell on the colorful pages and she leaned over, "Qu'est-ce que c'est?"

She reached for the book but at that blessed moment Mrs. Brandy cleared her throat, "Excusez-moi" and flicked the lights.

Out of the darkness of the flashing light came the two most beautiful figures a boy could hope to see.

Lillian flipped dark strands of hair over her shoulder and smiled at him. With his mind already transferred to French, he could only think, *Ooo la la.*

Promptly he slapped himself again, but in a reserved manner this time. But Esther saw him and smiled knowingly. *Shoot!*

Mrs. Brandy turned to Abigail and Lillian and asked, "I assume you do not speak French?"

The girls looked at one another, but Abigail answered, "Only the smallest bit, but we do speak some Arabic."

Mrs. Brandy nodded then looked around the room. "Well, it just so happens we have a wonderful French instructor. Esther, would you mind?"

Peter's sister nodded happily.

Mrs. Brandy ushered the girls to Peter's semicircle as she spoke to them. He'd been excited to sit in the same room with them but this, to have them join his group, was awesome!

"With Esther's help, I am sure you will be caught up in no time."

Not likely.

When Esther wasn't being completely ridiculous, she'd said Edenia's junior school was comparable to college on the outside. The obligatory hour of 'French only' for thirteen-year-old's, she used as evidence.

Mrs. Brandy went on. "Just make sure you get plenty of rest, you'll need it. And eat properly. You're water drinkers, aren't you?"

Again, Abigail spoke first, answering the rather weird question. "Uh, yeah."

"Well that's great. So many kids from the outside are hooked on the sugary soda pop, and they forget that water is the fountain of youth. Anyhow, it will help for sure." Mrs. Brandy smiled.

So, Mrs. Brandy was one of those.

Some Edenians thought because the river Eden came out of the garden and supplied life to the whole town that it was a physical explanation for Edenians Natures. You drink, you eat, you get superpowers. This idea was supported by the fact that if you left Edenia, with in a short time your Nature unraveled until your returned. Even Guardian eyes changed—back to their natural color. One more reason to keep the Joneses (and the world) far, far away from Edenia.

As desks were gathered, Abigail and Lillian shoved in on either side of Peter. They didn't seem happy about cramming their tangle of legs and skirts under the desk. The proper attire always was a problem for newbies. Still, they seemed happy to see him. Bright smiles met him on both sides, and boy, did they feel like the sun.

Harry Potter had inconspicuously found its way to the back of

Peter's under-chair basket and his French reader now lay at his elbows.

Esther looked down to his book and narrowed her blazing, bright green eyes at him. She wasn't stupid, and glanced down at his basket.

He was so busted.

Swallowing, he spoke, "Ne pensez-vous pas Abby et Lilly pourrait utiliser un lecteur." He asked Esther innocently.

"Don't speak French now Peter." Esther snipped. "The girls can't understand you." Still she bustled away. Going to get a reader for them as he'd suggested.

The rest of the room went back to business as usual but everyone in Peter's group smiled at the girls, who were smiling at Peter.

"Good morning cousins." He beamed at them. "So happy you could join us."

"It wasn't an accident." Lillian said looking over at her sister conspiratorially.

"Uh-uh, nope." Added Abigail, with a violent shake of her head and a smirk on her puffy lips.

"Abby told Mrs. Brandy last night that it was absolutely necessary to our happiness that she put us in your group." Lilly added.

"She was very reasonable. I hardly had to tear up before she was giving in." The smug look on her face seemed to take a little of the pretty away, but only for a moment.

"Yes, Mrs. Brandy is a softy." Peter looked over at Lan who was now glaring at the girls. Mrs. Brandy was his mother.

Peter looked back at Abby, inconspicuously placed a finger over his lips, and glanced out of the corner of his eye to Lan. "Let me introduce you to the gang."

"Great!" The girls said together.

PETER SET down his plate on the yellow-oak lunch table as Lillian went on. "Seth hated it. You could totally tell. He actually walked out. And I'll admit I was there with him. It just was totally weird; *Grandparents*. Honestly I don't know what I feel about it..."

Abby finished the thought, "Like, suddenly you have all this family that loves you and wants to know everything about you, but you couldn't care less about them because your dance-card is full."

Peter tried not to be offended when he asked, "What do you mean?"

The twins looked at one another but Abby spoke. "Seth is kind of left out in our family, and so he has this need to be connected to other people. He just about passed out meeting our grandma and grandpa yesterday. But we aren't like him, we don't need anyone. We have always had each other. So, our social card, or our need for other people is pretty nonexistent. As long as we have each other..." She paused and looked over at her sister and Peter watched some great sadness fill Abby's face.

At that moment, Lilly turned to him and much more loudly and exuberantly than necessary stated, "You really don't eat meat? Not at all? Not even a sausage?"

Abby sniffed and picked up her fork as she chided, "Eeew, that is so gross, Lilly. We don't really eat meat either, but not by choice."

"Sausage?" Peter wondered out loud.

"Yes, it's three ounces of goodness that I dream about eating again someday when I don't care how fat I get."

They looked at one another and it wasn't a normal glance, it was as if they were both about to burst out in tears.

Peter took the opportunity to bust in. "I wouldn't say I *never* eat meat, but here in Edenia it is meant only for times of great need, not for everyday use."

The girls' eyes left one another's and looked at him.

Abby answered, "That's where dad got it. I don't get it though. So, like, if there's a famine or drought or something? Does that even happen here? From what I learned Friday, your God person or whatever, controls everything in Edenia, including the environment."

She emphasized the name, God, in a way that felt a tad condescending to Peter, but he ignored it. "The Master is not God. They are different. But yes, I suppose you're right in a way, but doesn't God control the environment of the whole world?"

"So, you believe in God? I thought you didn't, like you weren't religious."

"That is a really big, personal question and we've only just met." He evaded and offered them a hopefully charming smile. No way was he going to go into all of that right now.

"You didn't answer the question."

Peter sighed and went with the lesser of the two evil probes. "Actually no, I've never seen a drought." But he did so begrudgingly.

"Did you see what he did there?"

"Yes." Abby commented and raised an eyebrow at him.

Lilly laughed, "I can roll with it. So, you really have never eaten meat then?"

Peter swished his water around in its cup, thankful she helped him pull the subject change. Besides, they were going to find out soon enough what kind of place they had moved too. "No, actually, I haven't."

"Wow."

"Like never, never?"

"Not even a tiny little sausage?"

Peter shook his head.

Abby's face distorted unattractively. "That is so...weird."

"Totally, off the charts."

"I never understood Dad's problem before."

Lilly nudged her sister and smiled knowingly. "Right. He was raised that way. Geesh, I feel like I am getting an education already."

"Besides, like all the Hindu people we met didn't eat meat, so maybe it's not that weird."

"For the USA it's weird."

"Yes, I guess. You are all supposed to be fat and have French fries hanging out of your mouths, right?"

He stopped with a carrot halfway to his mouth and narrowed his eyes at the girls sitting across from him. They had just about insulted every part of him and it felt very awkward for some reason.

"Before you disparage another person perhaps you should get to know them first. For starters I am an American, I think, and I have never eaten a french fry. I think you might be impressed to know that we in Edenia grow or make every single thing you or I will put into our mouths. We sew most of our own clothes and build our own homes."

After a rather loaded clearing of throats, and an uncomfortable pause that begged him to finish his comment and turn this thing around, Abigail said, "You sound proud of that, but to me it just sounds like a stubborn..."

Her sister cut her off, "Your dad, um, Uncle Hirum, said you use nothing that takes gas in Edenia." She sent a glare to Abby.

"Yep. That's right." Peter answered and looked around the rather large lunch area avoiding the twin's eyes.

"So, does that mean you've never been in a car or like on a motorcycle or anything?"

"I have never been in a car. I've never actually seen a running car. Sometimes they break down right outside of town but that doesn't count, does it?"

"Nope." The girls said in unison.

His usual lunch buddies watched him. He nodded toward them and noticed kids glancing at Abby and Lilly.

"But you have electricity." Lilly offered speculatively and almost sympathetically.

"Thank God." Abigail added. Peter glanced at her and she covered her mouth, her eyes apologetic. "Is that bad to say?"

Softening his face, he smiled and took a fork to his fruit dish. He didn't like the way this was going at all. Not only did he sound totally pitiful, but now, *he* was the goody-two-shoes? He gave up with a sigh and just answered. "It depends on how you meant it."

"I meant I'm really, really grateful. I don't know what I would do if you didn't have electricity."

Lilly butted in, questions all over her questions. "Yeah, so why is that again?"

Peter swallowed and just told it straight. "Well, ok so this is the way we see the world. It has smart things in it. We want to have all the smart things that are possible to have, but we want them here where we can be separate. And we don't want them to crowd out the distraction and satisfaction that hard work offers." He realized he sounded like he was quoting from like a mission statement or something. Perhaps he was. Sighing again, he went on. "As soon as electricity was invented, Tobias Miller, my, great-great-grandfather knew he could produce it with a dam and water wheel. So, he built one. Our wheel powers the entire community."

"Is that impressive?" Lilly asked innocently. As Abigail asked, "How many people live here?" They looked at one another and smiled, then, Abigail turned back to Peter, "We do that all the time."

With a smile, he glanced at Abby and answered both questions succinctly. "About one thousand people live here. And from what I understand, providing sufficient electricity for this many people with our tiny setup, is so impressive that *only magic or God* could do it."

"But you don't believe in either of those things?" Abby pressed.

Peter shrugged again shutting the conversation down.

The girls chewed in silence for a minute before Abby asked, "So tell me more about this community sharing thing you do. Are you all *forced* to share food and stuff?"

"No, no, no. *That* would be interesting though." Peter laughed. "You can't force people to *share*."

"Our parents force us to share all the time." Lilly stated and spooned in some bean casserole.

Peter put thumb and index finger to his chin contemplatively.

"And how does that make you feel?" His voice mocked as his eyes narrowed and his head turned slightly to the side.

Lilly laughed but refrained from spitting her beans on him. Instead, she threw a carrot. She got him in the chest, dead center. He caught the carrot before it bit the dust and took a ravenous bite out of it. Chomping loudly while snuffling.

"Were you raised, in a barn?" Lilly laughed and threw another carrot his way.

"Why yes, yes I was as a matter of fact, and I have the manure to prove it."

"Yuck, you keep manure?"

He wagged his eyebrows at them, "Better be nice or you might just find a bit of horse droppings piled in an unexpected place."

"Ew!" Abby protested as Lilly laughed, "Gross! You wouldn't do that. For real?"

"I won't say it hasn't happened before. Me and poo, we have an understanding. So much so that I have been compiling a list of poo-isms..." He proceeded to tell them all about his many poo-scandals and both girls laughed and tossed food at him in a most appealing manner.

CHAPTER 12

Seth

Everyone in Seth's class was preparing for something called a Sabbatical. It was all they talked about for the last two hours of school. Still, Seth was a bit dubious as to what it all meant. Maybe it would be important. So, at the first opportunity he asked Eve to explain.

"He's talking like that because next week he's supposedly leaving on sabbatical. He's trying to sound like an outsider." She laughed, "Like you, I guess." She emphasized 'supposedly' but there was an airy, absent mindedness to her other words.

This was why he was hanging out with Eve. Maybe she would absentmindedly tell him everything he needed to know so this day wouldn't be such a total waste. There were only four days until Lillian's appointment in Baltimore, and he planned on being there if he had to walk through fire.

Pushing back all the anxiety, he asked, "What do you mean by sabbatical? I thought that was something professors did to," he donned a spectacularly stuffy sounding English accent, "get a break from the rigors of academia." His attempt to lighten the mood worked.

Eve descended into a giggling fit.

"You're funny!" She exclaimed to her surroundings—which happened to be all the seventeen-year-old boys in Edenia—and laughed a bit more. Seth kept quiet, hoping she would realize he wanted an answer.

Finally, she did.

"Oh, that was a real question, um, well, it's sort of like that, except for the opposite." Eve giggled a little to herself again and pulled Seth into a room clattering with voices and silverware.

Still, Seth stayed silent.

Glancing at him from the corner of her eye and then looking away a bit uncomfortably, she flipped her hair to one side and shrugged her shoulders. "This is a dreary subject; can't we talk about you? You aren't too upset about the whole electronics thing, are you? You know, even if you had something it wouldn't work here. We're in a dead zone."

"So, you have to be outside of Edenia for electronics to work?" That explained Jeremiah's extreme measures.

"Yes." She said smiling, thinking she'd changed the subject.

This electronic thing was important, but he pretty much already knew that. He needed to know what this sabbatical thing was.

"Hey, I'm feeling so lost here. Help me out. We've been talking about this sabbatical thing all day and I have no idea what it is. If I'm going to have to do it, I wanna know what it is."

"Well, you won't have to do it since you already lived in the outside, but I guess you could if you wanted to."

"Uh-huh." Seth said encouragingly.

"So, we spend lots of time learning about the outside because, well, the history of Edenia is boring, so what else is there to learn in school? And we have to go to school, idle hands and all. That's actually a huge reason we do a lot of things we do, and the way we do them. All in the pursuit of keeping busy. For those of us who were born here, all that learning can make you curious. So, the elders started the sabbatical."

When her prattle came to an end, Seth asked, "So, what, do you actually leave Edenia?" He was sure his father said they could never leave Edenia once they came. *Surprise, this move is permanent.* Just another one of the awesome ways his parents betrayed them.

"Sure. For a few years actually."

"Seriously?" He said thoughtfully.

So, if by chance things didn't work out with the plan, he could just suffer in silence until he was old enough to leave, then he would never come back. Relief flooded through his body at having a plan B.

"Why?" Seth asked not feigning interest anymore.

Eve shrugged again. "There are lots of reasons to go on sabbatical." She turned to face him and stopped to stand in the lunch line. "So, well, first and probably most important, it's a test of sorts."

"A test of what?"

"Well, of what we believe in, of course." She smiled broadly and moved forward.

"What do you mean? How can going outside test your beliefs?"

The smile completely left Eve's face for the first time since he met her, and she looked around a bit nervously. "You know," she leaned in close, "living outside just tests our resolve to live here. We can choose not to come back from sabbatical if we want, but no one has ever..." She trailed off, her hands clutching nervously at her skirt.

It was at this point Seth put two and two together. "No one but my father, or doesn't he count? Kind of ruins the stats, right?"

He gathered from her body language that what his father had done was wickedly uncool. Would that negative perception affect him and his mission, he wondered?

She glanced at him and quickly went on in a placating manner. "It's not about stats. It's about choice."

"Okay, I think I get it. So, what you're saying is that all of you get a break from this freak show? And you get to choose whether to come back, but nobody but my dad has ever stayed gone. How is that even possible?" He realized his mistake the minute Eve turned.

Her blue-green eyes were narrowed dangerously. "Who are you calling a freak show?"

Seth tried to backtrack. "I didn't mean you. No, you seem really normal. That's why I can talk to you. I just meant...I don't know what I meant. This is all really weird for me." He stepped closer to her and said, "Sorry Eve. Maybe if I have someone cool like you to explain things to me, I won't feel so..."

"Freaky." She finished for him then laughed a tinkling sort of laugh, all anger gone. She started walking again. "'Cause you know, Seth, here in Edenia, *you're* the only freak show."

CHAPTER 13

When the sixteen-year-old lunch began, Peter caught sight of Eve and Seth—heads together conspiratorially—talking. He hoped Eve was keeping her mouth shut. He brushed away a flying cauliflower chunk—the girls really liked throwing vegetables at him— and asked, "So what's up with your brother?" Peter nodded toward the couple making their way through the lunch line.

Both girls turned, stared for a few moments, glanced at one another with that knowing look again, before turning back to Peter, faces serious. Abby dipped a broccoli floret in the sauce on her noodles. She eyed it hesitantly. "You never finished telling us about how this place works."

It wasn't even a tricky evasion. He took a breath to let her know as much, when Lilly touched his hand. "I need to know everything." Her cold fingers left him with a chill up his back. A good chill. Like a shiver. What was he thinking about? His voice came out a shaky crescendo. "What do you want to know?"

She left her hand on his for the space of ten more seconds, looking deeply into his eyes.

Abby interrupted, "This whole place looks like some kind of Amish socialism to me."

"Except with way nicer clothes."

"Yeah, for sure."

Though her eyes were on her sister, Peter was sure that Lilly, who still touched his hand, could feel the instant heat filling his body.

His mind worked through the sensations as he attempted to concentrate. Why did everyone choose to misunderstand? The fierceness in him demanded that he defend. "You obviously don't understand socialism then. Here, you *choose* how you want to live. We care for one another out of choice, not force."

Abby fed off the contention in Peter's voice and answered with venom of her own. "You see Pete," the name had a bite to it, "it doesn't look that way to us." Abigail's eyes bored into Peter's. "I choose to have a phone, and a T.V. and..."

Lilly burst in, "sausage and soda and, and snickers."

Abby turned to her, "Shut up Lil, you never ate that crap anyhow."

"Yeah, well, that was then." She turned narrowed eyes at her sister, "This is now." Her voice was pointed, almost snippy.

Peter didn't understand any of it.

"Okay, whatever. Just stop distracting us." Abby looked back at Peter, "I want some answers."

He looked between them and contemplated how to explain his whole way of life to these girls without sounding as pathetic as he did before. Nothing came to mind. All he could think of was, *I can conceal myself and you will have a superpower too, in about a week.*

Finally, after an excruciating silence, he copped out. "Didn't the council explain it all? Or your dad?" The girls shared yet *another* look, and all the fire went out of them.

Did they have a language hidden in those glances?

Finally, Lilly spoke up, "We aren't really on speaking terms with our dad."

Peter said, "Oh."

Abby rolled her eyes, "Do you seriously think we listened to anything the old guys told us?"

Lilly smiled. "Yeah, the rustic décor was a bit distracting."

Abby added thoughtfully, "Though, there was a lot of drama about some mysterious incident, like twenty-something years ago. And our dads left for a while to talk about something *super-secret*."

"I wanted to ask questions, but..."

"Yeah, but just lots of hushed discussion." Abby pause looking again at her sister. "And then there was, of course, conversation about the garden." She added hesitantly.

"Of course." Peter said disarmingly. "You would have to talk about that, because that is why we are here. Isn't it?"

Abby had heard enough. Her face went all stoney. Annoyed she flipped her generous sheet of ebony hair back. "Okay, Pete. Enough games. Do you really think that you bunch of zealous Amish-wannabe freaks here are guarding the Garden of Eden?"

Peter felt his feet itch, and suddenly he could feel his Nature inside him. It was obvious and large and part of him. It was big and it grew, gathering, and filling him. Knowing right away that this gathering was different from any he'd experienced before, he gripped his pant legs and braced himself. This is how it started, everyone said so.

Any moment his irises would shudder for the first time. His Nature was taking him now, in the middle of lunch, in front of Abby and Lilly and everyone.

Why? Maybe as a response to what he felt was a threat? The insult?

His mind raced. Not three hours ago he'd known that his Nature was waiting on the right timing. How was now the right timing?

The feeling got so big he felt it would burst out of him. This was going to happen! He looked at Abby's annoyed expression.

"Wouldn't that be a story for TNC." Abby added, and this statement felt like a slap to his protective sensibilities. "I can see the headlines now; 'Crazy, loners'..." Abigail's eyes, which were still focused on him, suddenly went wide with fear and confusion and she stopped talking.

Lillian touched his hand again, "What's wrong..."

"...with your eyes?" Abby finished with a loud shriek, just as his Nature burst forth in full force.

Both girls stood quickly and grabbed at one another's hands and asked in unison, "What...where did he go?"

Abby yelled something else and then there was scraping chairs, whipping hair, and running feet.

He put his concealed hands up to cover his concealed face and shook his concealed head. It wasn't until he heard some tentative claps that he opened his eyes and looked around. His relatives and classmates were, now openly, giving him a round of applause.

He heard murmurs of, "It's about time." and responses of, "Yeah, but he is so dead."

CHAPTER 14

Seth

"... I'm not sure if he said it to get me angry or to intrigue me. Boys are so crazy, ya know?" Mentally Seth leveled the same accusation at Eve. She laughed. "That's a silly thing for me to say to you, you are one." Eve continued smiling while she preened her gorgeous hair like a blonde peacock on a fashion runway instead of sitting at a cafeteria table.

This chica was loony. Beautiful, but completely bonkers.

Well, she fit right in here.

Seth rubbed at the back of his neck and then looked again at Eve. She had turned her attention to Gregory, who sat next to her. The table burst with boys, all of whom had eyes for Eve. It didn't seem to matter that most of them were related to her, they hung on her every word, her every move. She'd mentioned that things had improved since the betrothal, and if this was better, perhaps the whole plan was a stroke of genius. None of these boys would be getting an ounce of schoolwork done if they thought they had a chance with Eve.

He shook his head and sighed. What would her world look like if she weren't so giggly? Focusing his attention on his plate of plain homemade noodles, he tried to block out her animated chatter. She had a table of admirers listening, she didn't need him.

They called this dish white spaghetti; it just plain lacked in all departments.

Who in their right mind would go without as much as these people did? Who would separate themselves from the world, to guard something that God had seen fit to guard himself? He and his father had talked, and in this, Seth heard a repeat of his father's sentiments, which bothered him. But he was right. If the garden of Eden was here, then didn't there need to be those weird cherubim? Maybe that was something the Edenians hid, these strange creatures. He would keep an eye out for them, just in case.

For a few hours he'd considered that perhaps these people themselves were four faced cherubim but they only let you see their human face. But that would mean that his father was one, wouldn't it? And there was no way his father was any sort of heavenly creature.

The idea was a stretch, but perhaps it would explain their abnormal eyes. He found himself staring hard at the lot of them. All sitting around eating lunch like they had nothing to hide.

"So, Seth." Gregory said, pulling Seth out of his thoughts.

He moved his chin toward the boy in acknowledgment.

"How are you doing? How's Edenia treating you?"

Seth held up a fork full of his pasta and pursed his lips. "I'll be honest," he watched the noodles unravel and flop back down in his bowl, "not so great. How in the world am I going to survive here?"

Eve smiled at him, "Oh you'll get used to it, don't you worry. And just think, in a few short weeks you'll be so healthy and strong."

"I didn't know I was lacking in the health or strength department."

"Of course you are, I am a bit of a health nut and I can tell you the diet of the outside hasn't done your body any good. You'll see." She grinned at him and raised her eyebrows excitedly.

"Awesome. Thanks. I'm so glad there's a silver lining."

And they were off again chatting away about nothing, and Seth returned to the thought thread he'd been working on.

What he didn't get was the whole threat of a cherubim with a flaming sword. How was that not enough to keep people away and uninterested, regardless of the power of the fruit of the tree? Eternal life means nothing to the already dead.

Besides, people weren't meant to live forever in his mind, but that was him.

He thought of Jeremiah. That man was highly interested. Seth thought of how he would tell his employer about the garden. He wondered if that was all they wanted to know. He had a suspicion it was not.

Fear climbed up Seth's spine as he thought of his timeframe.

Feeling insecure about all plans, he felt for the thick cell phone in his pants pocket. Jeremiah told him not to use it in Edenia and he hadn't, but he kept it on him. The battery was almost dead though, and he had plans to sneak down to the little shed outside of town where Jeremiah had a charging cable set up. He would have called Jeremiah then, though he had nothing to report yet. Yes, he knew about the Garden, but he couldn't imagine Jeremiah not knowing that too. It was what he was after.

His stomach growled, and it brought his eyes and thoughts down to the bowl in front of him. He'd go and call right after he ate. The rest of school could screw itself.

Seth spooned the noodles up and tucked it in. It actually didn't suck.

While chewing, he glanced past his table. Abby and Lilly sat across the room with another one of his cousins, *that little pest Peter*, he thought. Of course, he didn't know the kid, but he just had that 'I'm trouble' look about him. Like a little imp.

Someone bumped into his back. He turned to see a sheet of white-blonde hair moving past him. A face he recognized half turned his way and Seth realized it was another one of his cousins. She sat a full table length away from him, all alone. She glanced toward him, but her eyes got stuck on his. Her bright violet irises visible even at a distance.

They gazed at one another for a moment before he heard screaming. A familiar screaming.

He turned back around just in time to see two things happen;

one, his cousin, Peter, melted into the cafeteria wall in a completely impossible way, and two, his sisters taking off out of the lunchroom.

Seth stood, wanting to follow his sisters out, but he couldn't take his eyes off the place where his thirteen-year-old cousin had been. It was like his skin—and clothes—changed, dissolved. Or, like he morphed into the most amazing human camouflage ever. Every limb, every inch of the boy's skin and clothing matched his surroundings exactly. Or perhaps he disappeared, like for real disappeared, like, gone with the wind. Whichever way, he was invisible.

Speechless and staring, Seth couldn't move. Then, a boy next to him began to clap. Clap. This pulled him out of his stupor. But there were more claps. All heads turned toward where his cousin *was,* assuming he was still there. Real shock and joy filled the faces all around.

Bulge-eyed, Seth embraced the urge to run for the hills without a backward glance for the freak show around him.

It was as he exited the cafeteria that he realized that now, he *had* something, something huge. He had information way beyond some crazy Garden of Eden fantasy. And Jeremiah was right, it was worth a boatload of money.

CHAPTER 15

Miriam

Seth wasn't ready. If he found out about Natures now, it would just scare him off. He was smart, for sure, but not ready. Eve told her how he figured Eden out, and what they were doing here, though he thought it was a joke and that they were all crazy. It wouldn't be the first or last time she'd heard that assessment. Lots of people figured out what was going on in Edenia before the week was out. But seeing a Nature...

The Johnsons were not ready.

So, Miriam followed Seth as he left the cafeteria. Though she was happy for her brother coming into his Nature, she couldn't linger. She had to catch Seth and talk to him. But what on earth would she say? What would she do?

Would she treat this like any other situation with an outsider and take the memory from him? Maybe, she would have to do his sisters too though. She would have to keep them apart as she did it. That would be messy, but it was possible. She had done it before. She would need help though.

She followed him as he moved through the streets, her mind beginning to formulate a plan of how to fix this situation but she kept getting distracted by the way Seth walked; quick, stiff, kicking harmless rocks, determined. Butterflies fluttered her stomach.

Ever since their conversation in the chapel, she knew the twist that had lived in her middle since Friday both began and ended with

Seth. As she watched his gait, which purposefully took him down the house-lined street, she couldn't help but notice how smoothly he moved. His head swiveled back and forth as he went, and she tried to ignore his chiseled face and his shiny black hair that swung slightly with the movement of his body.

He was unlike anything she had seen before; handsome and determined and worldly and vulnerable. A tingle swept up her body. She placed a hand over her stomach, willing it to settle.

Seth turned sharply to the west, down the Edenia road. Then he started jogging. This pulled her out of her head. Was he leaving town? Just leaving, right now, this very minute? She sped up her pace and was surprised when he didn't notice her, or at least the noise of her running feet.

Several yards later, he turned sharply into the play field and she breathed a sigh of relief. But he walked through the field and beyond toward an old dilapidated shed set behind an enormous oak tree.

Both were at least twenty yards outside of Edenia and Miriam hesitated. Seth did not. Ducking under a low branch, Seth stepped into the shed and pulled the latch shut.

Miriam looked at the town line, the place where she knew she would be out of the protection of Edenia and into the world. She stared at the spot on the ground until she heard Seth's voice. He was speaking to someone. Instantly Miriam felt her Nature take her, and with purpose she stepped outside of Edenia.

The shed's construction consisted of loose old oak planks nailed astride one another. Afraid of being spotted or heard, Miriam crept up slowly on cautious feet.

Even from five yards away Seth's voice was loud enough for her to hear.

"Yeah, well, I got something." A pause.

"Yes, of course I'm in the shed."

Her feet stopped and so did her heart.

"Yes, for real." Seth's voice jeered, but it held confusion...

"Okay, so, I don't think I can tell you now. I just don't know if I can say it out loud. My brain is too effing freaked! Plus, I need...I dunno, details. Jeremiah, I am wigging out! I need to confirm what I saw with my sisters. I just wanted to let you know I've got something. And if I have what you need, can you be ready to do what I need?"

Pause.

"'k, yeah that's exactly why I wanna make sure I get every detail."

"No, let me call you back later."

"Yeah, yeah. Good idea. So, let's say midnight so I cannot get caught?"

"Yeah, like blow your freakin' mind."

"K, later."

She heard a beeping sound and a click. She stepped around the corner of the shed as Seth opened the door and walked back the way he'd come.

Her pounding heart stopped. Her instincts froze, *her* mind *freaked* out. It took a full minute to realize what just happened. Seth had a cellular phone, and he somehow found a place just enough outside of Edenia for the thing to work. There was a major problem with that, yes, but...

Miriam squeezed her eyes in frustration, breathed out, and then entered the shed. There was nothing in it. She searched and hunted and found no cellular phone, though she did find some sort of wire. She pulled at it, and the dirt came up as the wire exited the ground. She followed it to the wall of the shack. She went out and to the back where she saw a wooden box. It was carefully made, and it matched the color of the shack perfectly. Miriam would never have looked twice at it. She pulled at it and it swung open on a hinge. Inside was a contraption Miriam could only guess at. There were wires coming out of it going down and up. She followed the wires up to the roof. As she looked up, she saw that the tree had been trimmed carefully, so that nothing blocked whatever was on the roof from the sky. She had nothing to stand on, so she decided to get over not knowing and closed up the box. Then she went back into the shack and reburied the wire.

So, Seth had that phone on him. A phone he brought into Edenia and then brought out again and then used just now. Why did it still work? The minute he entered Edenia the wind Natures interference should have killed the phones delicate electronic balance. One of the huge advantages the Guardians had in the conflict with the Joneses was that they couldn't bring anything electronic into Edenia. It immediately fried. The Guardians relied on this advantage so much that organizing the wind users into shifts that covered every second of the day was her father's biggest job.

So, what was happening here?

Miriam realized she was focusing on the phone because she didn't want to think about what else this meant: Seth had obviously been recruited to spy.

It was a typical Jones ploy. Not having a brain that ran towards intrigue and espionage, Miriam wasn't sure how they invited newcomers to spy for them; *'Hey the Garden of Eden's in there, can you tell us where to find it?'* It seemed like a precarious proposition.

However, they did do it. Edenia had seen its fair share of spies, which was why it was so important to keep Natures hidden until after the seventh day. If the Joneses found out about Natures, what exactly they were, they would figure out how to use them against the Edenians. Her father also worried about them telling other people or government entities. The list of dangers was long. So, secrets were best and had served them well so far. The Guardians fought daily against the Joneses and now had Miriam to help when the Joneses actually saw something.

Seth just didn't understand what was at stake here. He was uncomfortable. He was selfish and out of his element in this conflict. And he was freaked out. But she'd talked to him in the chapel. She was sure she could stop him from betraying them. But how? She was not a planner of nefarious plans. This threat did spark the Guardian in her but still, how could her Nature help her now? She had to be a Guardian in a different way.

Something whispered in her heart; *connect him.* But that idea scared her more than taking his memories.

She was well out of her depth here. She needed help. She needed a partner. But who?

CHAPTER 16

Peter

Sitting in front of the mirror was not something Peter spent much time doing. But as soon as he'd let go of his Nature, the students closest to him in the cafeteria freaked out over his eye color.

Yellow. His eyes were Yellow. And not even a good yellow, a dark yellow with tendrils of brown. Just exactly the shade of baby poop.

Close up they were pretty cool, the brown weaving through the yellow, but far away he looked like he had baby poop eyes. He couldn't help but feel like it was fate.

"And my obsession with poop comes full circle." Peter said to his reflection and smirked, deciding to embrace it.

Still. What did they mean? What Nature could it be? He closed his eyes and opened them wondering. What. Blink. Could. Blink. They. Blink. Mean. Blink.

It was like a puzzle. Blink. It was like a game of ultimate destiny. Blink. That little yellow tint changed the shape of his life's path. Blink.

Then.

For the space of a blink Peter was in a dark room, a room that felt as old as time and as vital as life. Blink.

He was in the bathroom at north school, blinking at himself in the mirror like an idiot.

Blink.

The dark room felt like it was the expanse of the universe and the closeness of a homemade quilt fort. Blink.

His irises were swirling. Blink.

The room pulled him more solidly into that other space. And he felt intelligence, and time. Blink.

The bathroom door opened up. Peter turned. It was Dean. "Peter, what in heck are you doing in here?"

Peter smiled at his friend. "Checking out my eyes."

"Oh, yeah, I would too. They are super creepy." Peter narrowed his creepy eyes at his friend who quickly amended his statement. "In a totally awesome way. You look like a wolf."

Peter looked back at himself. "Really?"

"Totally."

Peter smiled again. He was a wolf. A predator. A defender of his pack. He was an alpha. How did he get so lucky? He loved this Guardian stuff.

PETER WALKED IN THE DOOR, and his mother and father were all over him. News of what happened at school made it home before he had. He was sweaty and muddy from his chores, but he was happy for the attention. Though the question still remained. What on earth did the yellow represent? The Brown was obvious, he'd gone invisible, but what else?

All of his extended family brought food for the impromptu Guardian ceremony. While his mama, Aunt Willow, Aunt Sarah, and Hannah put all the food out, the rest sat in the living room while his papa began the history that was integral to every ceremony.

He cleared his throat and Peter smiled and settled into the floor cushions, so happy it was finally his turn.

"Long ago, here in this very grove of trees, the Creators spoke with our first father Adam and his wife Eve." Though they didn't do the ceremony in the actual Garden any longer, Peter still loved that beginning. The cadence of it, the set up. He smiled even brighter. "God the Father and God the Creator had to turn Adam and Eve out of the beautiful Garden they had created for them. As he did this, the Creator gave them one last gift. '*I will set Cherubim and a flaming sword to guard the tree of life lest you eat of the fruit and forever be sealed to your ignorance, damned to this estate and left behind.*' The word was spoken, and the cherubim came together. Formed from four different powerful Natures; earth, water, fire, air.

"There at the base of the tree the miraculous creature stood guard, violently turning away any desirous for the fruit of the Tree of Life. The world spun, and the floods came, but the garden was not taken from off the Earth as man was, and for many long centuries the Cherubim stood guard, seeing not even one of the sons of Adam.

"But then man again made his way to where the garden lay. Before long, stories and legends of the garden, it's Guardian, and the tree spread throughout the land, but most thought it a story for children. Until two brothers, Enos and Ramon, learned from a traveling healer that in a land not too distant, a man of purest white descended out of heaven. This man taught the people the legend of Adam and his wife Eve and told of a Tree of Life. This man brought love, and peace and many followed him and spread the words he taught. Enos and Ramon heard these words and hungered for the eternal life they believed would bring happiness to them. Thus, the brothers and their wives journeyed to find the tree and the mystical power it held.

"They did not find the tree, but they told the story to their children instilling a hunger for the tree in their posterity. Their family grew to a traveling tribe, and in the wilderness of pre-America they stuck together in the quest for the Tree of Life.

"They were a good and hopeful people.

"Eventually they found the Garden and the Tree. A beautiful cherubim stood watch, shining like a golden light. The moment the tribe saw the creature they bent to worship him and the creature taught them the same stories the native healers had so long before, and many more things he taught them, but this time they understood the truth of eternal life. How it is given to all, but not yet. They must wait. Once they correctly knew the Father's and the Creator's plan for their children, the tribe set up camp nearby wanting to stay near the Master of the garden, never presuming, only worshiping."

At this point his father's voice changed to a theatrical villain voice and Peter couldn't help but laugh a little. He loved this story.

"Before long the evil Josiah Jones came along. After a young American prophet harmlessly revealed the true location of the Garden of Eden to a few enlightened people, word spread, and when it reached this Josiah, it sparked a flame. Throughout history many treasure hunters sought the pre-Mesopotamian 'Holy Grail' but they naturally did it in other parts of the world. Who would think to look for the Garden of Eden in America? The Joneses decided to investigate the man's information.

"In the middle of the night, Josiah Jones and his twenty associates came upon the garden and the native tribe who'd made their home among the roots of the old trees. Thinking they were competition for immortality, Josiah ordered his men to slaughter the innocent natives in their beds. They killed many. With the blood of the helpless tribe still on his sword, Josiah entered the garden and went for the fruit.

"Several saw what followed, but only two people matter to the history of Edenia; a native named Ammon and Josiah's teenaged son Josiah Jr. They both watched as the Cherubim, officiating in his duty, took Josiah Jones' head from his shoulders.

"Angry, many of the Jones cohorts attempted to attack the Cherubim but a dozen men were nothing to the Cherubim who blurred and separated into many different forms, all with swords of light and the powers of earth, water, fire, and wind. These mighty protectors made quick work of the treasure seekers and calmly coalesced after their exertion ended.

"In this act of sublime power and terror, these two human observers were changed forever.

"Josiah Jr. watched his father, uncles, and friends be cut down by a shiny, mythical creature. He lost his family and gained a vendetta. He only hoped it would require the blood of a Cherubim on his own sword. So, he studied swordplay and worked his body and mind into a fine frenzy. He challenged the Cherubim many times but was never able to get past it to taste of the fruit, likewise the cherubim never chose to defeat Josiah Jr. Still, he never stopped attempting to fulfill his father's quest. I believe this is why the Cherubim never killed Josiah Jr., he did not want the fruit for himself, he only wanted to avenge his father.

"On the other side of this story, Ammon and those left of the tribe; after clearing away the bodies of the dead from the sacred ground and heavy with grief, they, the natives, found their mission. Their purpose. They chose to hide the very existence of the Cherubim and the garden, thus protecting other like-minded treasure hunters from the Joneses' fate and they did this with a covenant.

"It is the same covenant you will take tonight Peter."

Peter had seen all his siblings go through this and knew it was time for him to stand. As he did, all the other full-fledged Guardians in the room surrounded him and placed one hand on him. Peter had the words memorized, so he started the covenant, and all said it with him.

Power filled the room at their joined words and Peter cried tears of joy at finally realizing his dream.

His father beamed proudly at him, and as they finished the words a great cheer went up. His father embraced him, and his mother called to him to come and eat. Absolutely giddy, Peter sat and ate and talked with his fellow Guardians, finally feeling fulfilled.

CHAPTER 17

Miriam

There just hadn't been an opportunity to tell her parents yet. She'd decided they were the only ones she could tell. Maybe she would say something to Aunt Sarah or Jai.

Her home was a little distracting, though. Every relative descended on her house. All the talk around the table was of Peter's Nature fully taking him. This was a long time coming, and everyone seemed relieved.

She waited for the pow-wow discussing what they would do about Seth, Abigail and Lillian seeing the whole thing. That seemed like a natural segue to speak about what she'd learned. Of course, no one brought it up.

Even more distracting to Miriam's purpose than Peter's Nature was his new eye color. At least to Miriam's point of view. Yellow. Yellow eyes. Well in truth, they were more like a stone-ground mustard color, a yellow-brown. Everyone understood the brown, he'd been able to conceal (his feet) for a while. But what did the yellow mean? For the first time Miriam felt what other people felt around her. What in the world was his Nature, and how would it affect them all?

In the quiet, secret part of her, the part she liked to ignore, she hoped it was something invasive like hers, so she wouldn't be alone anymore. But that was not very kind of her, and she knew it

Conjecture about what it meant filled the entire conversation.

Then there was the story and the ceremony, which was so very distracting, but also more inspiring than it had ever been. Miriam wanted to be a credit to her ancestors who had given so much to be Guardians. How could she do that if she hated her Nature? If she didn't step forward and become a Guardian instead of a pawn her parents used. It was never her choice to take memories. It was what was expected of her. Perhaps she could be useful in another way. A way that was hard, still, but less devastating than ripping souls.

Her attention was diverted by her Papa's words.

"It seems scary for a time. Things are a little uncertain, but just like with Miriam, everyone calms down." Her Papa was talking about eye color and soon he started in on his famous lecture. "All the mixed eye colors were new at one point or another. Amber, blue, brown, and green were the only ones to start with. Gray, blue-green, light blue, black, white and now violet and yellow-brown have all come later."

"I've never seen anyone with black or white eyes." Simeon stated petulantly.

"Yeah, how could you have white eyes?" Joseph asked.

Her papa smiled at her two youngest brothers and began the history of it all. Of course, Miriam knew the story. Everyone made a point of telling it to her once her Nature took her. The problem with her Nature was not that it was new, it was what she could do.

As papa told the story, Miriam found herself fretting about Seth. What if she never told her parents because they never shut up about Peter? What if she decided to act instead of wait? What if she didn't do what she should do according to her upbringing and did something else? What if she chose to take on Seth herself?

Without her realizing it she constructed in her mind a detailed plan of how to get out of the house and to Seth's house without being seen.

And then what?

It would be so easy if his sisters wouldn't have been there to see Peter. But they were. She would...

She would knock him out with a brick.

Then steal his phone.

Then tell his parents what he was up to.

What if she killed him when she knocked him out? What if she got lost in his dreamy eyes, in the middle of the night and ended up kissing him instead? Hey, that would distract him, she hoped.

No, she couldn't do any of those things.

What could she do?

She thought.

She could go and listen to his conversation. Find out what the Joneses wanted, find out what Seth would tell them. She would gather information. Yes. That's it. That felt right. And possible.

Excited energy flooded through her. This would be the first time she would act the part of a Guardian without using her Nature. And it felt almost as good as when she used the calming part of her Nature on aunt Sarah.

As she listened to the oath Peter took earlier, she felt the words in her bones. She loved being useful, and perhaps she finally was. No one was demanding that she do this, she chose it. She would just take care of this herself. There was no point involving others. It was simple. She smiled.

CHAPTER 18

Peter

Not two minutes after hopping into bed, Garren moved into the room, the speed of his Nature on him. "Peter. Joneses. You wanna come?"

"Are you kidding me?"

"Nope, saddle up buddy. You're a Guardian now."

It only took him two minutes to get ready, and so much less than that to get to the outskirts of town. Riding on Garren's back as his Nature moved him through the streets of Edenia was like what he imagined riding in a car would be like, but with more bugs up your nose.

Garren dropped him with Jai and took off for who knows where, but not before he said, "Take your Nature and just watch for tonight. Okay?"

Peter nodded, thrilled to be involved.

It wasn't long before the headlights of several cars were slowing and stopping just outside of town. Peter watched in fascination until Uncle Jai's voice reminded. "Nature, Peter. I know you are very enthusiastic but please this is just for your viewing pleasure tonight. No getting involved unless you must."

Peter answered by pulling his Nature to him. It was so easy now, like pulling on socks.

"Good boy." Uncle Jai answered and patted him on the back. He looked at his hand on Peter's invisible back, "I will never get accustomed to that." He patted once more and then looked at the military men piling out of the vehicles. Uncle Jai blurred into motion as the Joneses moved in with their formations and silly plastic weapons.

In the end it just seemed comical, almost like an over-practiced production.

The Guardians took them out one by one, with simple tricks. Dust in the eyes, tree branches whacking them in the face and knocking them out and the such. It was so fun to watch the water Natures in action. They skootched the men backward in-between steps. Their timing had to be pretty flawless, but for the most part, all the soldiers felt was a lot of wind. They were very confused as to why they couldn't move forward.

Uncle Brian was among the Guardians tonight, and he was incredible. Something Peter hadn't known before was that when concealed he could see other Earth Natures that were concealed, which was so amazingly cool. To Peter's eyes Uncle Brian kind of glowed, but just enough so Peter could see him in the dark. The man moved through the group of intruders, ripping their weapons out of their hands, pushing them into bushes with awesome force. Peter laughed to himself at the confused looks the Joneses shared with one another.

Scared, one man got trigger happy and shot (blew) a dart-like projectile in Brian's direction but it bounced off of Uncle Brian as he was stone and earth and couldn't be harmed. The dart veered sideways and hit another intruder in the leg. That man went down fast, and it was at that point they retreated, pulling their wounded with them and piling back into their vehicles.

Tonight, they hadn't even gotten ten feet into Edenia.

Others had a role in the rebuff, but it was his pale-skinned Uncle Brian whom Peter had watched with reverent awe. The man made his way toward Peter now that the Joneses were leaving. As he stepped past him, he put a glowing hand out to pat Peter's head.

Uncle Brian let go of his Nature to say, "You like the show?"

Peter did know he couldn't be heard if he spoke while in his

Nature. So, he nodded and tried to let go of his Nature. However, something distracted him; the Joneses were back at their vehicles, but one of them had a weapon pointed into Edenia.

Peter heard a crack, crack, crack as a real gun shot metal bullets randomly into the woods. Suddenly it felt as if Peter were aware of every molecule of air, every leaf, every bug. The bullets, flying through the air, were little red and orange pricks of light in the darkness moving at great speed in many directions. One however, was heading directly towards Uncle Brian's rotating form. His uncle was in the process of turning and calling his Nature, but to Peter it felt outside of time and space. He saw everything. Peter knew the bullet was moving too fast.

Thankfully, he was in a good position. All he had to do was lean to the side just so and pull himself to tip toe. In his super aware state, he realized the bullet began to implode. The small ball of white-orange flame moved as though the air were viscous, trailing a more substantial streak of red behind it. As if the bullet of death were disintegrating from the inside and from the outside. Two feet from its destination of Uncle Brian—as it passed right by Peter's face—he watched the small vestiges of the ball of metal crumbled into ash. Its vaporous residue cutting a red line through the air.

When he turned his head to watch it, he noticed another set of eyes, amber eyes, close by. Aunt Sarah's hand extended toward the object threatening her brother; her focus unwavering, her fire Nature hot on the small piece of deteriorating bullet. Then as if the metal gave up the fight, it sparked, glowed red and crumbled into ash. As it dissipated, Peter realized the heat aimed at him remained and Peter felt his clothes burst into flame.

After a moment of shock, all went back to normal speed and Peter dropped himself to the ground, rolling.

"Do not let go of your Nature." Uncle Brian's voice demanded loudly.

He had the fleeting thought that being a man of fire was not all it was cracked up to be.

Barely aware of his surroundings, he heard Uncle Jai say, "Garren, help!"

Within moments, water Nature doused his rolling body.

Aunt Sarah's voice carried through the night. "Oh no. Peter. I'm so sorry." She yelled, "I did not see you."

"You were never sorry when you did this to me," His Uncle complained.

"Well, you deserved it, and I just saved your life, so quiet down."

Brian scoffed but then stated impatiently, "Calm down everyone. He isn't going to let go of his Nature, so nothing can hurt him." He ended the speech, his tone superior and unruffled and about that time Peter was done rolling and burning.

He assessed himself; shirt only partly burned, pants fine. He was still steaming, though, and that was really cool. Standing up, he let his Nature go. Aunt Sarah moved to him, taking his face in her hands, assessing. "Your mother would have my hide if I let anything happen to you."

He endured her critical eye for a few moments before turning to his uncle.

"That, was the best thing ever."

"I know, right?" His uncle hunched down; his eyes excited. "Didn't even get you warm, right?"

"Right!" His eyes flitted from one adult to another. "You guys were amazing, but Uncle Brian, you were the best. I am so glad you didn't die, because I want to be just like you."

Everyone laughed. But once that subsided, Uncle Brian got a serious look on his face and glanced up at Uncle Jai. "I saw something that disturbed me." He turned and walked several steps to the left, "I need light."

Aunt Sarah moved to his side, held out her hand, and Peter watched as her hand went lava red. It revealed her veins and bone and sinew, but it also glowed a red-hued-light bright enough they all could see the ground around them. Soon, he bent over and picked something up.

"I noticed that this," he held up a black rectangular box with a long antenna, "still had a glowing light on it."

"Is it a walkie-talkie?"

"I don't know, but we need to figure it out because..." He flipped the device around and Peter saw that it indeed had a green glowing light.

"Is that what I think it is?"

"If you think it's the Joneses figuring out how to use electronics inside of Edenia, then yes, it is exactly what you think it is."

They all looked over at Peter and he knew what they were thinking. They were thinking about his yellow eyes and how whatever extra tidbits his Nature offered would surely combat this new technology of the Joneses, because that's just how it worked.

Peter sighed. "Well, I guess I better figure out what yellow means, and quick."

"I guess you'd better."

Jai sighed, "I don't know about the rest of you, but I am beat. I'm heading home. Let's figure this out tomorrow, yah?"

Everyone nodded their agreement, but as they all began leaving Uncle Brian asked, "Peter before you head home, can I have a quick word?"

Peter nodded. "Yes."

Brian pulled him aside and said, "I am just so proud, Peter, to have you take earth Nature."

"Well, sort of."

He chuckled and motioned him to start walking in the direction the others had gone. "It's enough for me. So, I'm here. I didn't get to tell you earlier, but there are a lot of things someone invisible can do..."

"And not do." Peter smiled.

"The chores will not do themselves Peter." He touched Peter's shoulder. "Now I know that you are extremely competent and smart, still, I am here for you. We have a great responsibility as earth Natures."

"I know."

Uncle Brian stopped walking and took him by both shoulders. "Do you, though?"

Peter looked up at his Uncle confused.

Brian took a deep breath, "Peter, I don't know why it took you so long to get your Nature..."

And finally, he understood where Uncle Brian was going with all of this. He was worried Peter would use his Nature to do crazy terrible things. And yes, he would do crazy terrible things, but only to the Joneses.

Peter shrugged off his Uncles grip, "Why does everyone think the Master didn't let me have my Nature because I played pranks on people? None of you understand." Peter backed up and walked away from his Uncle.

But Brian caught up with him. "Peter, please don't be upset. I wasn't trying to..." He pulled on Peters arm. Peter stopped and glared at his uncle. "Tell me what you mean. How about we start there?"

The words calmed Peter. Not even his father and mother asked him what possessed him to be the way he was. "I play the tricks because all I've ever wanted was to be a Guardian. It is like, the most incredible thing. I couldn't wait. It was practice. It all was to be useful."

Brian was silent as he looked into Peter's eyes for a tortuous count of ten. Peter actually counted, it was so uncomfortable. Then he sighed and answered, "I understand."

Surprised he queried, "You do?"

"Of course, I do. And your skills, I am certain, will come in handy. But Peter, I'm confused. We were talking about why the Master withheld your Nature and you told me about the pranks. Why are they connected in your mind? And why did you answer the way you did? Do you know more about what happened today than you are sharing?"

No wonder Uncle Brian wasn't married. He reached into your

soul and grabbed the truth and pulled it out, painfully, through your nostrils.

Peter looked at the ground, sorting out what to say. "I just know... that...my Nature was supposed to come in the exact moment it did. Everyone knew I was bitter about it taking its time. And Uncle Martin hounded me about it regularly, today in fact. And it made me remember that I knew why. It was while I was sleeping. Like someone had whispered the truth of it in my ear, or like a warm wave of water crept it into my soul, or like I saw it in a vision. The knowing affected my senses, is what I mean. It filled me, sort of. But I forgot, then I remembered." Peter felt vulnerable as he told his Uncle this. "And its not the first time I knew something or understood something I shouldn't," he almost whispered.

Brian licked his lips and started to say something but instead he looked away from Peter, crossed his arms and swayed from foot to foot. After an eternity of contemplating, Brian asked, "Like, maybe, you could understand the future?" He paused but must have seen the fear in Peters face because he went on quickly. "We had someone before, who could do that. But he left us and I personally have been waiting impatiently for that Nature to return. It was epic. Though his eyes were black, not baby poop yellow."

The moment these words were out of Brian's mouth Peter understood everything. And for a moment it *was* as if he could see the future. He put all the conversations he'd overheard together. That was what ran Zeke off. His Nature. He understood how Zeke must have felt, being the one who could see the future. The implications of that Nature fanned out before him like a horrific dream. His stomach jumped into his throat.

He shook his head. "No," he whispered. "No." He took two quick steps. "That's not what it is like. It's not the future. It's...it's timing. I think." He said the words out loud and instantly felt panicked. He didn't understand his own reaction, except he kept seeing Miriam's face in a crowd of people who considered her a weirdo. Was he next?

Brian's hand gripped his shoulder. "It is okay, Peter. Do not get upset. Let us talk this through. What do you mean it's like timing?"

Peter turned, looking at the concern on his uncle's face. It almost looked like pity. That was it! He ripped his shoulder out of his uncle's grip and started walking toward home. "I need to think." He hesitated in his speech but not his feet, which were moving fast now. "I'm going home. It's late. I'm sleepy."

"Sure. But Peter, we're not done with this conversation."

CHAPTER 19

Miriam

Miriam was three steps away from the back door, and she just knew she was going to faint. All the Guardians were quietly dispatched to their own homes, and Papa and Mama were snug in their bed, snoring.

Her foot creaked on a floorboard. She paused, listening.

Nothing.

But she couldn't stand the tension any longer. This needed to be over. Hurrying, she took the last few steps as quickly as she could, lifted the latch, and exited. Taking a few deep breaths, she leaned against her house, trembling.

Knowing it was almost midnight, she shook herself and forced her poor shaking limbs to move. There was a chill in the air, and it didn't take a full minute to feel cold all the way to her bones. Knowing how squeaky the gate was, Miriam decided to go over the back fence which wasn't too high. Still, her numb legs almost didn't cooperate.

She felt a bit warmer after her swift walk, but still, shivers plagued her. Not to mention the incessant urge to use the toilet. She was certain she would wet herself if Seth caught her.

If this was how being sneaky felt, she could not fathom why Peter did it all the time. And even if he liked the sensation, how he'd not ended up with bladder problems was beyond her.

Arriving at her grand-aunt Bilhah's house—it was the one across the road from the Johnson's—she stepped behind a bush and waited.

Not five minutes later, the front door of his house opened, and

Seth slinked out. He walked straight toward Miriam. Her heart jumped into percussion mode. Without knowing why, she ran her tongue over her teeth and pulled fingers through her hair. Why had she not twisted it into a braid?

She pushed against the house as Seth moved toward her, trying not to be seen, when a dog barked roughly into the night.

Miriam looked around for someone else, perhaps a patrol.

When she saw no one, she looked back to Seth and found his running feet taking him far down the street. She stopped breathing. Staring, and petrified with dread, she anticipated the moment she would have to stand and follow after him. The dog barked again, helping her mind catch up to her adrenaline. She pulled herself up, and forcing one leg in front of the other, she ghosted along behind Seth.

CHAPTER 20

Peter

The darkness all around him was not bothersome, but it surrounded him fully. He felt nothing on his skin as if he had pulled his earth Nature to him. This darkness was familiar now. It was comfortable.

Then something changed.

From far away, he saw light. It pierced through the darkness like a spear. He moved closer and soon what he saw looked like a ribbon. A ribbon of lights and colors and energy. He felt the vastness of time and space in the gentle bends and curves of the ribbon.

Interested, he moved again. As he came close, he saw how miles and miles of ribbon lay below him; flowing in a dizzyingly massive display of light and darkness woven in masterful splendor. He looked up and saw that the ribbon was not done weaving. The skeletal structure of the future ribbon—the warp and the weft which were also equal parts light and darkness—flowed outward into the darkness of the room in three directions up, right, and left. They were never-ending.

He saw the threads of time, or existence, or sentience, as they slowed to a snail's pace, as if they knew he desired to comprehend them. As he did so, the threads twisted, and his perspective changed. Now from a different angle the threads were connected in a tapestry of interactions. Some were bright colors, others were dark colors. Some places burst with many bright threads all together. Some groups were so dark they were deeper than shadow itself. He knew somehow that these clusters defined events, some full of good choices, some littered with pain.

His consciousness considered a cluster within a cluster which was so bright and significant it dazzled. He zoomed closer until the threads became large to his sight, like pillars or streaks of brightness that went on and on forever. There, he found that each pillar of light held quintessences he recognized. It was his family.

And more, he found his own column. It winked with a yellow-brown light. He traced it downward to the place it met the weave which looked like a jumbled mess.

Wanting to understand better, he pulled himself out of the forest of light pillars so that now the lives looked like threads again. He zeroed in on his one tiny life strand, examining the short centimeter it held, woven into the ribbon. That section of the ribbon was light indeed. He reached out with his finger and touched the edge that had just been woven.

He suddenly saw himself from above, he was in the cafeteria, his Nature was taking him. He saw Lilly and Abby and Seth, their faces full of fear, shock and disgust. He saw Miriam's determination. He felt the idea of timing once more. Then the moment paused, and he saw the threads bend horizontally as if a new life-pathway forced the thread to mingle elsewhere. He followed the threads out of the weave upward and noticed that threads of light now mingled unwoven with threads of darkness.

He touched the loose threads as they stretched into space. Energy burst out of his core and flooded his insides. The moment this happened, he saw something. A possibility.

Peter sat up, heart pounding. He'd been dreaming. Strangely, he remembered the dream perfectly. And stranger still, he understood what the dream meant. Sort of. His action today, his Nature coming right when it did, started something. Something he could not have fathomed by way of its effect on everyone around him.

For a long while his thoughts kept his eyes wide open in the semi-dark room.

Turning over in his bed, the sound of rubbing sheets and creaking wood almost drown-out the floor squeaking outside his room. But a louder groan of floorboards happened a few minutes later. Then he heard a footfall. A shiver ran up his spine and he pushed his covers back before sitting up.

Something brushed against the door. The assumption of Ma or Pa checking up on everyone was there in his mind, but they did not try to hide their steps in the hall, as this person did.

Adrenaline rushed through him at the thought, *it might be a Jones,* and in the space of a moment his Nature took him. Again, it was a reaction without forethought or control.

Out of habit Peter rolled out of bed as stealthily as he could, hoping his bed wouldn't make noise, but of course he could not make a sound when his Nature was upon him.

Without thinking too hard about it, Peter moved to the door and cracked it open. The hall was as dark as pitch, and though his eyes were accustomed, he saw no one, not even movement. Swinging it open, he stepped out into the hall, and that was when he heard the back-door latch.

Whoever it was, they were leaving. He moved to follow, but he hesitated instead. If they were leaving, why would he chase them down? The smartest thing would be to check on his family members.

Lifting the latch on Gabriel and Garren's door, he peeked through. He heard the breathing of his sleeping brothers. Turning back around, he crossed the hall to check the girls. The bed Eve and Miriam shared was right next to the door. Tentatively he reached out to where his sister should be. But he kept reaching and reaching. He noticed that the bed was still warm, and next to it, on the floor, a pair of boots were missing.

Either Eve or Miriam was gone.

His first thought was to rush to his Pa, but his feet took him silently to the back door. Still, he wondered why his Pa hadn't wakened at all the noise.

When his hand reached for the latch, he stopped. He should go get his Pa. But his hand went to the latch again, and this time the metal hinge was free before Peter stopped himself. He turned toward his Pa's room, thinking what he would say. But when he blinked, he was out of his house on the back porch just in time to see a stream of silvery hair slip over the back fence.

That had to be Eve, Miriam always wore a braid to bed. Peter wondered what on earth she could be doing. As far as he knew, he was the only person in the whole history of Edenia that'd snuck out in the middle of the night.

Seriously, it only took one time. Edenia was even more boring in the dark than it was in the light.

Where in the world could she be going?

Invisible, Peter followed his sister from a discreet distance. Curious. She didn't go far. He watched her duck behind a bush in front of Grand-Aunt Bilhah's, which just so happened to be right across the street from Abby's and Lilly's.

Seeing their house caused his mind to calculate the repercussions of this afternoon's misstep and how it would change their friendships. Would they be able to face him tomorrow? He assumed the reason he wasn't in trouble had to do with Zeke, how he could talk to his family about what had happened. So, the Johnsons knew now all about Edenia presumably, and what a cool place it was.

He hoped so, because how it happened was unavoidable. He understood that now.

He waited and watched and thought about his new friends. He wished so much that he could go up to their door and knock. He would apologize for scaring the pants off them. And he'd talk to them.

Movement from across the street caught his attention. Though part of him knew that no one could see him, or hear him, instinct took over and he made a run for it. He crossed two backyards before he slowed down and realized there was no need for panic.

Looping around, he moved between the Tanner's and his Aunt Sarah's and just about tripped over Lazy, the Tanner's chocolate lab.

Scared, Lazy moved in a manner unbefitting his name and barked harshly at Peter.

Unafraid of the dog, Peter continued on his way hoping Lazy hadn't woken anyone. He reached the street just in time to watch Seth Johnson run down the street and turn. Lazy barked once more, but no one paid attention to him.

For some reason Eve, or maybe it was Miriam, didn't even bother to hide that she was following Seth. Strange, but his sisters were Guardians. They knew their business. Peter stopped walking as a thought occurred to him. What if they were meeting up? Alone, in the middle of the night? There's no way. What could they possibly do?

Before he could work his mind around any possibilities, a light caught his eye. He looked toward the window and saw a perfectly beautiful face peek out of the curtains. It was Lilly. He wondered what he would say to her when he saw her next.

He felt curiosity draw him to follow Eve and make sure nothing untoward was going on, but glancing back at the face in the window, he forgot his interest in Eve. He couldn't help himself. His legs pulled him toward the Johnson house. Why were they awake at this time of night? Maybe he could talk to them right now. With no one around. Have it out with them. Help them understand.

He would do it. He would go and talk to them.

CHAPTER 21

Miriam

He led her out of Edenia to the shed just as he'd done before, and after looking around, he went inside.

Luckily, she'd stayed behind a tree so he didn't see her. Now she hurried to catch up to him. She looped behind the big tree. He was already talking, and she was close enough to him there to hear.

"Mr. Jones? I'm sorry sir, I was expecting Jeremiah."

Fear rippled up Miriam's spine. Seth *was* talking to a Jones. They *had* recruited him.

"No, no this is fine."

"I was worried it wouldn't turn on and then I couldn't get a signal, but we are fine now."

"Yes sir, of course, sir. I'm standing in the shed."

"Yes sir, I am..." he paused, his voice apprehensive. "Okay, but I just want to make sure that our arrangement is..."

"Yes, of course, I remember." His timbre changed and got firm. "I just need your word, sir. A life depends on it."

After a long moment she heard him blow out a deep breath like he'd been holding it, and Miriam wondered what he meant by *'a life depends on it.'*

His voice was all business as he spoke his first words of treachery.

"Well, keeping that agreement in mind, I must say that these freakin' crazy people definitely believe they are guarding something, and that something is, wait for it...the actual Garden of Eden. Like from the Bible." He stopped.

"With you giving me practically zero info about what I'm looking for here, I'm assuming you're interested in the tree of life? Or more specifically immortality. Or are you interested in their, like, superpowers?"

So, they just recruited Seth and gave him no information. Weird.

"Both makes sense. Well, I haven't heard much about the tree, except I know that it's here and it is a big deal to guard it."

"Yes, right in the center of town. I tried to go in but..."

"I'm sure I could. All I would need to do is figure out which is the right one. Does it have some kind of special description that would help me?" Seth paused, listening.

"Well that information might have been helpful. I will give it a go."

"I see. Okay."

"I saw one go invisible. It was, to say the least, freaky."

"So, according to my sisters, when they asked about the garden... are you sitting down sir...k good. So, the kids irises began to like, shake, and then he just vanished. Not like, poof! he was gone, but like we couldn't see him! Like his skin morphed into perfect, cafeteria-colored...camo. I don't know how else to describe it."

"His eyes? Um, Peter's eyes are...I think they are blue." His voice went up with uncertainty.

This made fear strangle her heart. Eyes, what could they possibly know about eyes?

But Seth went on. "No, no wait, they're brown. I think. Does that matter?"

Wait, wait, wait, Miriam thought. The Joneses couldn't possibly know for certain about their Natures, could they? She'd hoped that they assumed the Cherubim did everything. Anyone who saw too much got zapped by her. But she hadn't always been a Guardian. Perhaps they know more. How could they know of Edenia's evolution? A herculean effort to keep that bit of info under wraps occurred every day. Furthermore, if they somehow did understand, how did they know it correlated with eye color?

"Whoa. One can take memories. Like mind control? Seriously?"

"So, that's the dangerous person."

"I can see how that would be a problem."

"Do you know who this person is? What they look like?"

"Yes, Jeremiah told me that the person was probably my age."

This sentence stopped Miriam's heart. Fear gripped her. *The Joneses know about me?* She took a few steps away from the tree.

"What they eat? Um, veggies, fruits, grains, no meat though. I'm confused sir, why is what they eat relevant?"

"You think that kid can go invisible because of something he eats?"

"Hey who am I to deny what I've seen. I'll tell you, I am totally terrified of these people now and I never want to eat another thing they offer me. But I saw it."

"Is that something you want me to find out?"

"Um, holy crap. So, you think they all have strange abilities and that the color of their eyes tells you about what they can do? So, they are just like, elemental abilities?"

"I still don't see that as proof, but I will make some notes and watch it closely. Man, I didn't know they were such freaks."

"I can see how that might be a problem. So, this memory stealer, how do you know there's only one of them?"

"Ya know, sir, this is freakin' my brain out. Are you sure they're not like aliens, or something, because one of them looks..."

Each heartbeat slammed in Miriam's chest. Was Seth about to say one of them looks like an Alien? He had to be talking about her. He had to be. She knew that she was not the most attractive person in the world, not like Eve, but she assumed that Peter only called her an alien because he was a meanie, not because she actually looked like one.

Now she knew what Seth thought, and to her shame his admission hurt her heart deeply. Tears came unbidden to her eyes and soon overflowed onto her cheeks. She bit her lip.

"No sir, um, I am most definitely not an alien. Just because..."

"Yes, but I don't have any abilities."

"Are you suggesting that my father does and that I could..."

"Yes, yes sir I need to find out more about that. I most definitely do not want to become some freak of nature."

"No way, I do not subscribe to that. Heroes are not weirdos with special abilities, they are real people. They are soldiers, police officers and firefighters. They're Joe Schmoe who tackles the bad guy trying to rob an old lady. Or doctors who..."

"Okay, sir. Yes."

"Wait sir, I have one more thing to tell..." there was a bit of a pause before he finished, "...you. And a pleasure talking to you too. Bye." This last was said in a very different tone than the rest of the conversation, it was snide and sarcastic.

Turning her face away from the sound, she slumped against the old tree trunk. Her head flopped to her knees as tears poured down her cheeks in a silent stream, fear and sadness ripping at her mind.

Why did she have to hear that conversation? The words went over and over in her mind. *Seth thinks I'm an alien, a freak.* She barely knew this boy but his words cut. His disgust wrenched at her heart and immobilized her. Fear and shame and hurt tingled up and down Miriam's entire body.

She heard him walk away, and she cringed at his footsteps. Part of her, the non-self-pitying part, demanded that she acknowledge that from the sound of it, Seth was the one that got the education, not the Joneses. Which was a topic for further reflection, but for later. Right now her pride demanded a bit of soothing. But soothing didn't come.

In a town of supernatural beings, she was a freak. That was Seth's word wasn't it? She covered her face. Feeling such a bone-deep rejection, made it impossible to breathe.

The crippling waves of shame for her alien face and invasive Nature hit her over and over again and she braced herself against the shack to stop from collapsing into the dirt.

A thought came back to her; *connect him.* She ignored it, big time now.

Her hand reached up and wiped at her wet cheek. She hated Seth. She wanted to rip his face off. She hated herself. She wanted to rip her own face off. She hated this place. She wanted out of here.

But most of all she hated all the little wisps of soul she had inside her. She hated her Nature and what it did. She hated how she was a coward. How she didn't tell her family about Seth. How she was prideful and thought she could do this on her own. How could she face her family when Seth's betrayal went down? How could she look at them knowing she was to blame?

She had to get out of here. She couldn't watch it all happen. Sniffing, she rose. If she left, she wouldn't have to explain anything to anyone. Her feet started moving. She decided she would leave now. This very night. Head for the hills and never come back. Never. Never see this place again. Never be assumed to be an alien, or some grotesque monster again. Never have to suck out a piece of anyone's soul again. Never have to feel guilt for being a terrible Guardian and not stopping Seth from betraying Edenia.

Her fear left her, and determination rocketed with her blood through her veins. She was already outside Edenia. How far could a person walk in a night? She was healthy and strong. She probably could get ten miles down the road before morning.

That wasn't far enough. She started running. Her brain caught up with her emotions and she realized if she kept going parallel to the Edenia road she'd end up at the Joneses. She turned sharply east and made her way around the outside of the town and toward the hills to the northeast.

She ran, and tears poured out and down her cheeks, and her stupid hair flung behind her in the night breeze. She ran until she thought her heart would burst and then she ran some more until there weren't any tears left in her eyes and then she ran until she was moving up the side of a hill and her legs would no longer go quickly.

She breathed and clutched at her side looking at how far she'd come, and the pain of failure was a little less. Sniffing and wiping at her nose, she sniffed again and the suffocating feeling was a little less.

She dug her fingernails into her palm and clenched her jaw and the anger and shame were a little less. She crested the hill and understood that she was, in fact, outside of Edenia for the first time in her sixteen years and the bone-weariness of alienation was a little less.

She tried, she tried, she tried. She had tried to find a purpose. To find a way to be a Guardian without using her dreadful Nature, and where had it gotten her? Here. Bumbling through her encounter with Seth and then abandoning all she'd ever known. For what? Where was she?

She walked a circle around the top of the hill breathing and looking in all directions. There were lights far off in the distance but nothing else. She looked up to the black sky. There was no moonlight, the cloud cover was too thick. Just her luck. She wanted to see. She'd been shielded from the world for too long.

At the thought of the darkness it seemed to close around her. But then the wind came up, and the clouds moved off, and it was as if she had wished the golden shape of the full moon to give her light and it obliged. She looked around. Hills, trees, hills, river, something else...

White, angular shapes filled the valley below her. They were tents. A great number of them. They confused her, but then she smelled campfire and as she walked along the ridge of the hill, she could also smell human waste and animals.

She wondered what they were doing here and if they were friendly. This made her pause. What would she do if she ran into unfriendly people out here in the dark? She turned her face back toward Edenia, a different kind of fear tingling up her back.

That moment, the light revealed her home; the fence that surrounded the fields, the peaks of rooftops and the large trees in the center of the town. Her home was beautiful, she would never want it to be destroyed or damaged. But that was exactly what the Joneses would do if they got the chance.

The moon went behind a cloud again, leaving her in darkness.

Seth would get them what they wanted; she knew down to her

toenails that he would. There was something in the way he spoke about the contract they had made, something about the desperation in his voice.

She finally understood why her belly was in knots over him. He was chaos. He was her enemy. He was the antagonist in her story.

If she understood him correctly, he and the Joneses were searching for her specifically now.

Would he hurt her?

Cradling her sides, she felt so alone. Singled out. Hated. Even by the Joneses. All because her Nature could affect people on the inside instead of on the outside. Tears streamed down her face. She needed help! She felt broken and lonesome to her bones., "Help." She whispered to the darkness.

The moon emerged once again from behind a cloud, leading her eyes back to Edenia. Instantly, her mind felt like it was taken over by a force outside herself. The force brought to mind memories long forgotten and neglected; her making bread with her mama, her aunts Sarah's terrible singing voice, her papa telling her stories, her friends combing her hair. Then there were thoughts of all the people in Edenia. Yes, some were wary of her, but all respected her and would fight with her, die for her. She sniffed and pushed back her hair as she allowed the images to work through her.

However threatened she now felt by the Joneses or by Seth, she knew that her father and mother, her siblings, and all of Edenia would protect her until their last breath. They were Guardians.

She thought of Seth's face. His sleek form and tortured eyes. The facts she learned tonight would define all of her further actions toward Seth. She had to take back the advantage. An advantage, by the way, they had no idea they'd lost.

In that moment she felt something strange. Timing, timing was everything. She thought about Peter and what had happened with his Nature. She knew instantly how that was a matter of timing. It was as if she knew without being told with words that events were destined to go as they had thus far, that it had been out of her hands. But now,

now things were different. She didn't have to proceed down the path she'd been led down.

She did not need to be what she had been before. She did not have to use her Nature the way she had done before.

Her Nature was a multi-faced gem. A tanzanite.

Stealing souls was not in Miriam's *character,* regardless of what her Nature was. She had never been able to do so with confidence or satisfaction. A thought occurred to her: her Nature had recently manifested itself in a new way; calm. The calm she passed to Aunt Sarah, her mother, and to Seth in the chapel felt wonderful. She loved it. She helped them, and it felt exactly right. Perhaps, like Peter, her Nature needed the right timing to manifest completely.

The moon went behind a cloud again and the feelings left her.

The sadness, wanting to take back possession of her, whispered; her entire Nature was about controlling what the Joneses knew. Obviously, she'd failed. They knew about the eyes, the Natures (though details on that seemed slim), and they were at least at the cusp of figuring out how to use electronics.

"No!" She shouted. "No, I will not listen. I will no longer wallow." She balled her fits and flung the words at the sky. For a moment, the doubt, guilt, and sadness left, and she was filled with the knowledge that she was a Guardian. She was a Guardian! And though she might always regret not having outside experiences, she would never allow Seth or anyone to destroy Edenia. She would never become a lamb brought to the slaughter. She was powerful, her family was powerful. She could act and not be acted upon.

She needed to act. She needed to move. She paced around the hilltop like a caged animal wondering what to do.

First, she made herself a promise to never take memories again, unless specifically told to do so from the Master. She hated that part of her Nature, yes, but if the Master asked her to do it, she would not deny him.

Second, she promised herself she would tell her parents her

promise and they could spread the news so that all knew to not ask her to do it any longer.

Third, she would attempt to use the other parts of her gift. She knew she could sort of mesmerize people into doing her will like she'd done Dorothea when she wanted her to stop crying. Maybe there was a way to use that instead of taking memories. She'd never tried. And if she hated all the parts of her Nature, she could be a Guardian without them somehow.

Last, she refused to let Seth win. She would fight back.

The thought of the little box outside the shed came to mind with the idea to throw it in the river. "Yes, that is something I can do." But she thought she would also see what happened when the barrier touched it. She made a plan and started walking.

The clouds parted and Miriam looked once again toward Edenia. Was she going *back* back or was she going to do this thing, dump her info to the nearest Edenian and head back out of town?

Sure, she had a purpose for tonight, but what happened when she ate lunch alone again tomorrow? Leaving also had the benefit of being out of the Joneses' way. If she was no longer a Guardian what could the Joneses want with her? She would be free, at least in theory.

Her heart thudded, not knowing what she would choose.

Would she act? Save herself? Live her dream? Be free? Or would she cower back to Edenia expecting to outwit Seth and the Joneses, honor her Guardian covenant, and get married like a good daughter. Hoping that the town would one day not be scared of her?

Miriam thought hard as she walked; she considered this all carefully. It was her time to choose.

She never had a problem being a Guardian. In fact, before she got her Nature she was as zealous as Peter. She remembered her feelings inside Eden, looking at the Tree of Life. She knew, with her heart so full that it overflowed, how much she loved the place, how she would do anything to protect it.

She just hated her particular Nature. But maybe, she could do something about the little pile of souls in herself. Maybe she could be different.

As she fought back and forth between these two things, something occurred to her; what if the only thing standing between Seth and the Joneses getting into the Garden, was *her?* The knowledge she'd just acquired was valuable. She knew it. What if all the pain she'd felt for the last two years had purpose; what if it led her to that shed, to listen to Seth?

The idea would not leave her mind. It kept rolling as she walked. Finally, she justified all the little grievances she had within herself against the probability that the Master knew what he was about, and that, somehow, her Nature was exactly suited to this predicament.

Once her perspective changed, the questions evaporated like the dew, and purpose settled over her like a blanket. She shoved the last bits of tonight's grotesque situation—in which Seth wounded her pride and heart—aside. She would have to deal with them, but not now. Right now, she had a job to do.

The weariness of her flight and the need to do what she could right now bogged her down, but still she moved forward, her shaky legs jolting her down the hillside. She wished she were a wind Nature sometimes. She was so far from the shed.

Her thoughts and her progress went up and down. Once she got down to the level of the river, she rounded a bend and halted at the sound of a whinny. Startled, Miriam turned and saw a man on a white horse moving into her path.

"Miriam?" he asked.

She jumped at her name and backed away.

"Do not be frightened." He moved slowly toward her. "My name is Noah, and the Lord wakened me out of my sleep and said, 'Go, find Miriam. She needs to know I am by her side.' He also put the idea in my head that you might need a horse." He dismounted. "So, here I am, and here you are."

The man was tall and strong in the moonlight. He had short hair and a clean-shaven square face, though the rest of his features were unclear. "Who are you?" He was very close now, but Miriam did not feel afraid. He smelled of campfire.

"A servant of the Lord, just as you are. But I keep his sheep." This startled Miriam, and she wanted to back away, but she couldn't. Then the man went on. "The Lord also wanted me to tell you, he is pleased with your choice."

"Who is this Lord you are talking of? And my choice? What choice?"

He looked puzzled for a moment but then answered her. "Why, to go home, of course. That is why I am here. For you have an important mission to fulfill. Now, would you like to use Buttercup to be on your way?" He thumbed at the beautiful white horse.

Miriam looked between the animal and its rider and wondered what in the world the man spoke of and how very strange he was. However, instead of asking him again who he was or how he would get his horse back or what he meant by all he said, or if he came from the tent city, she felt compelled to do as he bid her.

Before she knew it, she was astride the animal, heading toward the shed, and her duty, with gratitude for the strange man and his Lord in her heart.

CHAPTER 22

Peter

It surprised him when he felt pebbles dig into his feet. He looked down and realized that his Nature had left him again, without him doing anything.

The material point was, he walked toward Lilly, in the middle of the night, in his nightshirt. Before she saw him, Peter ducked behind a neighborhood tree.

Turning his back to the tree he clenched his teeth. There was no way he was talking to them. He hadn't decided what to say yet. *Sorry, I can go all invisible. It's rude and a bit strange but can we still be friends?* He turned back around to see if she was still at the window. She was, but now Abby had joined her.

They both looked awake and open, and somehow forgiving. That had to be in his mind though. However, the thought made him wish he had pants on.

This house was his Uncle Brian's. Maybe he would let Peter borrow...Peter rolled his eyes as he struck down the idea; it was the middle of the night.

And yet...

Uncle Brian was single and not at home. It was his shift in the field house, he was sure of it. Peter smiled. And his mind started concocting what he would say to the girls. This was going to happen.

Peter took one last look at the lit window next door and ran for his uncle's dark porch. Cracking open the door, he walked into the dark space. The shutters in the main room were closed so Peter took a chance and switched on the piano light.

There was junk everywhere; tools, papers, a saddle. It looked more like a tack room than a front room. There were a few jackets hung by the door but that didn't do him any good. He would have to go snooping around.

He thought of looking in the cellar for some old clothes that might actually fit him. Peter flicked the light on once down the ladder and blessed his good luck. Right in front of him, amid a huge mess, was a pile of clothes. It didn't take him long to find several pairs of suitable pants. Carefully he slipped a rather pathetic brown pair on. They were big, but not too bad. There was something stiff in one of the pants pockets, though. He pulled it out, and surprised, examined a photograph. The subjects instantly made him feel awkward. He ignored them at first in favor of examining the background. There was a huge bridge and thousands of buildings. The detail of the picture was astounding and the scope of the city it portrayed, enormous. It could be the other side of Mars for how alien the whole thing looked to Peter. The huge structures, all smooshed together. He stared and stared and couldn't make heads or tails of it all.

His eyes moved to the people whose faced filled the right corner of the photo. They were involved in an almost frenzied embrace. The man's lips pressed firmly against her cheek at the corner of her mouth. His large hand wrapped around the other cheek, pressing the two heads together firmly, fingertips clutching at her desperately. Her hand covered his hand, her eyes closed, her forehead wrinkled as she leaned into him; cementing her acceptance and desire.

His eyes went back and forth between the two people, and suddenly he knew both faces. As realization hit, this image blew his mind for the second time.

This photo told a story that filled in all the gaps of the conversation between his father and Zeke. Just then, an idea sparked in his mind. He could use this. Abby and Lilly were desperate to know why their father forced them to come here. They were in anguish over it. Maybe Peter could steer them to look into this little bit of history. Maybe it would satiate them for a few days, or at least maybe until their Natures took them.

And it would break the ice between them after the lunchroom debacle.

Peter put the photo back into his pocket and began to move up the ladder when he heard a noise from upstairs. His uncle must be home. But he wasn't allowed to leave his watch. Peter paused knowing he would need to get out as soon as his uncle cleared the hall. But that did not happen. Instead the cellar door opened.

Adrenaline pumped through his body, it only took Peter one moment to scuttle behind a few boxes and piles of clothes, and he was glad he did. If Uncle Brian caught him down here in the middle of the night, he probably would have scolded him, then laughed at him. The men coming down the ladder would not be so amenable.

Hirum Miller, his father, and several members of the council scuttled down the ladder one by one. Peter had no intention of embarrassing his father in front of the council with his mischievousness. Carefully he sunk further back into his hiding spot.

"Wasteful of Brian to leave lights on all over the house, Hirum."

His father grunted. "Yes."

"Jeremy, what's the time?"

"It's time. Interference should be silent."

"I do not agree with this, Hirum. What if the Joneses attack again tonight?"

"I know you are concerned, Wallace. But in light of what Garren reported tonight, we must figure out the scope of our problems. Besides, they rarely attack twice in one night."

"What if they hack us, or whatever the kids call it? We never should have gone wireless."

"That dial-up modem was so slow, and the upkeep was getting ridiculous."

"Hirum, why do we continue to send our children on sabbaticals if we do not use the skills they glean to secure Eden?"

"For heaven's sake Wallace, we do use them. I am not in the mood to argue this right now. The council voted, it's done." Peter peeked through the boxes and watched his father sit down at an enormous box with a glass front. Lights went on as his father touched things Peter could not see. It took Peter a minute, but soon he realized it was a computer. Peter had never even seen an actual computer, just a picture during his *Outside Studies* course. Edenia used all kinds of electric devices in moderation: ovens, refrigerators, clocks. Things from the outside they felt they couldn't live without. But the hard, fast line was drawn on communication devices—so he thought.

"I remember what you were like when we wanted to put electric lines in. You thought it was the end of the world, but I'm sure you enjoyed your wife's perfectly cooked meal this night. Stoves are a marvel and so is wireless internet." He heard some clicking noises.

Wireless internet? What? He should have paid better attention in class the day they discussed computers.

"There are about ten thousand articles on what is happening in the Middle East right now. Which one am I supposed to read?"

"What are the topics?"

"North Korea producing an atomic bomb. That one sounds pretty important. It says that Chinese leaders are convinced North Korea has secretly developed a new kind of nuclear bomb..."

For several years now our ally, China, has pleaded with United States to once again broach nuclear negotiations with North Korea. But not even the bloody Korean conflict of 2025 tempted US leaders back to the Korean table. Now Americans have reason to feel threatened. It has taken them five years, but North Korea has followed Syria and Iran, and gained micro-nuclear warheads and the capacity to use them to bomb their enemies.

"Wow, that is scary."

"American enemies having micro-nuclear warheads is very disturbing."

"Who are Korea's enemies? I thought we were friendly with them. And how does this concern us in Edenia?"

"It is just information Wallace."

Peter's father clicked around and every so often reported. "Yes, Russia and Syria are in bed together. They hate the United States as well as most capitalist countries."

"That cannot be. Look up the stuff Garren told you about." There was clicking.

"I see it. It *was* an earthquake. That is where all the people are coming from. The earth just swallowed up whole cities south of us. They told Garren the truth."

After a time, he broke the silence. "I feel violated by all this devastation and death and hatred. However, I see that Ezekiel was right. The world is ripe for destruction. I just looked up the so-called signs of the times. There's a man who combined all the earth's religions; he has it all laid out. What it is and when it happened. I don't tend to put stock in that sort of stuff, but he makes a compelling argument."

"If you take those things seriously."

"What in the world does any of this have to do with us, Hirum?" Wallace's voice stated pointedly.

"Nothing. We have no control over what happens out..." his father cut off mid-sentence. "Now this is interesting. Listen. Um, okay right here."

Many of this faith have followed the command of their leaders and gathered in tent cities. Large white tents are shipped into the area and members gather their necessary items and move from their homes to live in third world conditions in a tent city. There are about twenty of these cities across the United States and thousands live in each.

Why, you may ask? Is it preparation for the end of days? Doomsday, the apocalypse, Armageddon, the end of the world? Yes, people, that is what they claim. According to their leaders the end is upon us...

One of these tent cities lay in Adam-ondi-Ahman which is located in Jackson county Missouri. It has been prophesied by church leaders that not only is this the area where The Garden of Eden was, but that it is where Jesus will come to gather his warriors for the last battle, Armageddon. It is also said to be where Adam will return as a being of light to the earth before Christ comes to organize his people and bring the power of God to many. Very interesting nonsense if you ask...

"Well, anyhow, he goes on to be very condescending."

Peter felt his ears burning. Was that article saying what he thought it was saying?

Jeremy echoed his question. "Is that saying there are people setting up a tent city right over the north hill from us?"

"How old is that article?" Wallace butted in.

"It is saying exactly that, Jeremy. And it looks like...yes it says this article is six months old."

"Six months! Well they would more than have a tent city set up and functioning by now. So, we have an entire community of people living a few miles away, and we didn't even know they moved in?"

His father looked up at Wallace, "Many of us have known about them for the last two years, but at your insistence that we keep to ourselves, we chose to keep this to ourselves." The words were pointed.

"We have no need to let our children..."

Peter's father cut him off, "We don't have time to rehash the decision. You know now. The facts are that they live near us and they have never bothered us."

"Except to steal food."

"Yes, they do take food on a regular basis but that is to be expected and we have plenty."

"Though we must be careful."

"I am always careful Jeremy."

"I know. I'm just saying."

"What we need, now that we understand their purpose, is to find out their intentions."

"I feel like it is fairly obvious. Their leaders are inspired men who told the people to gather in places of safety, and prepare for, well, all the things that are happening in the world that we just read of. Bombs, financial crisis, I saw an article that we didn't click on that spoke of natural disasters that have happened in the last year alone."

"Where?" His father asked and maneuvered around on the computer.

"It was on the last page. Yes, click. Go up. Right there." Jeremy directed.

"I can't believe it." His father exclaimed after only a few minutes. "Floods, fires, earthquakes, hurricanes, volcanoes. Oh, look. It says here,"

The largest volcano in the world is located in Yellowstone National Park, and park rangers and seismologists have reported a record high in activity over the past year. They feel the time has come, and they are expecting moderate volcanic activity to begin any day as a prelude to the main event; the desolation of the northwest via massive explosion.

Nay-sayers complain that they have heard this story before, but never before have all but the most dedicated scientists abandoned their posts in the National Park. That has happened here.

"What I can't believe is that we have been sheltered from all these disasters."

"I can. As I've said, we do an important job." Wallace chimed in.

"Speaking of which, you only told Micah and the interference team to keep it down for an hour and it has been that. Any moment we will lose our internet connection and this computer will be ruined if it has power."

"Yes, I know the rules, my dear man. Is there anything else Ezekiel said that we should look up while we can?"

Peter's father was quiet for a moment and Peter, suddenly conscious that he'd been crouching in the same position for an hour, shifted around a bit. It made a shuffling noise and it wasn't until then that Peter realized he could pull his Nature to him to be silent.

He wasn't used to thinking that way.

Hoping against hope that it would work Peter closed his eyes and did so just as several men in the room turned to look. It must have worked because his father wasn't growling his name and pulling off his belt. Peter opened his eyes and looked around. He'd done it, and done it fast.

Oh, the awesomeness that was earth Nature!

A few uninteresting minutes later, the men rose from their positions and moved up the ladder, chatting all the while.

"I will send Garren to check out this tent city." His father sighed. "Yes, Wallace I know, regardless of the laws, he is my son and if I want to ask him to go, I will do so." Father was not to be argued with when he talked thus, so when none commented he went on. "Well, I think we all should spend some time in reflection about what is ahead of us and our families. Jeremy will go to the border and stand guard the rest of the night. Sam, you get home to that new baby of yours."

Unbidden thoughts and doubts crept into his mind. He didn't want to think about the world at war. He didn't want to think about bombs killing innocent people. He didn't want to think about what would change in Edenia if the apocalypse were to really be here. Many people would die.

And what about these tent cities? It seemed like the leaders were inspired, but would they be on the right side when push came to shove?

Peter knew about the apocalypse the way everyone knew about it. It supposedly was when Christ would come again. He didn't know how he felt about all of that. He believed in a lot of things. He liked the teachings of Buddha, and Martin Luther, Carl Jung, Plato and Jesus. He embraced it all. Just as many in Edenia did.

According to the stories he'd heard, things in the world would get really awful and from what he heard tonight, earth was there at the brink of pretty awful.

The good thing was that he lived in a place where everyone watched everyone else and where moral rules were agreed upon and followed. There was perspective here. The very Nature of the Guardianship demanded a certain level of sacrifice and dedication that naturally led to obedience and a moral life.

So where would this apocalypse leave him? He didn't know.

Then the question had to be; was he going to let fear of the outside world ruin the world he'd made for himself here in Edenia? Didn't he still have plans and motivations and desires, that as of yet, were not touched by the outside? Yes. Yes, he did.

Peter decided to keep all of it to himself. There was no reason to worry everyone, because the Master would protect them if they could not protect themselves. The absolute certainty of that thought nestled in his soul, and he felt no fear. He let go of his Nature, stood and shuffled from behind the boxes.

He set aside his worries in favor of making plans for tomorrow. How would he talk to the girls?

CHAPTER 23

Miriam

This four-legged beauty, Buttercup, was a masterful beast indeed. Miriam seemed to fly through the woods. When she reached the shed, she made quick work in achieving her goal. First, she ripped out the device, then she used the horse to carry it a mile or so out of Edenia where she threw it into the river. It was exceptionally gratifying. But after that work was done, she shrunk from the next task; telling her parents.

What would she tell them, exactly? She pondered if she should tell them about Seth. In the back of her mind she realized she had budding feelings for Seth. Did she really want to ruin any hope of their blossoming friendship by telling her mother that Seth was even more of a threat than she already perceived him to be?

Probably not.

If this worked out how she hoped it would, she would get Seth's phone, his Nature would take him, and no one would be the wiser that he had made a deal with the devil.

She felt right about this choice.

After leaving Buttercup in the barn, she stole into the house and sat on the edge of her papa's side of the bed.

He didn't gradually wake. He woke instantly. With ten kids and enemies attacking at all hours, he was used to it.

He sat up and touched her hand, "What is it? Where are they?"

Miriam didn't know how to begin. Her papa took her hand. "Your trembling Miriam, what is it?"

Her mother was awake now also. She propped herself up on an elbow.

Miriam closed her eyes, took a deep breath and spat it out. "Papa, I cannot use my Nature to take memories any longer, unless the Master asks me directly. It makes me very unhappy and the only way I feel I can continue as a Guardian is if I am not required to use that part of my Nature."

Her mother of course broke in, upset. "Miriam, I do not like your gift, but I trust the Master to give us what we need, and your Nature came just as it was becoming harder and harder for us to remain unseen."

Miriam rose from the bed and turned away from her parents. She took her forehead in her hand and breathed.

"Lu, we must listen."

"What is there to listen to? She is a spoiled child who thinks she is above her duties."

That was it, Miriam spun back around in the dark and faced her mother. "I have done everything you have asked of me. I never act above my duties. Regardless of feeling that they were wrong. Stealing memories is not my Nature. It makes me feel unhappy. It pricks my conscience and I will no longer do it."

"What are you saying Miriam?" Her father asked kindly. "You no longer wish to be a Guardian?"

"No papa." She said, her anger defused by the love in his voice. "I am a Guardian. I think I have finally accepted that that is what I want to be. I am just going to find a different way to use my gifts. That's all. And I would appreciate it if you would let everyone know. They need to be more careful. They need to not be seen. Because I will no longer be using my Nature to take memories."

"We will do no such thing." Her mother said as her father took her and smiled and nodded to her. "If you want to tell them yourself, go ahead, bring shame onto your family."

"Lu!"

Miriam bit her lip. She considered what telling everyone herself might look like, and she instantly knew she didn't care. "Fine mama, I will do it. Please ask at least one member from each family to meet in the Divided Hall tomorrow night. I will tell them then."

"I will do it." Her father said, "Now go on to bed." He squeezed her hand once more.

Miriam breathed a sigh of relief and made her way to her bed.

CHAPTER 24

Monday

Peter

Picture in pocket, Peter headed to school. He had all the excuse he needed to tempt the girls into a conversation, and what a conversation it would be. This was the first time ever he wished he could un-know something. His mom and their dad. Yuck and weird. He wondered if the relationship had somehow caused Ezekiel to not come back to Edenia and then to *come* back.

Once at school, he searched through the hall and found the girls standing outside their first class. Lillian looked pale, and she had her hand to her head.

Peter snuck up behind them and slithered the picture between their shoulders. They both glanced at it and then at him and then quickly back at the photo. He watched as the girls examined it. Both faces held confusion.

"Okay, weirdo." Abby said in a whisper and turned toward him. "Oh my heck, what is up with your eyes?"

"I have no idea what you're talking about." Peter said casually.

"Oh my gosh, do you have another superpower, like werewolf power or something? And it makes you need to skulk around at night and howl at the moon," Lillian asked, excited by the idea.

"And gives you yellow eyes?" Abby added with condescension verging on disgust.

"I like them." Lillian said, "They're glowy."

This was a bit ironic but Peter kept that to himself. "No, I am not a werewolf. Will you just look at this?" He wiggled the photo. "I know that you've only met her once but the lady in this picture is my mother. Do you recognize the man?" He held it still.

"Of course." Lilly answered, "It's our...dad." Her voice started out incredulous but ended with surprise as realization dawned.

"I was snooping around in my uncle's house and found this. I thought maybe it might help you understand why you're here."

Before he could finish, Abby broke in. "Why, in this place, would you have any reason to snoop?" She snapped the photo out of his hands and examined it closely. "This is Manhattan. I recognize the skyline, though this picture is super old.

"I don't know, it seems like *several* people have the need for snooping around, or at least being out in the middle of the night." That recaptured Abby's attention. He raised an eyebrow at them, and that shut them up for a minute as they shared a furtive glance.

He literally saw their trajectory shift.

Just like that, there was an understanding. There would be no questions about why he was snooping or there would be questions about why Seth was out in the middle of the night.

Lillian put on a flirtatious smile just as Abigail narrowed her eyes at him.

Abby spoke first, "Ya know Pete, I'm not sure I can look at you. I am just too freaked out. What are you? You...you can..."

So maybe their father hadn't talked to them. So how in the world were they dealing with this? One thing was obvious, they were both pretending nothing had happened, until now.

He knew from his dream, which came to his thoughts just then, that this moment was an important one and that being honest was the only way to get through it.

So, he blurted out, "Turn invisible, I know. It's totally rad right?"

"No," Abby burst out her face contorting with repulsion. "It's wrong, sick and..."

Lilly broke in "That's not the worst thing he can do. Is it true that you rigged a bucket of cow crap to drop on anyone coming into the barn?"

Why was she changing the subject? It kind of felt like they should talk about the whole invisible thing.

Peter went along with it simply because it was a more comfortable topic. "Who's asking?" He inquired, feigning a guilty glance around.

"And that you regularly put rotten eggs in people's boots. Or that you find it hilarious to hypnotize the chickens? Or that you spent an entire month only communicating with people via pea-shooter."

"Ok, who have you been talking to?" Peter asked concerned. "There were very good reasons I did all those things."

"Reasons?"

"Yes. It's research. And that pea-shooter thing made me an exceptional aimer."

"Research? That's the excuse he gives? Research." Lilly's eyebrows rose, but the corners of her mouth still went up in a very pretty way.

Abby looked from her sister to Peter and remarked, "You know Pete, I'm trying to decide if you're the creepiest boy I have ever met or just some kind of super evil genius I should admire." The bell tolled, and they walked into the classroom.

Lilly chimed in, "I am voting for option two. If he can find trouble here, where everything is rosebuds and lollypops, he has to be an evil genius."

Peter smiled. Finally, they understood. Well except about the evil part. They sat down at their desks.

"I guess every family needs a black sheep." Wagging the picture at him she changed the subject. "If this isn't trouble, I don't know what is."

Peter saw his chance. "Exactly. Remember how you said that during your meeting with the council there was lots of talk between my dad and yours about some horrible betrayal or whatever."

"Attention sortir vos cahiers de travail." Esther called to them.

Lilly smiled at him and whispered, "We'll talk later." They looked at Esther for their lesson.

You're talkin' to me now. Peter thought to himself and smiled. His work was done here.

CHAPTER 25

Seth

Before last night he'd felt like Edenians were nice people. A bit odd with weird beliefs, sure, but nice, good, salt of the earth kind of people. Now he felt like he was on the set of Invasion of the Body Snatchers and Edenians were welcoming in the same way the pod people were welcoming. *Save me from the pod people!* Kept circling in his mind.

Seth moved determinedly through the cafeteria line, gathering his aromatic tray of vegetable goulash. There was no way he was sitting in here again. Not with all these freaks. It was bad enough to sit next to them in class. All he could think about was which freaky ability each had and how he could *not* become one of them.

He caught sight of his sisters with Peter, the little weirdo, across the lunchroom. Lillian had been so sick this morning she could barely get out of bed. She barfed from her meds and she said her head felt like it would explode. But Mother got some food into her and now he never would guess how sick she was. Those meds, they were a miracle. Her, smiling and laughing hurt his heart.

Focus. He told himself.

So, this morning, after their first class, Lilly chased him down and made it clear that Peter had brown eyes until today. Now they were golden.

Seth made a point of walking right by them now. Peter looked up at him as he passed and gave him a mischievous grin. The boy's eyes were just as much brown as they were yellow in Seth's opinion. They were freaky looking. Seth shivered and kept circling the lunchroom, uncertain of where to go.

Earlier, he'd jumped to the conclusion that everyone with brown eyes could do what Peter did, but now he forced himself to be objective. Peter didn't have brown eyes anymore. *How could someone's eye color change?* He shivered.

So only people with yellow eyes could do what Peter did? If all his assumptions were correct. He would figure out this eye thing.

The problem was how to get started. He only had seen Peter's freak out, and none of these kids had eyes like Peters.

Mr. Jones only said they *thought* their powers were determined by eye color. Peter's transformations seem to confirm this theory.

On his second lap around the lunchroom he realized all the vivid irises were on him. He felt like he had a target of some kind painted on his forehead. It was time for flight, and he spotted his exit. He left the lunchroom behind.

The smell of mulch was in the air, with the sound of rustling leaves in his ears. He stood under a semi-covered porch dotted with a few picnic tables. Completely empty of freaks. Great. For a third time, he shivered. Either he was getting a cold, or he was truly creeped out by the mutants inside.

Seth placed his tray on the nearest table and buttoned up his coat. He looked around at the yard that lay beyond the porch. Play-yard equipment stood to the left. Children covered the metal as thick as ants. They laughed and yelled. Seth was sad for them growing up here.

He looked away to his right toward several mammoth trees. It was quite pretty here. Those trees were so huge and ancient. Under the arching limbs of an antique oak, wrapped in a coat and sitting on a blanket, sat someone else.

The person, for whatever reason, wanted solitude too. Her hair was pale and very long. He knew it could only be one person, his odd cousin, Mary or something. She was the one the twins accused of being an alien. Their visceral reaction to her—mixed with the whole alien thing—intrigued him.

For a moment he thought, and realized the twins weren't the only ones who reacted that way. He saw her on his first night here, all alone but for a few adults. In the lunchroom when it happened, she sat alone, and now she sat alone again. How could she be strange to these people? What would make you freaky among freaks?

Not being one of them.

And for a moment he contemplated Eve's scathing remark yesterday coming back to him. *"You're the freak show here."* He was the oddity here. But he had the perspective that in the real world of seven plus billion people, he was normal. It could keep him warm at night. What did this girl have? She was out of place here where normal people were out of place. Maybe she was normal, and that's why she was odd.

Suddenly an overwhelming desire to speak to her grew in his chest. Despite her purposeful separation, he needed to sit under that tree, on her blanket, next to her. Before he was certain what he was doing, he'd picked up his tray and began walking her way.

On the way, he realized that he'd gone about this in a bass-ackward way. Eve was not who he should be prying info from; this lonely, unattractive, unpopular girl, was. She would probably fall all over herself if a boy paid attention to her. Even if he was her cousin.

Putting on a smile, Seth's step lightened as he approached her. Her back was toward him but when he was about three steps from her blanket, a high, quiet voice asked, "How's your head, Seth?" and the girl took a bite out of a huge red apple as if she didn't have a care in the world.

Seth's feet stopped as his hand went to the rather sizable goose egg he'd gotten at the chapel. Confused about how she knew about his head and how she'd known it was him coming up behind her, he asked, "How'd you know..."

The girl turned violet eyes, so large and round they did seem alien, toward him. They held censure. Like he should know everything she knew and not ask such stupid questions. Maybe he'd made a mistake. Maybe she was just freakier than the rest and that was why she was alone.

He thought for a moment about leaving, but then she turned back around, and her pale sheet of hair fluttered a bit in the breeze. A few things clicked. She was the girl he'd talked to in the church, that's how she knew.

Didn't he promise himself that he would thank her, if he got the chance? Sucking up his uncertainty, he asked, "Can I sit with you?" The cocky smile of a moment ago gone from his face.

She didn't speak, just flourished a hand out, as if to say, 'Be my guest'.

Carefully he placed his tray and sat. Looking over at her solemn and thoughtful observation of the playing children and her obvious unaffectedness at his presence, he rethought his plan of wowing her into sharing all of Edenia's secrets. "Thank you." He said simply.

She turned and raised her eyebrows.

"For listening to me in the church and making me laugh. I needed it."

"Sure." She said without a bit of emotion and turned back to watching the children.

He felt a tad dejected by her one-word answer. It was weird but a part of him hoped that bringing up their earlier conversation would break the ice. For some reason he wanted to talk to her. He wanted to open up the way he'd done with the wood partition between them. He wanted a friend. A very short-term friend. Why not this girl? She'd been really helpful. And it might just be possible that she wasn't like everyone else which was why they all ignored her. That suited him just fine.

A thought occurred to him. He wondered if he'd hurt her feelings when he laughed at her silly question: *'Is that how you get on a boat? You hop.'* Even now it made him smile, but he wondered if she were serious. Maybe this girl had never been on a boat. "And, I'm sorry I laughed at you, about the boat thing...it just..." but he knew that if he justified the action it negated the apology, so he stopped himself and repeated. "I'm just sorry."

She turned more slowly back toward him this time. Observing; those fascinating, huge eyes squinting at him as if she were mystified by his comment. "Okay." The word exited her mouth slowly and her brow wrinkled. Her mouth moved, but she stopped herself and looked away, rocking back and forth almost anxiously.

He stayed silent, and having nothing else to do, tucked into his food. The now frigid vegetables were not distracting enough though and his eyes kept returning to the girl with the white-blonde hair as long and straight as a being out of a mythical story.

Finally, the energy of her movement boiled over into her voice. "So, are you going to answer my question then?"

He swallowed. "The boat question?"

She nodded with quick jerking shakes, as if she were uncertain she wanted to know but would force herself into the truth of it all anyhow.

He bit his lips to stop a smile. Then used the excuse of clearing out his mouth to give him time to settle down. Laughing again would not help his case with her. He cleared his throat once more and answered, "Sure. Um, you don't hop to get on a boat. You just walk on."

She nodded. "So, what if you don't want to get wet?"

He sniffed his laugh away, "Well, they have like a gang plank, not like in the pirate days like; 'walk the plank, ye scurvy dogs' but like…" he struggled. "um." He paused because she was looking at him so confused. "It's like a bridge over the water from the port to the boat."

"So, you saying hop, it was just a colloquialism?" She half stated, half asked.

He turned away from her and smiled, "You could put it that way. Yes."

"Well," she said straightening out her skirt. "I must say that relieves my mind. I was having the hardest time imagining it."

His head whipped back around toward her and he couldn't help but smile. "I imagine you would."

She examined him openly with no pretense, almost as if a child were looking at him. It didn't make him feel self-conscious—it just, was.

"I'm sure it all might seem silly to you, but there are many things we don't learn about here, and if we have no practical experience, then…" she left it hanging.

"You're lost. I get it. It's sort of cute," the word made him blush, "I mean like cute like childlike or innocent." He clarified.

She did not blush, she just examined him. Again. Her mind working at a million miles an hour. He could see it as he studied her right back.

Everyone had brightly colored eyes here—he now knew there was a reason for it, though he didn't understand the particulars—but he had to wonder at hers. They were like nothing he'd ever seen before. Such weirdly colored irises had to signify something. Like a certain type of *power*. A shiver went up his back at the word.

He considered her. No one else he'd seen looked like her. Not to mention everyone avoided her. Her father was extremely protective of her. She had to be different from the rest of them. Perhaps she didn't have any *power* at all.

Scraping his plate clean he told himself he would speak to her, but before he could, she broke the silence.

Her round face turned a bit red, her knowing eyes so bright and intelligent. "Did you find what you were looking for?"

Startled by the question—he felt like a little boy with his hand in the cookie jar—he wondered what she knew. His mind flitted through all his contraband info. The deal he'd made with Mr. Jones, all the secrets he'd learned and shared. Lilly, her doctor's appointment, how he couldn't let her die.

Even if she knew any or all of that stuff, he couldn't talk about it with her, could he? He considered it for a millisecond, of course he couldn't.

At the last second before not answering would become uncomfortable, his brain came up with the only possible thing she could be referring to that he could answer. "You mean in the scriptures? No, not really. But what I did find helped." He looked down at his hands a characteristic bit of shame slinking up the collar of his shirt making his skin feel flushed. He pulled at it and trained his eyes on the playing children.

Out of the corner of his eye, he saw her nod and turn her head away. The moment her large eyes left him, he felt chilled. They sat in silence for a few moments while Seth gathered himself.

He thought back to their conversation in the church and decided to throw her off the subject. "So, your sister Eve told me that you all get to leave here and do like a work study sort of thing. Do you know where you'll go for yours?"

Her amazingly alien eyes flashed at him, then down to the blanket where she picked at its ties. "I won't be going on sabbatical." Emotions a mile deep were contained in those words.

"Why not?"

She shifted, but kept quiet.

Finally, she conceded the silence to him and offered. "I have a predicament, similar to Eve's, yet in a different vein of life." The formality in her words could be cut with a knife.

Yet Seth laughed, "I wouldn't exactly call having every boy in this place crushing on you a predicament. From the looks of all the sad mooning faces, I'd call it an epidemic. One I would say was unwarranted, well, I suppose, unless you like to talk to a girl and not just look at her." Once he said it, he bit the inside of his lip wondering if he'd again put his foot in his mouth.

But Miriam surprised him when she turned to look. Some sort of realization grew quickly in her face, then, slowly, a smile formed on her watermelon-red lips. Seth watched the attitude alter her face. It seemed to tilt all her features up, color rushed to her cheeks, and light danced in her astonishing violet eyes.

In that brief moment; she. was. gorgeous. It was as if the feeling required by a smile transformed every feature of her face from alien to perfection.

She was the most amazingly angelic human he'd ever seen, he admitted to himself in shock. He would happily spend every moment left in his life staring at her face. Monuments should be made to celebrate beauty such as this. It forced his heart to accelerate and made his palms sweat. Eve was an ugly duckling compared to a smiling Miriam.

That was her name. Miriam.

She graced him with five very solid seconds of her joy and then her face turned away from him, though she held the smile.

He felt the loss of her pleasure instantly. Like the way you feel when the sun moves behind a cloud on a cold day.

"Miriam," he said urgently, needing her to look back at him.

It wasn't until she looked that he realized he had nothing to say to her. He fumbled through ums and uhs while his eyes watched her amazing face. The smile slipped, and she began to look annoyed.

Spell broken.

"Well, spit it out Seth Johnson. I was positive that articulation was one of your talents." One eyebrow rose.

Now that he knew that smile lived in her face, he could see the beauty even when she looked cross. Had he been completely blind before?

"I, um, only asked because you said in the church that you would never go anywhere." He remembered in a brilliant bit of luck. "In fact, you seemed pretty upset about it."

She looked away again, dejection like a mask on her lovely face. "It's called the Divided Hall, not the church or chapel, by the way, and sabbatical was my only chance," she whispered. "So, no, I won't." She turned to him, angry. "And you know how crappy that is?"

This was a rhetorical question, he hoped. He didn't want to open his mouth for fear that he would laugh at the way she said 'crappy'. She was so formal. Or so intelligent maybe? Still the word sounded a bit out of place.

She was going on, so he tried to pay attention.

"Because if there is anyone here that wants to know about the outside, who needs to smell it and touch it and see it, it's me." Her bitterness was real and overwhelming. "The ability to choose for myself what life I lead, and the lessons taught by experience, I can confidently say, are necessary, nay foundational, to my very soul." She paused sucking in a breath, for she'd said this all in one.

"Eve said it was the time for you to decide if this," he motioned around him, "is really what you want. That going outside was a test. Is that what you are trying to say?"

Her cheeks flushed scarlet, and she nodded her confirmation that he was correct.

"I may be stepping out of bounds here, but you don't seem like this is all about having outside experiences." He scooted closer to her, "Maybe it's about you not wanting to be here. Are you trying to tell me, Miriam, that you wouldn't choose this life if you had the choice?" He whispered tentatively. Then he laughed, "If that is what you are saying, believe me I get it."

Miriam eyed him. There were actual tears gathering in her eyes. They had not fallen, but they stood there as a testament for how important this topic was to the girl. She sniffed, placing her chin on her shoulder, she closed her lashes. The tears toppled down her cheeks. Then she looked up at him. Leaned toward him.

He could actually smell her hair now. It didn't smell like perfume or flowers, but it did smell clean and light. He liked the smell, though he didn't know what it was.

"No," She finally spoke. "I used to want to leave and not come back, but things have changed." Her cheeks flushed again, "I cannot believe I said those words out loud and in front of you no less."

Seth smiled at her, "I'm easy to talk to. Sisters. You have to do a lot of listening. What do you mean used to?"

"It does not matter. I think I found a reason to stay." She looked down breaking his mesmerized gazing. "I think right now I just wish I could go out there for a little while. You know. Pick a city and go exploring for a few weeks. Or heck, maybe just one week, if that is all I can have." She wiped at her nose and added, "Just something all-encompassing and exciting that shows me what the real world, the world we'd be in if we weren't..." She stopped and clicked her mouth shut.

"...here." He finished.

She nodded and moved her chin from her shoulder to rest it on her knees. "I just want to see it. Taste it. Smell it all. For a little while."

Wanting to help her feel comfortable, to share, and wanting another smile, he quipped, "Well let me tell you from firsthand experience, wanting to smell the outside is just plain crazy." He laughed, but she didn't, so he hurried on, not wanting to offend her. "Let me just concoct a little picture for you. Take urine, animal doo, vomit, sweat, and grease, shake that all together, add a dash of dirty human, a smidgen of mold and a helping of death, bake at approximately 100° for 2000 years and I imagine that dandy of a cocktail smells rather better than many streets I've strolled down in Cairo or Quebec."

Her nose wrinkled up while he spoke, but by the end she was *smiling*, and Seth thought he might die. Who cares about her IQ when she can smile like that! How was it possible something so small, such tiny movement of muscle, could take his breath away? It just altered her into the exact replica of a goddess.

As that thought formed, he wanted to punch his own head. How super cheesy was that? Still as that smile held, his eyes were dazzled, and his brain couldn't be rational. He smiled back at her.

"You really don't paint a very tasteful picture. It makes me a little ashamed for the dreams I've had." She looked away again.

Wanting her attention again, he went on. "Don't get me wrong." He had her eyes again. "There are places so beautiful, and sweet smelling, so filled with life and color, so full and messy that no picture could—wait, I have pictures." Seth said excited to please her. He reached into his pocket and took out his cell phone. He flipped it open before he realized what he had done. Not only was this not his cell phone with his pictures of Egypt but it was the burner phone from Mr. Jones.

Miriam squeaked and went pale. She eyed the phone and for a full ten seconds Seth was not sure what to do. But then her eyes lifted to his and her face slowly lit up like a neon moon. "Oh my, is that a cellular phone? Does it work? Can I touch it?" Her hands shot out and hovered inches away from Seth's phone. There were lights on, so she could see that it worked. "How is it working?" she wondered and scrunched up her forehead.

Mesmerized by her happiness and her smile, and basically all the expressions she was revealing to him, he dumbly handed the phone over to her. She took it so gingerly he knew she'd never touched one before. She kept muttering, "Oh my heck, oh my heck, oh my heck." as she examined it from every angle.

After a few minutes she asked, "You said there are pictures in here?"

Seth watched her with wonder, but shook his head at her question. "My other one has the pictures. I forgot."

"You have two?" Her excitement ratcheting up another notch which shot excitement up his spine like a jolt of electricity.

"Oh, no. Not anymore. I had to give my other one to your dad, when we got here."

"Yes," she added looking a lot less excited, though she still continued fiddling with the phone. "I suppose you would have, wouldn't you? Well, how did you keep this one?"

Seth thought quickly. "Um I don't, you see I, uh, didn't know we were coming here, to Edenia, and that we would be staying, and I had business, um I mean a friend that I needed to finish some business with. So, when that's all taken care of, I'll get rid of it." He reached over and pressed the home button so it would light up again. Unfortunately, it chose that moment to not cooperate. When she looked at him to question his action, he knew he needed to convert her. She needed to not do anything about this. He had to convince her to keep this quiet. "Miriam," he said and deciding to tell as much of the truth as he could. He pulled out his most convincing tone ever, "do you think we can keep this a secret, at least for a few more days? I have this person in my life. She needs help and I'm the only one that can help her. She's counting on me and I just don't want to get in trouble before I can finish doing, what I need to do."

As usual, she was completely unaffected by his charming attempts.

"It is literally life and death. I wouldn't ask you otherwise." He added for good measure.

"I feel like I need to know more. This is a big no-no around here." Her voice and eyes innocent, asking her questions, expecting truthful answers. No games no gimmicks, just Miriam.

Seth struggled with what to tell her. His brain wouldn't think and lying wasn't his forte. With the CIA always checking your stories, what was the point, and practice does make perfect. So, a true statement came out. "Um, I can't really tell you any more than that." His voice rose in pitch with each word.

Her eyebrows knotted all up and her mouth pinched.

He went on quickly with an idea. "I'll tell you what. If you can keep this a secret until Friday, I will tell you anything you want to know about the outside. Use me and abuse me baby." He smiled broadly at her.

She turned away quickly, pulling the phone to her chest. "As fun and potentially compromising as that sounds, it's probably better I don't learn too much. I mean I already know a lot. It's just the practical aspects of things, like getting onto boats that I guess I don't understand. And who needs to know that stuff."

How could she deliver some of the things she said with a straight face? He paused to appreciate how artless she was before gently asking, "Are those your words, or your parents'?"

She looked down at the phone, her hands white from clutching it. Then, she regarded him, her face uncertain yet desperate. Somehow their glance stuck together. As he searched her face, he realized that a quiet intensity lived between her eyes and his. A yearning, a belonging he'd never felt before. But it was more than that.

She was so beautiful and open. Her face perfect, and like a window into her soul.

He shook his head. Holy crap, had he really just thought *window into her soul?* There were so many ways in which his thoughts were antiquated and cliché. At the top of that list: she was his COUSIN.

She spoke, and reality hit. "Tell me, is this really actually life and death? Of someone you know?" The words were intense, but her gaze probed for the slightest hint of a lie.

"Yes."

"And how will this life and death business be done on Friday? Will someone die on Friday? How could you know that?"

He saw her analytical mind working. "This person has a life-changing doctor's appointment on Friday and with this," he pointed to the phone "I am going to do everything in my power to make sure she gets there."

She thought for several moments. Seth waited, knowing that his mistake had put Lillian's life in Miriam's hands. "Seth, on Friday you will have been here eight days." Her face held insinuations and questions he did not comprehend.

"Yeah. And?"

"I am uncertain what to say. The course ahead of me seems treacherous either way." She almost seemed like she was talking to someone else.

Confused he asked, "What?"

She shook her head and huffed. "I don't know if I can do this." She stood up, brushing crumbs off her skirt. She picked up both of their trays and put them to the side, before yanking on the blanket which was still securely under Seth's butt.

Moving out of her way and thinking quick he said, "My dad told me about the seven-day thing." He smoothly let that hang in the air. It wasn't a total lie, but he wasn't even sure if seven days was a hard and fast rule since his dad had also mentioned ten days.

Miriam stopped folding up the blanket and stared at him.

He picked up the end of her blanket and tightening the corners together, then brought it up to her. Though he was a good six inches taller than her, when he came near, their faces were closer than ever. He couldn't stop looking into her eyes and he couldn't stop imagining what it would be like to touch her silky cheek.

However, when pushing the blanket corners into her fingertips, he felt that she was still hanging onto his phone, this brought his mind back to the important business he had. Just barely.

He easily slipped it from her cloth-filled palm and put it back in his pocket. Bending down he grabbed the bulk of the blanket and pulled it up to put into her hands.

But she'd dropped her side, her hands outstretched toward his head. Just as she lunged forward, her face pale, her fingers twitching, he bent again for the corners. She ended up almost knocking both of them down. Seth fell to a knee and caught her around the waist effectively stopping her from going bottom-up over his shoulder.

He pulled her sideways, in a sort of dip, her hand on his shoulders. He only had a few moments of being so close to her, but that's all it took to be spellbound. Her skin was absolutely the most perfect cream. Not a freckle or blemish. Her eyes were lined with white lashes he could have taken a ruler to, and those glorious violet irises...

They were so large and clear and—rotating. Her irises were, like, rotating.

She scuttled back from him, and once she had her balance, turned around, her face seemed red and pale all at the same time.

He stood slowly, unnerved and yet intrigued. Was this her gift? Eyes that moved, maybe she could hypnotize people. He felt pretty hypnotized. Though whatever he'd seen was gone now. He ripped his gaze from hers and stared down at the blanket, shaking his head. He'd have to consider that possibility later when he wasn't so befuddled.

Looking back at her he saw she was trembling. "You okay?" Seth asked and bent to pick up the blanket again. "I don't know how you do this..." he held the mess of a blanket up, "...around here, but can I teach you my way of doing it? It's sort of fun."

She paused, her eyebrows knotting up in confusion for a split second. Then she licked her lips, nodded, and took a step toward him, a small smile on her face.

He just wanted to stare at her for like an hour straight. He wanted her to talk to him. He wished she would, in that serious way of hers, part her perfect lips and tell him what a fool he was.

But she didn't. She did nothing.

Shaking his head again he cleared his thoughts. This girl was his cousin. How many bloody times did he have to tell himself that? She obviously remembered because over the past two intense silences they shared, her face did not alter, her eyes gave nothing away. This meant, in his experience, she felt nothing, and why would she? He was the only idiot mesmerized. He was the only weirdo awed by his own cousin.

But this wasn't a purely physical thing, like, she wasn't just some beautiful person. If he were honest with himself, he felt something for her in the chapel, long before he knew who she was. No, despite its early stage, this was a multi-dimensional attraction; instant and full, not frantic. The question was, why was he feeling something?

He pushed the corners of the blanket into her palms. Slowly pulling his fingers from her grasp he stepped away and started his explanation.

"So, you take those corners. Then the other person bends down, lifts the bottom and gives it over." Doing this he couldn't help but get a zing in his stomach as their hands once again touched. But this time he didn't agonize over it, he pushed it aside and went on. "And you repeat." Which he did. "Until it's folded into a nice square. Military brat." He thumbed at himself and stood awkwardly smiling at her.

But her face held humor.

Uncertain of what to do next, he pulled the blanket from her arms and cleared his throat. "Uh, you knew exactly how to fold a blanket, didn't you?"

She did not speak, only kept that adorable half-smile going.

"Well, why did you let me go on thinking I was teaching you?" Seth asked, biting the inside of his cheek, embarrassed.

But she left the question hanging between them, forcing his glance from her mouth to her eyes. He shivered and decided he was a little too excited by the chill this whole scenario sent running up his spine. He wanted to step closer to her.

Parting her lips, she asked. "How much did your father tell you?"

She asked this as if the last two minutes never happened. As if they hadn't touched and connected in a way Seth felt a little lightheaded about.

Clearing his throat. His mouth was uncommonly dry. He spoke without really thinking. "About Edenia?"

She nodded.

"He told us just about everything."

"Well, if that's true, then you know that having that thing is ridiculous, pointless." She motioned vaguely at his pants pocket, her eyes darting there fearfully.

However, her face led him to believe that she might know more than he thought she knew. "I don't see it that way." He answered with a quiver in his own voice.

She didn't pause in her response, "How else can you see it? If you know." There was censure again in her tone and she turned away from him.

Seth reached out a hand and pulled her to him, not completely to him, but enough that when she spun around at his pull their sides pressed together for a moment. She looked him up and down slowly, lingering on his hand on her arm and when their eyes met, he said, "Please. Can you just trust me? There's something important I have to finish before I make this place my life."

"I do not think it is me that needs to trust, Seth Johnson." It was said in such a pointed, yet sincere way Seth's head spun. Miriam stepped back, and he dropped his hand. Then her eyes—the violet irises almost seeming to stir—penetrated him. She looked away from him. He would swear those eyes had pulsated, moved, and then seemed to spin dizzyingly.

He felt something cover him. Like peace and assurance that things would work out if... what? He trusted? For a sliver of a moment he trusted her completely. He trusted everything around him. He trusted life to work out exactly as it should. He felt compelled to vomit out all his secrets to her right then and there.

But the bell sounded, and her eyes went to the doors that were opening.

She took one more step back, and to his utter shock nodded, once. "Fine, I will do what I can to help. I will meet you under this tree tomorrow at lunch." She turned and walked toward the school, but turned in a circle. As her walking twirl took her face toward him again, she met his eyes and said softly in acquiescence, "I want to know everything about the outside." Then over her shoulder she added, "You forgot our lunch trays."

He smiled to himself and knew that the pod people were not the only people living in Edenia. Miriam, the most beautiful, most interesting, most charming girl on the planet also lived here. And just like many of his sex before him, he admitted that a beautiful girl could steal all motivation, bulldoze all dreams, reroute all needs and wants. A beautiful girl could change the whole world.

He took a moment and savored how he felt. He felt accepted. He felt excited. He felt expectant.

But his logical mind broke into the dreamy fog of mesmerism. Why had she had such an effect on him in the two conversations they'd had? It could not only be her beauty, because the first time they'd talked, he hadn't seen her.

He analyzed himself as he ignored the warning bell and gazed toward the doors Miriam had left him through.

He had a mask he wore; he knew it. A jack-A persona he presented. 'Aloof glare, I don't care' was kind of his motto. Sometimes he worried he played that role so much that it was beginning to be who he was.

This persona was a direct result of the life his father had chosen for their family, for the person his father was—aloof and distant himself—and because of his father segregating them from family members (i.e. people obligated to give him love and tough love). Seth needed both.

It also didn't help that every place he'd lived the kids his age considered him a temporary implant, someone always on the verge of leaving, a 'sort-of' friend.

That all changed here. Here in this place, with his cousin Miriam, he felt pulled in. Unable to be aloof.

With her directness, she cut through his bull crap and she did not get offended when he put his foot in his mouth. With her open, childlike ways, she completely disarmed him. With one glance of her immutable eye she eradicated the jerk. He was more himself in the few minutes he was with her than he'd been with anyone, including his sisters, in what felt like an eternity.

And he felt better, like, a better person. He had exposed himself and was vulnerable; two things he never did, and it was liberating.

It was a seriously bonding experience.

He wondered if she felt the same; he hoped she did. He couldn't wait to find out.

Seth picked up the trays, and with a smile on his face, a jauntiness to his step, and hope in his heart, he reentered the lunchroom.

CHAPTER 26

Peter

Peter's eyelids closed again and again, slower to open with each breath.

His *Western Government and Politics'* teacher Mrs. Marcy had a talent for boring people to tears, or snores. Peter succumbed halfway through class. No sooner had he closed his eyes than he saw the ribbon filling that strange dark expanse. He noticed this time that he felt contained like he was in a room, and yet he felt dwarfed by the blackness.

The ribbon moved to him this time.

As his consciousness zoomed into the mire of color and threads that became huge pillars of light, he felt a whisper of knowledge come over him. He knew he was standing in front of Miriam's pillar of light and life, and he knew that his pillar was now next to hers, entwined with hers. An admonition reverberated through his soul; *Say yes. Say yes. Say yes.*

"Peter Miller!" Mrs. Marcy thundered "It is not nap time."

Shocked, Peter sat up and blinked at his teacher. The kids snickered and Peter would have made a smart remark, he was sure he had one somewhere; but his mind was filled with confusion over what he had just seen. And more, what it meant.

He was certain about one thing. He would soon find out.

Abby and Lilly said they would drop by his house after school today, and he could not wait.

His mother sat at their kitchen table, and when he came in the back door she stood. She had not been herself the last few days. Yelling and snapping at everyone was not her normal behavior.

Perhaps having the Johnson's here was why his mother had acted so weird. Maybe it was hard on her to see Ezekiel. Maybe she was embarrassed or ashamed. He would be. Someone other than your spouse kissing you was bad, but having it captured on film…

Still, he didn't want a lecture, so he hurried to put his books away.

"Peter," his mother called.

Stopping on his way down the hall he sighed. "What did I do now, mother?"

An exasperated huff came from the kitchen, "Peter, please come sit with me."

Her tone intrigued him, so he moved toward the kitchen. He sat. He looked at his mother expectantly.

"I just wanted you to know that I am proud of you." She said simply.

Peter's eyebrows shot to his hairline. "What…for?"

"Well, not only did you wait so patiently and faithfully on your Nature to emerge, but by my reckoning you have—for the first time in your life—gone two days in a row without a whipping." She wiped a hand on her apron and continued. "I decided long ago that if you could go at least two days without an infraction I would use the energy I normally use disciplining you to do something special for you instead." She leaned over and produced a pie from the seat of the chair next to her. She placed it in front of him.

He slouched down in his chair to hover over the blessed offering and sniffed. "Is this for me?"

"You know it is. For whom else do I bake apple pies?"

"Everyone."

His mother laughed as he took the fork she handed him and stood to lovingly cut a generous slice. He wondered as the aroma hit him—

and he watched the steam of the baked apples rise—why, oh why, hadn't she told him about this little arrangement long ago? He would regularly restrain himself if it meant getting an apple pie for his trouble.

She talked as she did so. "However happy I am with this lapse in misbehavior, you must know that it begs a question." She carefully plopped the pie slice on a plate and asked, "How are you dear?" As she put the plate in front of him, she reached over and ran her thumb over his cheek, like she always did when he was a child.

"I am fine, mother." He said through apples and cinnamon and flaky, buttery crust. The pie was perfection. He pulled away from her fingers, just a tad. "Although it seems I might have some emotional problems because I am so close to crying over this delicious pie."

She sat down and reached out for his arm. Then she moved her chair closer to his. "It is more than that. I want you to know that I love you. You are such a smart, gifted, young man, and I am so proud about your Nature. Earth is truly one of the most important Natures to our family and to the garden." She squeezed his arm and their eyes met. "I know how much the Master trusts those he gives that particular gift to. He has to, because you are above men's judgments. You can hide anything you do. You are your own judge. He has such faith in you Peter, and I do too."

These words filled him with something he didn't know he was missing. He really did feel like crying. He dug back into the pie and ignored the sniffs that came through his nose.

"And more, he gave you a mixed Nature. I am excited to see what the future holds for you." She patted him. "I also wanted to talk to you about something else important," she said, and her cheeks flushed a little. "I know the Johnson girls have caught your eye. I just want to remind you that it is very important who you choose to invest your feelings into. Those girls were not raised here and if you want to pursue one of them, we need to make sure they accept our way of life first."

What is even happening right now? Peter thought. So, this was not a reward pie, it was a procreation pie. Great!

"Mom, please stop. Pa and I have gone over this."

"I know, I know. But since you are hanging out with girls, I just thought we could review."

He got up from the table. "Mom, they're my cous..." His mother's eyes flashed at the contraction. He calmed his voice down. "They are my cousins, mother. And I know that does not matter to most people here, but I am a man of science." Emphasizing the separation of words, then he added, "Be serious. And may I remind you, I am only fourteen." He didn't even feel bad about using the lie to hide how he felt.

She put up a finger, "*Almost* fourteen."

He let it slide.

Her eyes went distant, and she took in a deep breath before saying, "I was fourteen when I fell in love. Besides, do you have any idea how many people marry their cousins?"

"That is just revolting. It causes birth defects."

"Not in Edenia it does not. And someday that may not matter as much as it does right now."

"What? To me, that is always going to matter." He picked up his plate and took it to the sink. "Always." From this comment he knew his mother knew that the Johnson's weren't blood, that was obvious. But just like much in Edenia and in the Miller household, these little bits of information that could connect and unite were used to separate and mislead. He shoved his plate in, metal knocking harshly on the fireclay.

There was a knock at the back door. Peter went to answer it, knowing it was Abby and Lilly. His saviors.

Abigail looked him right in the eyes and asked, "Would you like to take a walk?"

He eyed his mother, who looked frustrated, but nodded all the same.

"Uh, sure."

The girls walked arm-in-arm in front of him without looking back to see if he followed. They walked through the neighborhoods to the quad and Main Street, then past First House to the bank of the river Eden. There they followed the river until they came to East Bridge.

Walking to the middle of the bridge, the girls stopped and waited. They did not talk, only looked at the swift moving water. Peter rarely came here, for good reason. The moment his feet touched the thick planks of wood his mind took him back six months.

That day his father brought him to this bridge and told him he would not be going into the garden for his birthday as everyone else did. He had to wait for his Nature to take him completely. His feet slowed as he thought of how hard he cried that day.

Finally, his feet moved him to Lillian and Abigail's side. The girls turned to him. Their faces never looked more similar, holding the same expression; calm, lovely, but guarded.

Abby reached into her pocket and took out the picture she'd snatched and handed it to him. "I think there's a story here. And I think we should find out what it is." Then she looked behind her at the entry to the Garden. As brazen and fearless as always, she asked, "Is that it, then?"

A bad feeling started in Peter's gut and wiggled its way to his heart. He felt the tingle of his Nature in his toes. But it did not move up. Not yet.

He examined the girls. Their masks had dropped. He saw how confused and angry they looked. Part of him was sealed as solid as a crypt, but a small part of him just wanted to explain everything and make it so that everyone was happy again.

Lilly moved next to him. She threaded her arm through his and kept silent. After he calmed, he looked at Lilly and then at Abby, then back at the river. How could it hurt for them to know? "Yes." He said quietly.

Lilly's body stiffened at the single syllable. He'd never been so close to a girl. It seemed like she pushed herself into him, and in one heartbeat a sensation Peter loved and hated filled his veins. He looked into Lilly's eyes and his heart raced faster.

After a moment, the intense glance between them was interrupted by footsteps. He turned and saw Abby walking straight for the Garden. "Abby, stop!" He yelled just as she stepped off the bridge and into the Garden wood.

Instantly, Peter's Nature took him. He ran to protect the garden, all thoughts of Lilly, gone.

Before Abby was five steps into the woods, Peter stood, invisible, in front of her, blocking her way. As she shifted around him, he moved with absolute silence, obstructing her. She crashed into him again and again, left, right, left, right, as she tried to step further into the garden.

She was getting frustrated, but she didn't speak to him. She couldn't know he was there. She pushed at him, but he didn't budge. The earth held onto his feet. He was a wall. He was a rock. He was immovable. He also wasn't alone. Henri, another earth Nature, the one on guard inside the garden wood, stepped to his side. His fuzzy Nature form raised its eyebrows and hands in a questioning gesture. He was asking if Peter needed help. He was certain. Peter smiled confidently and shook his head. Henri nodded and stepped back into the trees.

That was when Abby started beating against him. His body instantly went rigid to accommodate for her blows.

"What. Is. This. Thing?"

Her attack seemed to reverberate through him and into the earth. The sacred ground drinking in the power of her assault like water.

Then Lilly was there. She touched Abby's shoulder and pulled her away. "Stop," she said in a quiet voice. Then more firmly, "Stop it Abigail. Stop it now!" the beating slowed, "Can't you see? It's Peter. He literally is protecting it. He has become exactly what it needs to keep us out."

Abby stopped and looked at her sister and then looked at the negative space that was Peter. "That's him? But he's so strong." She looked at one of her knuckles, it was bloody. "And hard."

Lilly took her sister's bloody hand and led Abby over to the water to wash it. "You know what this means, Abby."

"It means that these stinkin' crazy people aren't just crazy, they're freaks of Nature too."

"Stop it." Lilly's voice was harsh, something that Peter hadn't heard from her. "Think. Calm down and think." They were silent for a minute.

"The water is really cold." Abby finally said. Then a few seconds later, "Do you think any of this is possible?" She took her hand out of the water and pressed it to her lips.

Lilly laughed, she seemed kind of excited. "I know you always like to pretend bad things away, if you can't argue them away. But face it, how else can you explain an invisible boy that blocks you as well as any wall? And he does this at the very thought of you entering this wood." Lilly stood and looked behind her, right through Peter. "This is the Garden of Eden and Peter's family guards it. It just has to be. Right?"

Peter was interested in her battle, her mind trying to understand what her eyes and heart told her. Lilly was so amazingly beautiful when she concentrated.

Abby cradled her hands protectively to her chest then turned and raised an eyebrow critically. "I thought the Garden of Eden would be prettier."

Peter smiled at the girls. Just as he was about to let go of his Nature and tell them to get back on the bridge, he heard something that made his heart beat faster than even Abby walking into the Garden wood had.

"Peter!" It was shrill, it was hysterical, it was Miriam. "Peter, where are you?"

She came at a run to the middle of the bridge. He could see her now and she could see Lilly and Abby.

Even from here he could see her violet irises begin to swirl. Letting go of his Nature he shouted "No," and waved his arms.

"Peter!" Miriam's voice condemned.

"I've taken care of it." He answered defensively.

"It doesn't look like you've taken care of anything."

Abby stepped forward, "Chill out, chica. I tried to go into the Garden there and Peter stopped me, okay?" She turned so she could see both of them, "Now..." She looked back and forth between Miriam and Peter. "I want some answers, and I want them now."

CHAPTER 27

Miriam saw her predicament. She would not take memories. She could not take memories. Though it was her default, she would not do it. During her lunch with Seth she realized just how much of a default it was. Her instincts had almost completely taken over. Her Nature had pulled at her and she'd fought it fiercely. Still, she almost broke her covenant. But she hadn't. And she would not do so now.

In her mind, she acknowledged that at some point, if the Master needed her to use her Nature in that way, she would have to do it. But she promised herself again, that she would not use it as a default any longer.

She had to figure this out another way. She could use her other gifts to get the heathens out of the Garden wood.

Two facts confronted her: First, for all she knew, these girls could be just as traitorous as their brother. Second, Peter obviously cared for their friendship. Miriam in general wasn't the heavy-handed type but she could see she needed to tread lightly here or things would get ugly fast.

Also, after mulling over what happened last night, she knew if she were to protect Edenia she needed Peter's help, and the absolute failure today at lunch taught her she was no match for Seth and his charcoal eyes, his perfect angular lips, and his dimpled cheeks. She sat there like a hypnotized chicken in his presence.

Besides all these evidences, there was the fact that she was not even a little bit sneaky, nor could she be blatantly combative. She just couldn't.

However, she thought she could get their feet moving.

"Before anything else is said, let's step out of the Garden wood and back onto the bridge. Okay?" Miriam could not believe Peter let it get this far. These girls stood in the foyer to the Garden. Miriam knew Peter had not even done that yet. Her Nature swirled within her. Her instincts snarling for defense.

But Abigail fought back, just as Miriam suspected she might. "Garden wood?" She narrowed her eyes at Peter, "I thought we were in the actual Garden."

Her Nature rose up within her. If these two girls did not step off the hallowed ground of the Garden wood...

"No!" Peter shouted again and stepped between Abigail and herself. "Miriam, they'll come. Just don't, okay?"

Lillian paled at Peter's words, but Abigail only got smarter. "I'm not going anywhere. I'm not scared of freak-girl here."

No one could know how those types of names hurt Miriam. Pulling courage like a cloak around her she tried to not let her anger and hurt change anything about her determination. It did change Peter's.

He grabbed Abigail by the arm, "You really have no idea," he paused to focus. His breaths were coming fast as well. "Stop being so arrogant and get on the bridge." Miriam was impressed because Abigail's foot actually moved in the right direction. With some unexpected prodding from Lillian, the group started walking. Once they were really moving, Peter glared at Abby, "Why do all of you outsiders have a death wish?" His tone was no nonsense, and Abigail said nothing, but glanced uncertainly at Miriam. She stood straighter, proud of her brother's confidence in the Master's ability to take care of business if needed. Peter was *literally* saving their lives. Which was the very essence of what a Guardian did. In this tense moment Miriam couldn't help but feel the dignity of Guardianship.

The minute her feet hit the wood planks, Abigail wrenched her arm free of Peter and stopped walking. Her eyes had daggers for everyone, finally she said in a quiet, scalding voice, "Tell me what I want to know, now!"

Peter stepped in. "Now hold on Abby..."

"I will not. You can go invisible. Your eyes have changed color. It might be hard for you to believe, but both of those things are outside the realm of normality. I know you think that is the Garden of Eden, but what is the big deal about it? Why is everyone so interested in it? Why do we have to be here? What are you protecting so fiercely? And what in the name of all the saints is going on with my parents?" By the end of this little speech she was screeching and breathing hard.

Miriam's eyes went wide. She took Peter by the arm. "Peter, I need to talk with you and there is no point in trying to discuss anything with her, she is too upset. Let her calm down. Come with me, now."

Peter looked at Miriam confused, but took a step toward her.

That was when Abigail threw herself between them and protested loudly, "Peter, you promised we would talk about this." She touched his arm. After a moment of Peter fixated on Miriam's eyes, and not answering her, Abigail pulled on that arm until Peter looked at her. "I'm sorry I ran into the garden. I'm sorry I got so mad. I am just sick to death of being in the dark here." She wiped a tear from her eye. "You know how I told you we aren't talking to our dad..." Peter nodded at her, "...well, we all sat down to figure this thing out and he wouldn't tell us a single thing. Pete, we left our whole lives, everything, and I still have no idea why. I know this sounds selfish, but there were...are...some important things happening. Some scary things, and my dad just ripped us away before we could deal with them. And now," She took her sister's hand, "And now those things are ten times worse." She wiped her nose on her hand and sniffed. "I have to know what is going on around here. I just have to. I need to know this is all worth it."

Miriam noted two things from this story. One, Seth had told her differently and said his father told them everything, so who was telling the truth? Second, Seth and Abby both shared this over-the-top-urgency, this life or death emergency about them. For some reason—that had to do with doctors and medical treatment—they were all very motivated to help the Joneses out. Seth's words about a life at risk and of a matter of life and death repeated in her ears. She'd totally thought he was lying, certain in fact that he was. That it was his cover story. But now she wasn't sure. Unless it was as she suspected, and all the Johnson children were working together.

Okay, and third, wow, Abigail was a master of manipulation—which sort of confirmed her second thought. Miriam knew what was going on here, how they all needed information and even she felt sorry for her.

She looked closely at the girls. Abigail clung to her sister; Lillian had this sad almost-guilty expression on her face and a limpness to her body like she'd just been through an ordeal. It started something in Miriam's mind, but she couldn't put it all together.

She hated this confrontation. It felt all muddled and incomprehensible. One fact remained. It didn't matter what the girls had seen or what they thought they knew, no one owed them an explanation.

Miriam pulled her courage around her as best she could. "Girls, I think it would be best if you went home and talked to your parents about this."

Abby glared at her. "Were you not listening? They won't tell us anything, and Peter promised to."

Miriam sighed. "I'm sorry but Peter cannot answer your questions. Besides, he needs to have a very important conversation with me."

"Nothing you have to say can be as important as this." She motioned between Peter and herself.

Peter burst in, all solicitude. "Abby, trust me. It's worth it. Don't be scared." He turned to Miriam his voice quiet, but proximity to the girls made the effort moot. "Hey, what's so important? Can't it wait?"

He raised his eyebrows and motioned toward the pressing need of the girls.

"I'm sorry, but no. I must talk to you now." Miriam turned to go. "Please come."

"But what about them?"

"Let someone else deal with them." Miriam looked around and it didn't take her long to spot Henrietta Covey not far off watching the interaction. All she had to do was wave and she could avoid the rest of this mess. "Look, there is Henrietta." When he hesitated, she added, "Peter, you must let things unfold naturally. You must."

She walked away from the twins knowing Peter would come. He followed her a half a dozen steps, but then whispered, "That's already messed up. They know. I don't understand why it has to be a secret anymore. I'm just going to tell them the bare minimum, just to keep them off our case." His face turned toward the girls.

"Peter, no. You can't tell them anything." But his eyes were all she needed. She could see defiance and knew what she had to do. He moved back toward them and her instincts kicked in. Quickly, she allowed her Nature to change her and simultaneously she pulled at Peter the way she'd done a fussing Dorothea a week ago. The poor dear was tired and Miriam couldn't get her to sleep. She got frustrated and demanded Dorothea stop. And she did.

This was her doing things differently than she'd done before. So, she tried. Peter would not go down easy. She put her mental weight into it and pressed on his mind until she saw the blankness. Once his mind was supple, she waved at Henrietta, who ran over without hesitation.

She pulled on Peter's arm. "Peter, you will come with me now."

"But..." He muttered. Miriam tightened her hold and pulled him along before he figured out what happened.

The girls chased after them. But then Henrietta was there, and she knew how to deal with newbies.

"They need to go home." Miriam told the older woman, who nodded.

The girl's faces paled. Their bottom lips trembled. Rage seethed in Abby's eyes, but they went with Henrietta.

She pulled Peter into the first place she could find; the cellar doors of the Mason's. Shoving him down the steps Peter started resisting her in earnest. "What," he shook his head, "What are you doing, Miriam?" He pushed her away.

"Listen to me Peter."

He interrupted, "What did you do to me?"

"Peter..."

"How did you even do that? You used your Nature on me, didn't you?" He brushed her outstretched hand away. He shook and rubbed at his skin in fear and revulsion. "No. No, no. How dare you? I can't believe you can do that! That's false, Miriam." They stood staring at one another in the semi dark. When he went on, his voice was quiet and angry. "Threatening the way mother does is one thing, but to actually use it. On me? You forced me, took away my will. I...I can't believe you." He moved toward the doors.

"Peter, they are working for the Joneses." She spat out.

Peter stopped; his face twisted into a different kind of anger. "What is this?" He asked, squinting his eyes and shaking his head, "How do you...That's a lie! You're just upset that you aren't the center of attention so you're making up lies to get your fix." He sputtered out half-heartedly.

"Shut up and listen." She walked toward him, "Last night, I followed Seth."

"That was you?"

"Yes," she said without hesitation, then realized what he asked. "What do you mean that was me?"

He rolled his eyes and took a deep breath, "Never mind. Tell me what in the name of all that is good and holy you are talking about."

"No, what do you mean? You saw me? Do you mean you were out in the middle of the night at the Johnsons..." She paused and in the matter of a second so many scenarios played through her mind.

None of them good. "Peter Phillip Miller, you tell me this minute what you were doing out in the middle of the night."

Peter shook his head stubbornly, "I am not telling you a thing until you explain yourself. You're on trial, not me. Because believe me, I would just love to tell mother and father that there is a new little caveat to your Nature, and you used it on me."

Miriam knew she owed him an explanation, "Alright...but I am not letting this go either." She took a step back. "After your unfortunate scene in the cafeteria, I decided I would do some damage control. So, I followed Seth."

"Damage control, huh? More like you wanted an excuse to be alone with a boy for the first time in your life."

Miriam shook her head, "What are you talking about?" But then her hand cut threateningly through the air. "Whatever. Just listen, okay? So, I overheard him talking on a cellular phone. At the time, I didn't know who he was talking to, but he said he had some information and they made a plan to talk at midnight. He said it was about you, so naturally I snuck out and followed him."

Peter was shocked, she could tell, but it didn't stop him from making a rude comment. "It didn't look like you were sneaking when I saw you. More like a bee when it stings."

She narrowed her eyes at him, how could he be giving her a hard time when she just told him that Seth had a cell phone? She went on. "When he made his midnight call, it was to Willis Jones."

It was satisfying to see his jaw drop.

"They talked about an understanding of some sort between them, and Seth received orders. He must get information about...well, you know." Miriam's eyes went down, her anger flopping out of her with all the words, but the exit caused a vacuum in her mind and it was replaced by fear. The fear of this situation caused her hands to shake. There was a reason the details of other kidnappings and such were kept secret. What would the Joneses do to her if they got her? What tortures would they inflict? Her Uncle Brian had been one they'd gotten, and her mother was convinced that was why the man didn't get married. He was too emotionally damaged.

She was going to puke.

They stood silent for a long moment while Miriam got her gag reflex under control. It wasn't until a wet droplet fell on her hands that she realized she was crying. She looked up at Peter and saw his face transform from angry confusion to concern.

"What? What else?" He paused, then asked again. "What are his orders, Miriam?"

She breathed out heavily, "Well, the usual of course. Where's the Tree? But they surprised me. They know about our Natures. And eyes. In fact, they seem very interested in that..." She looked down again, and drew her toe around in a circle in the dirt of the cellar.

"What else? Miriam, you're freaking me out."

"It's a little more personal, because..." She sighed, "Because they specifically want me. Or, they want to find and take the one that can control minds." She lost it a little and grabbed at his shirt. "They want Seth to give me up, so they can take me."

Peter patted her awkwardly on the shoulder but was silent for a moment. Finally, he smiled. "I guess you've annoyed even them."

Despite herself, Miriam laughed. It was a nervous laugh, but she was grateful for it.

"How do you know that Lilly and Abby are involved? That it's not just Seth?" He asked sincerely.

"I'll let you be the judge. Think about your conversations. What have they consisted of?"

His face was thoughtful. "But that could have to do with...well, a lot of things."

Miriam shook her head, "She herself said that her father won't tell her anything, and if he is being as tight lipped as she says, then how do they know anything is going on at all?"

"Because my Nature took me in front of them."

"No, think about what she said on the bridge. If she didn't know of people interested in getting info on us, would she have said it like that? Plus, they were nosing around way before that. Way more than normal, anyhow. Why would they have reason to do that?" It was at this point that Miriam realized that before following Seth she had no real reason to suspect him of anything. If it weren't for the reaction in her stomach to his arrival, she would've treated him as any other outsider. But that feeling, a simple twisting in her gut, brought her to hear what she heard.

Peter went on. "I see your point. Most new arrivals assume we are some zealous branch of Amish." He ran a hand through his walnut hair. "Of course, no one has been stupid enough to use their Nature in the open either."

With this comment Miriam suddenly understood something. She needed Peter on her side, so she had to go all in. "I think they also have a motivation of some sort. They are scared. I can't be sure, but they are worried about someone they love. Maybe the Joneses are holding a friend captive. Threatening them. I know you can't fake the concern on Abby's face or Seth's. They are desperate. And what do desperate people do?"

"More reason to tell them the truth."

Miriam understood his point, but there was a big problem with it. "Yes, and have them tell the Joneses."

Peters brow furrowed. "Right. We can't trust them."

"I'll tell you what. You help me get the phone from Seth and I will not tell anyone what you choose to tell Abby and Lilly. After we get the phone."

Peter smiled. "Secrets, Miri? Intrigue? Who are you? Don't ever go away, I like you better like this." His yellow-brown eyes were playful but genuine.

Rolling her eyes, she nudged him, but ignored his flippery. "I kinda have a plan but I need your help. If we can get that phone, then how can they tell the Joneses anything? And once they gain their own Natures, they will be all that much better equipped to help whomever they want to help. Right?"

Peter got a look in his eye, a far-off look like his mind was somewhere else for a moment, but then he nodded. "My answer is yes." His face turned conspiratorial. "Right. So, getting the phone is priority number one."

She couldn't contain her relief. She almost pulled him into a hug, but stopped herself at the last moment. "Yes, getting that phone is basically all my plan consists of."

"Well done, my little fledgling. That is the place I would start, because if we get the phone, it won't really matter what they know. They won't be able to tell anyone. Then the week will be up and they'll be like; *awesome, I can turn invisible too,* or whatever their Natures are. And they won't want to tell anyone anything."

The devious little wheels in his mind really turned now. She recognized the slightly constipated look. He wore it a lot.

"So, let's come up with a more detailed plan. Are you with me? Because you need to be one hundred percent at my back."

Peter didn't even pause to think. "Of course, I am. This is what we do. This is why we live here, to protect the Master's garden and to protect one another. It's all I want to do. It's all I care about."

Miriam could see the eager zealousness in his face, and it surprised her and made her feel even guiltier for that lingering desire to leave Edenia one day.

More, though, it made her think perhaps papa was wrong about Peter. Perhaps she was wrong about Peter. Perhaps everyone had mistaken Peter's intelligence, craftiness, and talents as mischievousness, when really, he only boiled inside with a desire to help, and had no outlet to do so before gaining his full Nature.

Well, he had an outlet now, and boy, did he have the perfect skill set for the job.

CHAPTER 28

After mucking out the barn, a disgusting, smelly job filled with near misses of flies in the eyes and manure dust in the face, Seth headed home for dinner. Once there, all it took was one look at Lillian's pale face for Seth to be filled to the brim with guilt for thinking about himself and daydreaming about Miriam all day.

He rectified the situation that night in their room. To his surprise they had done some investigating of their own.

"So, our first attempt to obey your command was a failure, but we will try again." Lillian concluded the story of their adventure into Eden.

"And we won't be stupid enough to actually bring one of the Edenians with us next time." Abby added.

"Yeah, classic misstep."

Seth shook his head, amazed at his sister's gumption. "But you actually pounded on him? That's kind of awesome, Abby! So, you couldn't see him but you could feel him?"

Abby nodded, "I have the busted-up knuckles to prove it." She held up her hand. "It was like I was hitting rock, literally."

He stood up from the girl's desk and headed over to the bed where they both lay. As he walked, Lilly commented, "She was fierce. It was so awesome, well, except the part about it being Pete. I like Pete, he's funny."

"Shut up Lilly, he's a total idiot."

"He's not, he's cute." Lilly whined.

Seth took his sister's hand, which she'd held suspended in the air awaiting his examination.

"He is cute. But he's creepy, too, and creepy outweighs cute any day."

"Yeah, this whole thing is freaky."

Seth examined her hand and then grabbed the other one while she talked, but now he interrupted her. "Which knuckle did you hurt?"

"Come off it, Seth, not even someone as unobservant as you..." Abby jerked her hand out of his and looked at it for a full five seconds before sitting up. She smacked Lilly and held her hands up. Lilly came up and examined Abby's knuckles, a look of horror on her face.

"What the actual..." Lilly grabbed Abby's hands and held them closer to her face.

"You aren't visually impaired, Lilly, the cuts are gone." Abby's face was thoughtful. "The only thing I did was put them in the river. But I don't think I even noticed them after we washed them." Her voice had a far-off quality about it.

"They probably just weren't as hurt as you thought. You can be a bit of a drama queen."

But then Seth caught her inference. "Abby, you don't think...do you think that water healed you? I know that sounds crazy, but think about where we are." Seth voiced the wild thought slowly and looked over at Lilly awkwardly.

"No," Abby said, her eyes coming back into focus. "I probably just didn't hurt myself as bad as I thought."

Lilly looked as white as a sheet. "Yes, that has to be it."

The girls shared an incalculable look.

Seth offered, "Could one of the abilities be healing? Did anyone touch you, or maybe even look at you in a way that made you feel...weird?"

"Oh my heck! Yes. That freakier-than-them-all freak Miriam did." At the mention of her name, Seth's heart beat extra hard. "What if she could heal you, Lil? Maybe that is why they brought us here, for that freak girl to take the tumors away." Abby started bouncing up and down, "I knew mom and dad wouldn't just bring us here for no reason. Lil, they can heal you."

Seth looked at Lilly's face and knew that it mirrored his own. Shock, thoughtful shock, yet there it was.

"Aren't you all just a tiny bit curious about this place? I mean like why are they like this? Do they all have powers? What's in the garden? I really want to figure that mystery out, don't you?" This came again from Abby. "And if they can heal Lillian..." She let that hang.

He had to rein this in before it got out of hand. "Okay, okay. Let's not get ahead of ourselves here." Seth said but he couldn't help but hope that is exactly what his parents thought.

Lilly ruined the hope by being reasonable though. "If they could do that, don't you think they would have by now? I mean, don't you think that would be, like, the first request dad made when we got here?"

"Maybe he's being careful because of the whole, *'him abandoning everyone and betraying their whole way of life thing'*." Abby offered with finger quotes all over the place.

Seth couldn't help it; he threw some fuel on the flame. "She does have a point. You saw how he acted when we got here. Like he was forced to come or something. And then he wants all the secrets."

"Maybe that's why they asked for us to act the part. As a test or something. Maybe after a few days, if we prove that we are willing to stay and play along and keep our mouths shut, we could be healed if we needed it." Abby went on. "And daddy would know that because he lived here before."

Lilly was still unwilling to get her hopes up. "Let's not get all giddy, Abby." Lilly said hesitantly, "Think about what you're saying. It is completely out of the range of normal or possible. If we wanted to believe that someone here could have the power to heal me, then... then we would have to buy into this whole way of life, this whole guard the Garden of Eden crap, like, for real." She looked again at

Abby's hands, "Like...God, actual God, has people on this earth guarding something for him and he's given them special powers to do it. I don't know if I'm ready to buy into that."

"What the crap, Lilly? You were making just the opposite argument on the bridge. Remember, *'Peter can turn INVISIBLE, he is doing exactly what is needed to keep us out. What other proof do you need?'* Those were *your* words."

Seth disagreed. Just because someone could do that craziness did not mean Lilly could be healed. Though logic would suggest that this was exactly why his parents had brought them here. But why wouldn't they just tell them?

"We could fake it." Abby got up. "We could just pretend we buy into it all, then, if there's no healing, we do it Seth's way."

"I don't know a ton about him, but I think it's a basic assumption that you can't fake out God, Abby."

Seth couldn't process all the ways his mind was bending this information. Abby's idea explained so much, but it also left so much unknown. He knew right now that the trust well between him and his parents was as dry as a bone. As he analyzed his opinion about the insanity that was Edenia, he knew he couldn't put his faith and the fate of his sister solely in it. He still couldn't rationalize what had happened. And who knew what powers existed here.

It seemed his choice was made. Edenia was his parent's route. And two escape routes were better than one. He would have to continue down his course.

Plus, he didn't know what help from Edenia would cost. Would he be paying for it his whole life? On that front, Jeremiah's deal was way better, in his opinion. Get info on the Edenians, and have all medical bills paid when he got back to the real world with real doctors, versus live here and be a freak and maybe, just maybe, Lillian can be 'healed'. It wasn't even a contest.

Abby protested, "But we have seen a boy who can turn invisible. You can't just explain that away, Lilly. This place, there's something about it. Maybe everyone here does have some kind of superpower and one of them is healing. We just can't know. But it makes sense."

Seth knew it was time to share his secret. "It makes no sense, but I think you're right in a way. I think they all can do something unusual."

Both girls turned to him, but Lilly responded, "What?"

Seth took a deep breath, "I'm in contact with a man named Jeremiah Jones, who, by the way, is another one of our not-dead cousins, he knows things about these people, but he and his side of the family want to know more."

Abby cut in. "Wait, what?"

Seth rolled his eyes. "I'm not even to the important part of this little revelation Abby, I'll explain Jeremiah to you later." He looked intently at Lilly. "The important bit is that I've made a deal with them, the Joneses. They have promised to take care of all your medical bills, no matter how extreme they become, if I give them what they want." Seth swallowed and watched his sister closely. "I called Dr. Lillehei after I made the deal with Jeremiah and un-canceled your appointment for Friday." Lilly looked super pale as she licked her lips and searched his face. "Baltimore is not that far from here. We can do this, we can make it work."

Abby jumped up, tears flooding her eyes. She ran to him and squeezed him tight. "Thank you, thank you, thank you." She cried into his shirt, "How did you even...how could you...you are the best brother in the world. I'm so sorry for every mean thing I have ever done." Just like that Abby was again thinking clearly.

Lunacy set aside, they could really plan a way to save Lilly.

Slowly, Lilly came over to him and Abby pulled them both toward her in a hug. Her eyes would not leave his, even though tears streaked down her face.

He had to make this realistic, though. "Nothing is for positive. We have to find what these people want or none of it even matters." Seth's voice betrayed his fear that all his effort might be in vain. "In the last day I've gathered nothing useful. Well, nothing that they didn't already know." Frustration couldn't tint his voice any more than it did. "We've just got to get the information they want. Your appointment is on Friday, so…"

She nodded.

After quite a bit of crying, Lilly pulled back from him and sat back down with Abby. Then she reached out and pulled him onto the bed with them. "I can't believe you would do this for me."

"We are all doing something for you Lilly. Mom and dad are doing what they think is best and I am doing what I think is best," he said resolutely.

After several minutes of silence, Abby spoke up. "So, tell me, you said all the Edenians have superpowers?"

Seth separated himself from his sisters. "Yes. Good, let's get down to it. But I have no idea if healing is one of them." He clarified before pulling out his notepad and his cell phone from his pocket.

Abby freaked out, "How did you get a phone? Give it over. I am going to call Garai and Amunet right now." She grabbed for the phone.

"No." Seth batted her away. "This is a burner phone with only the Joneses' number programmed in, and that's all we use it for. It's our security. We have no other way to get a hold of Jeremiah if anything happens to it. Besides, it only works in this little shack close to the edge of town. One of the other crazy things about this place. It isn't only 'no electronics,' its 'broken electronics', unless they are special, like this one."

Abby backed off, but she kept her eye on the coveted phone. He handed the girls the list he'd written down of the Joneses' demands. "They think that each eye color means a different power. They want to know as much about that as they can, but they are looking for one in particular; the color that allows memory control. They seem to want that one as much as they want the tree. And they do want the tree, as much information as we can get them."

"Tree? So, what, like the tree of good and evil, or of life?" Lillian asked.

Abby said, "Someone here has memory control?"

"Exactly."

Abby pushed the notebook away, "I can't get my head around this."

"Come on. Two seconds ago, when a superpower could heal Lilly, you were the most faith-filled believer ever." He touched the hand she claimed she'd torn up punching Peter. "You have to realize that this is the only way to get what you want. Accepting these things for fact and then finding out more about them—like you would a new amazing cosmetic procedure." He turned to Lilly, "And you have to separate yourself completely. No attachment, no attraction. You are doing a science experiment with fictional characters and you need to find out these things about them to fulfill the requirements of your assignment." He nodded at them.

Abby gave him a sly look. "You're kinda smart, huh?"

"Yeah, he sorta has us down to a -T-, right?"

"Not likin' it."

"A bit stalker, if you ask me."

He rolled his eyes, again. "Focus, girls. Nothing else matters." He smiled at Lilly. "So, let's make a plan."

CHAPTER 29

Peter

Knocking on the Johnson's door was a bit intimidating after the scene by the bridge. But he and Miriam had decided to flush out the Johnson spies. There was never a better time to encourage a spy than right after they almost succeeded. And if they were all working together, perhaps he could tempt them all by tempting the girls.

Abby opened the door, raised her eyebrow at him, and almost closed it again.

He put a hand out, "Please, let's just talk about it."

"You abandoned me today, Peter." Abigail whispered still closing the door but slowly now.

"I know. I'm sorry. And I'll prove it if you'll let me." Peter rushed out.

The door stopped before it touched his hand, her eyes moving back to his. "Prove it how?"

He looked around conspicuously. Then he whispered, "I'll answer one question, any question you want."

Lillian came up behind her sister in the now more open doorway.

He made eye contact with her and nailed home the bait. "Every single person in Edenia would kill me for this, but there it is. I really am sorry, so ask away."

Miriam and Peter had thought of three questions they might ask. What do each eye color mean? Where exactly can I find the Tree of

Life? What are you? To his dismay the girls did not go where he wanted.

Abigail, who had been silent, immediately asked, "Can the river Eden heal people?" as Lillian simultaneously asked, "What will happen to us on the seventh day?" Each question showed where the girl's true hearts were.

Peter was silent for a long time. Thinking, weighing, connecting with the Guardian inside him to find out if he could answer these questions. He felt no warning bells. In fact, that ribbon of light and time and choice came to his mind, and he knew they were weaving something right now.

Finally, he said slowly "One each. I suppose that's fair." He cleared his throat and proceeded with caution. "Abby, I don't know exactly what the river can do or if there is anything it can't do. That water is the life force of this whole place. Its origin is in the garden. Many here think our wisdom and power come from that river. Do we know that for certain? No. Is it possible? Sure." He wanted to remind them what the world would look like if it knew how to get powers. But he understood the rules. Warning them would red-flag the exact thing they did not want the Joneses to know. He had to play it cool. Act like it was all conjecture. "Good enough?" He asked.

She nodded, but she also narrowed her eyes at him, unsatisfied.

"As for what happens on the seventh day…" He paused for what felt like a minute. "This really is something that should come as a realization of one's own Nature, a process of change and self-rediscovery, instead of a lecture from me or anyone. Are you certain you want to know, because there is no going back." They looked at one another, things passing between them he could never understand. But they both turned to him and nodded at the same time. "Alright, well I will say it this way. Because you are of age, it will only take approximately a week for the Master to remake you. Staying for that amount of time obliges you to the will of the Master. Thus, you will become fully adapted to guarding his Garden."

These words registered with the girls subconscious before it did their conscious. Peter knew this because even before their eyes bulged with confusion, their breathing became labored.

Peter's voice rang out one final sentence, like hammering nails in a coffin. "Basically, in a week or so you will enjoy all the mental and physical privileges I do."

Lilly burst out, "Does that mean anything wrong with us will be healed?"

As Abby said, "I will suddenly be an invisible dork?"

Peter laughed, "At least no one will be able to see you in all your dorkiness. Well, that is, if that's your Nature." Peter felt his teeth snap closed, not of his own volition. He turned to Abby and the answer he had for her dried up in his mouth. He was not supposed to tell her the answer, and because the Master stopped him in such a profound way, it drew his attention. Why did they need to know about being healed? Maybe Miriam was on to something.

"Our Nature?" Abby asked in a harsh voice, pulling his mind and gift of speech back out of him.

"Yes, you take on abilities that are already naturally a part of you. Stealth belonged to me long before my Nature took me."

"So, it's not organized in any way? The doling out of these abilities?" Abby pressed.

"We are talking about a supreme being here," was Peter's purposely vague answer. He had to be careful.

The girls nodded, but they obviously didn't want to go off on a tangent. "What other abilities are there?" Abby asked again.

"Wait now. I have been more than fair with you. Answering two questions when I said one."

Abby interrupted. "One and a half." There was a pout to her lip.

He went on. "Besides, I think that should be a surprise. I can't ruin everything for you." Again, vague on purpose. "Now, am I forgiven for scaring you half to death?"

The girls nodded their eyes wide with shock and uncertainty.

"I can't believe this. So just living here will give us these freaky superpowers?"

"Yes."

"How?" she asked, concerned.

"It is a mystery. Really, it is. There are theories, but we don't know for certain."

"And no one has ever tried to figure it out, ya know, test tube it?" Abby wanted to know.

"I don't know."

"Wow, you aren't the fountain of information I'd hoped for, are you?"

"What is that supposed to mean?" Peter asked feeling now more than ever that Miriam was right about his 'friends'.

Lilly answered him, "She means we haven't any friends..."

"...here. Yeah, no one to talk to, no one to answer questions." Abby clarified.

"...except you." Lilly finished and smiled sheepishly.

Nicely played girls, Peter thought. "I see, well, I hope I have given you some hope, or some consolation. All is not terrible. You're needed here and soon you'll have proof of that fact." He cleared his throat quietly, "I need to get going. But I hope tomorrow we can start fresh and maybe talk about that photo."

"Hey, can you just clear up one more thing for me?" Lilly asked in her sweetest voice.

"Perhaps," was Peter's cautious reply.

"Abby's hand, where she hit you when you went all Mr. Stone man on us. It was bloody, and she washed it in that river, and well, now it's totally healed." She left the question implied but unasked, which made Peter doubt everything he'd just decided. Could this simply be about a hand?

"I think we covered this. I promise I'm not holding back. I really am not certain."

"What do you believe?" Lilly pressed.

"I don't know. I'm not a man of faith. I'm a man of science and so...I'm not the one you should talk to. But my sister Esther, now, she is faithful. Maybe she will answer your questions." He left that hanging for a second but had to add, "She's also a real goody-goody so I wouldn't ask until you've been here a while." Totally not a lie.

"Yeah, well, thanks Peter. I'm so glad you came by. I feel much better about all this..." Peter caught the slight condescension in Abby's voice. "But I still think you're a freak." She added quickly and he could tell she was attempting to sound playful.

"Don't worry. Soon, you'll be one too." Peter decided that was his cue to leave. He hoped he did enough. This had not gone the way he planned. But this river thing, maybe that was enough to get them out of the house so Miriam could search for the phone. "See you tomorrow," he said, and turned and walked away.

CHAPTER 30

Miriam

One member from each family was enough to half-fill the Divided Hall. Miriam stood before them on the dais and cleared her throat. She'd practiced how to say this but had no idea if that would help her or not. All she knew was she had to spit it out quick or she might not be able to say it at all.

Once everyone quieted, she began. "Hello everyone. I am so grateful to you all for coming on such short notice. I have been spending a lot of time in thought and I have decided," She cleared her throat again and took a deep breath, "that I will not be using my Nature to take memories any longer."

The quiet of shock only lasted a few moments before there was a rush of whispered conversation and that turned into louder voices asking questions and making statements such as, "You are a Guardian!" "You took an oath." "That is your Nature you can't just ignore it, can you?" "It is your job to do it."

Miriam felt blood rush to her cheeks. She felt her anger over the last two years build and bloom and before she could stop herself, she burst forth with.

"How dare you? All of you. You have no idea what it is like to be me, what my Nature costs me. You have ostracized me and hated me for my Nature, but you have used me for it, nonetheless. Now you are surprised that I don't want to use it? That I hate it? Not one of you can judge me for this, because you have no clue what it's like to be me. But if you do judge, I will not care. I have spent two years getting over what anyone thinks about me. Getting over the fact that I have no friends. That my own family doesn't understand my Nature or what its purpose truly is. Still, don't mistake that I do this to gain your love back. I do not. I do this now for myself. I hate my Nature. If I could get rid of it, I would. If I could leave Edenia and never come back, I would. But I can't. The Master has made it clear he still has a use for me. Until I figure out what it is, I can do but one thing to protect myself; I can choose not to use it. And that is what I have chosen." Miriam took in a deep breath and with it released the remnant of the anger left inside her. Once done, she concluded calmly. "Now, though you have not supported me for two years, I ask you to support me now. I ask that you be more careful in your defense of the garden, and that you not show yourselves to the enemy, for if you do, I will no longer clean up your mess."

Aunt Sarah stood in the shocked silence that followed her speech. After a few moments she spoke. "Miriam I am so proud of you for standing up for yourself. I know how difficult it must be." She paused in thought. "Perhaps we have used your Nature too liberally. You are right, it is not like the rest of our Natures. For one, it has unique consequences. Perhaps more consequences than any of us know. Because of that, I pledge to you that I will be more careful in my duties. I will go back to the thinking of two years ago, before your Nature. I will keep my doings a secret. Not exposing our Nature's to Joneses is pivotal, so I will do better to be stealthy. All of us can." She looked around and nodded encouragingly. "We all know how to be careful. We have done it most of our lives. Right? We can do it again. It is not that difficult."

Suddenly there were nods of agreement. Murmurs of consent. And before long, most everyone seemed amenable. When they all settled back down, Miriam found that she had tears in her eyes. "Thank you." she said and opened her mouth to say more but stopped herself.

Miriam had planned to tell everyone that she had other facets to her Nature, that she could still be of use in the Master's work, a fact only her family members knew. But it was better this way. As it was, the Guardians would expect nothing from her, which was just fine for now. She could learn to harness the calm and the compulsion, first, then perhaps, if they began to treat her differently, she might share her secret. Maybe.

CHAPTER 31

Seth

The girls spilled the whole conversation to Seth then left him alone with his thoughts.

Seth couldn't help but let the words affect him. *'You'll be one too.'* His body shuddered, and he went cold. What exactly did that mean? Just by being here, they would change, morph into Edenians. And be altered in a way that made them different from every other human on the planet? These thoughts ripped through Seth like lightning. His skin began to crawl. He scratched at himself until his skin was red and welted.

Standing up, he paced, his hands clenching and his shoulders curling in. He was right. His parents' plan had too big of a price tag.

The thought of becoming a freak, being forced to become a freak made his mind race to think of the quickest way out of here. He couldn't stay cooped up in this room a moment longer. Grabbing his phone, he slipped out the front of the house. Not looking left or right, he just walked, not thinking, not planning, just moving.

How could his parents want this for him? They knew him. They taught him. As a kid, when his dad read him comic books, he always followed the fantasy with reality. Action-packed stories of real-life men and women who risked their lives, not only for other people, but for what was right. When he got older, he realized his dad was one of them, and the likelihood that most of the stories he grew up with were actual things his dad did, made him so proud. All he ever wanted was to be like his father, and if *he* didn't need superpowers to be amazing, Seth didn't, either.

In that moment, he felt it in his bones. No amount of power could entice him to be a freak, an oddity. Seth remembered Abby and Lilly's faces, their horror, when they saw Peter turn invisible in the cafeteria. What they must have been thinking about Peter in that moment. *No,* he shouted inside his head.

This major aversion was all the more reason to get out of here. There was no reason to even think. No way was he going to hang around here seven days, regardless of getting the needed info. He just hoped he could do both, because what would happen to Lilly if he failed? He just couldn't fail Lilly or himself. On that note, finding the tree would solve everything. No way the Joneses would deny Lilly's care if Seth told them where the tree was.

Seth couldn't stop thinking about going into the Garden. It was decided that the girls were in a much better position with Peter to get the information they needed—tonight had proven that—so that left him with the job of finding the tree. Not with the intent to get the fruit like they had on their first attempts. Now it was just to see how to enter the garden and to see if there was a tree.

He had assumed there would be traps or alarms to stop people, but according to the girls, they just walked in. If Peter hadn't been there, who knows how far they could have gone?

Looking up, he was surprised to see that his feet had taken him to the bridge across from the garden. Pulling in a deep breath, he took one step onto it and heard girls giggling softly. Ducking behind a bush, Seth waited and watched.

A moment later he saw his sisters sneak down to the water's edge. They waded in ankle deep.

Walking onto the bridge he leaned over and whispered, "What the heck are you guys doing?"

Both of them shrieked at his voice, but Abby answered, "Just testing a theory. Now go away."

"I was going to sneak into the garden, but you two are making so much noise someone is going to come out and get you."

"If this works Seth, you won't need to go into the garden."

Easy for them to say. They didn't seem as upset about turning into a freak. They had one-track minds.

Out of the corner of his eye Seth saw a blur of movement, and a wind picked up, blowing his hair from behind, so it covered his face. Flicking and brushing it back he looked behind him. There was nothing there.

But an Indian accented voice came out of the darkness from the direction of the garden. "You girls better stay out of the river. It moves quickly, and you will be swept away."

Seth glanced toward the voice but was distracted back toward the girls when he heard a shriek. Abby and Lilly were both neck-deep in the water, as if they'd jumped in the second they heard the man speak. He watched them struggle to stay on their feet, but they lost their balance and were drawn under the bridge and down the river. Seth had been on this journey before, and knew how cold and fast the river moved. Immediately he began pulling off his shoes, but the man moved out of the shadows of the Garden woods and onto the planks of the bridge.

"Don't be concerned. They will be fine. Mattis is in the wheelhouse tonight. He will pull them out." The walnut skinned man, with his eastern accent spoke but did not take his eyes off the girls. "Go home." He jogged through the garden in the direction of Seth's floating sisters.

Seth looked at the garden. Did they have people just waiting inside in case someone decided to wander in? It must be the case. And if there was one, there had to be others. How would Seth ever get inside? A moment of hopelessness filled him. There was something about that deep dark wood that made him uneasy. He didn't want to go inside. But he had to do this for Lilly. The girls had distracted everyone. Maybe this was his only shot. He took a step toward it and then another and another.

His trepidation heightened, but before he knew it, he stood on the far side of the bridge. He swallowed down the fear and moved forward. Five steps, ten. He looked around, the trees were large and gnarled. The earth fragrant. Huge multi-colored autumn leaves littered the damp ground.

And then he felt it.

He felt peace. He felt time. He felt his heartbeat, his breath, his eyes. He blinked as if in slow motion. A breeze blew a strand of hair into his eye. His hand lifted to brush it away, and at the apex of his arm's movement, his hand disappeared with a small flash of light. His mind caught up with what he'd seen, and he slowly moved his arm back down. At the apex it disappeared again, only a silver circle mid-air to indicate something was there. Seth held his arm steady and leaned to study the slight silvery outline that sparked in the darkness just as he got yanked backward by the scruff of his shirt.

A familiar voice said, "I told you to go home."

Seth was moving at a velocity that his mind—calm and peaceful as it was—couldn't comprehend, and before he knew what was happening, he was on the other side of the bridge.

He looked around himself. Confused. He was alone. He spun in a circle, his heart finally catching up with what happened to him. He moved back toward the bridge, but the same voice echoed over the water, "Don't even think about it." Once Seth stopped moving, he said, "Go home Seth. You will have all the answers in due time."

Seth stood in stunned silence for several long moments, processing.

Finally, he understood the man was right. Seth had done all he could do. He knew what he knew and now he would never get into the garden again, he was sure. They would have it guarded even more tightly. He'd cast his die. At least he had something to tell Jeremiah. Now, if he could find out more about what powers were what, and if he could find the memory stealer, he'd be golden.

He thought about the girls' river swimming escapade and wondered if in this strange place, that actually meant anything.

Would it heal Lillian? If it did, great. This could be the test. But with one task behind him, Seth was more committed than ever to his plan. They could play along, but he was determined to do his part. And again, two plans gave twice the opportunity for success. And there was no way he was staying here. Not even God could convince him.

CHAPTER 32

Tuesday
Miriam

Miriam had pried Seth's window up after he'd taken Peters bait. Peter was an absolute genius. But there was no phone in his room.

Miriam told Peter about it on their way to school. "I checked everywhere."

Miriam's fingers riffled through her straight tresses and then rubbed her eyes, hoping to wipe away the fatigue. Two nights of interrupted sleep were not good for her. She wondered how adults did it. "I feel like a zombie."

"You look like one."

She stopped to glare at him.

"What? I'm your loving brother. Aren't I supposed to tell you things like this—just so you're aware?" He asked innocently.

She shook her head at him.

"It's this quest we are on, it's stealing my sleep." She yawned, and it took the gravel out of her voice. "And I'm stressed out," she said, through another yawn.

"So, our first mission failed. No phone." Peter put out a hand, stopping hers from brushing through her hair again. The action brought emotions to the surface for her. "You know," his voice rose conspiratorially, "you do look really bad today. You could skip school. Play up the tired."

"That wouldn't be a lie, but I have an appointment today with Seth." She whispered the name.

"Point. But if there's a time to search the Johnson's house again it would be now. I guess I go search and just pretend I'd been in class the whole time, but that I had my Nature on me. Then pop! It would scare the pants off Esther." His grin was so naughty Miriam actually took her fingers to his face to pull the grin down.

"You're scaring me." She said. Once he relaxed his face she added, "It astounds me how easily you can just think of deceptions Peter. But still, that is exactly why I need you. I'm sure at some point today all the Johnsons will be gone from their home."

"Miriam, I am astounded! The very thought…"

Here Peter was. Miriam wondered if all the responsibility she'd placed on him had changed his need for sarcasm. Obviously not. "If anything, it seems you should be proud; your despicable ways rubbing off on me and all." she sniffed.

Eyebrows moved up and down as he croaked in a strange accent, "Very good grasshopper."

"Huh?"

"Nothing. It's something I heard Garren say. Anyhow. Sneak in, sneak out. No one the wiser."

"And what if he takes the phone with him. Like he has it on his person. He did the other day."

"Again, astute, Miriam. Astute." He thought. "I check there, you check here. You already have an *appointment* with him." He lingered over the word appointment annoyingly.

She hoped her cheeks were not heated. Peter wagged a finger at her, but she nodded her assent.

Miriam tried to recover. "Aren't you worried about a whipping?"

He shrugged noncommittally and absently felt for his bottom. "This is a matter of highest security, and with the earth shading me, no one will be the wiser."

Miriam nodded again, worried for her brother, but trusting in his practiced debauchery.

"Can you take care of Seth?"

"Of course. I can try."

"*Really?*" he sing-songed the words again. Implying that something was going on between her and Seth in a way only an annoying little brother could.

She wanted to tell him to be quiet but decided to use a phrase she'd heard the twins use. "Shut it, Pete. I'll take care of it. Now, go take care of your part." She added a commanding tone to her voice just to irritate him.

He shoved his books into her arms and scrunched his eyes, but Miriam thought of something, "Wait, Peter."

He opened his eyes back up, "Yes."

"Any signs what the Yellow is all about?"

His face drained to white. "Geez Miriam lay off. What is this, are you eager to not be the only extra-specterrestrial in town?" He glared at her and pulled his Nature to him.

It was fine, because she had nothing to say to him. First his irises shook, then his feet went to the earth. The elements of the Master's ground cloaked her brother's entire frame with their power. He was the earth's, and she took his form and hid it. No sound, no hint of warmth...just gone. Miriam grunted with jealousy, but finding herself alone on the path to school, she worried about how she would get close enough to Seth today to get his phone.

CHAPTER 33

He beat Miriam to the tree. He shoved his food in, not wanting to waste his precious lunch time. He had no plan. He knew he should try to connect with her. To have a personal conversation and then entice her into opening up about Edenia. He knew all this. And maybe that's what would happen, but not because he manufactured it.

He wanted to be here with her. He wanted another smile.

So, he spent his time deciding on the most interesting thing about the outside that he could tell her. He'd traveled a ton and could describe any number of beauties. The pyramids. The David. The Taj Mahal. Sand dunes. The Northern lights. The ocean. Sports. The Louvre. The Pont de Grenelle Statue of Liberty. Bubble gum. Pizza. A luau. Driving in a car. Surfing the ocean and the internet. Animals. Watching TV. Going to movies and eating popcorn. Skiing. Riding on a train. Mountains. A comfy hoody and jeans.

Once he bent his mind toward what Miriam hadn't experienced, he felt overwhelmed.

"You're pensive." Her voice blasted through his thoughts and sent a shiver down his back. When he looked up at her, the sun shimmered through the branches of the big oak and hit her in strobe, glittering off her blonde hair and her dazzling eyes when she gave him a small smile. He felt his heart race. She was...wow. He smiled back and patted the ground next to him.

"I was thinking about you."

Miriam paused mid-throw of the blanket. "Me? Why?"

Her voice held such shock and oblivion that he answered with more fervor than he had the right to feel, having only just met her, "Yes, you. I don't think you see yourself properly."

She eyed him skeptically. "I think I see myself exactly as I am, but no one else does."

"They're all just jealous."

Her face went from skepticism to incredulity. "No. No, that is not it at all."

"I think it is." Seth reached over and touched a lock of her white-blonde hair and looked deeply into her eyes. "I'm positive it is." His voice was low, and he saw a slow warmth creep into Miriam's perfectly pale cheek.

The tingles of energy between them were loud and clear. He let her hair slide between his fingers.

It confused him as it overwhelmed him. He'd never felt this way before. He was afraid he was weird. He was afraid he was a pervert. This girl was his cousin. But having no experience with familial relationships, he wondered if he was mistaken in his adoration, or if that's how people connected by blood felt for one another.

He decided to ask her about it. "You've always had relatives all around, haven't you?"

"Yes, I guess." Her pale eyebrows knotted up as she looked at him.

"Well I haven't."

She nodded. "I know."

"Yes, I suppose you do. So, it stands to reason that I'm a little confused about how to act. In one way you seem like any other girl to me, meaning not related to me, but in another way you seem..." he stopped himself from saying 'like the person I want to be with forever' and instead said, "...like a million times cooler than any other girl I've ever met." He clenched his teeth. "I hope that doesn't sound weird. I just need to talk about it with someone. Is this..." he motioned to the space between them, "how cousins feel toward one another?" He looked into her beautiful eyes, "I mean I look at you and I don't see you as my cousin, but my head keeps telling me that you are, and then there's this, like, tension." He touched her hair again, but only because it was pooling on the blanket between them. "Do you know what I'm talking about or am I just crazy?" He rubbed the silky strands of hair between his fingers and noticed how his heart raced. Letting the hair go, he looked into her eyes.

She stared at him intensely. Their eyes locked, and Seth swore if she wasn't his cousin, he would lean down and kiss her right then and there. That's what this felt like. It was exactly what you see in all the movies, the moment where conversation stops, the tension builds and then the couple are kissing.

Seth looked away, knowing he had to.

When he looked back up, his eye was drawn to her mouth, or more specifically, her lips. They were not smiling now, they just sat there like two peach slices, juicy and perfectly symmetrical. All he had to do was lean in.

She broke into his thoughts by saying, "I hadn't really dissected it before."

His eyes moved back to hers. He stopped breathing, wondering if she would admit that she felt it too. "But yes. It's normal. I feel strongly toward all my relatives. It's like a fierce protective love that burns here." She placed her hand over her heart. "There is a bond that comes from sharing traits, features, memories, summers. My grandmother and I have the exact same shape of eyes. Strange little things like that bond people in unique ways."

Seth breathed. "I know, I met her." Seth noticed how the timbre of his voice turned the words down, sadly.

She eyed him. "You don't sound like that introduction was all you dreamed it would be."

He laughed, "You can tell that, huh? To tell you the truth, I felt nothing for her. She seemed to have all the right ingredients but in the wrong amounts."

"I see." Miriam looked away. "Expectations; sometimes they can harm you just as much as they can help."

He turned toward her. "There you go again making sense of my crazy."

She didn't look his way, but she added, "It probably didn't help that you look nothing like us. Not with your dark hair, eyes, and skin."

He nodded. "It certainly was obvious. Why is that, by the way?"

"I have no idea. You are the image of your father, and my father and your father do look alike. Sort of."

Seth almost said something about how Jeremiah looked just like his father but at the last second, he remembered and didn't. "So, this connection I feel toward you?"

"Probably has everything to do with our ability to communicate in a way that feels comfortable. I have an aunt. Her name is Sarah and I feel like she is my best friend even though we are twenty years apart in age and she has a totally different type of personality." She fingered the edge of the blanket. "We just click. I don't feel that way with anyone else."

"Perhaps you are my 'Aunt Sarah'."

She turned to him and smiled, barely. "Perhaps."

"Does that mean that I get to call you Auntie Miriam?"

Her face did that amazing morphing thing as her smile turned full and true. "I suppose, if you must." She turned away again, and he felt the disappointment of it. "It wouldn't be the worst thing I've been called." This was said quietly.

Seth was just about to ask her what she meant when she noticed how Miriam's hands trembled. He grabbed the back corner of her blanket and pulled it over her shoulder. "You're chilly." When finished, he put his hand on top of hers, wrapping his hand around her cold fingers.

She looked down at their hands and then at him, her eyes full of questions.

"Hey, I thought we just decided that being cousins meant we felt things for each other. Right now, I don't want you to be cold, so I'm helping."

Miriam slid her hand from under his and pulled on the corner of the blanket he'd carelessly draped over her shoulder.

"Seth, I have taken many classes on outside relationships and I understand that in the culture you've been raised in they have strict ideas about cousins and intimate relationships. For genetic reasons it's a faux pas on the outside, but we do not hold to those strictures here. In fact, if anyone saw you sitting so close to me, looking at me thus, and holding my hand, they would assume we have an understanding, that we are courting." She cleared her throat. "and that we are on our way to be wed. For no such liberties are acceptable otherwise."

Seth knew that these words from any other mouth would have had him scuttling back in revulsion. But he did not. He stayed and looked at Miriam, wondering how in the world he'd found someone that appealed to him so deeply and so quickly. And how she delivered the most harsh rebuffs with a formality that didn't offend. It was quite a talent.

She went on, "And of course that would be a very stressful problem for my family, for they have all but promised me to Foster, and he would not like me being so free with you, cousin or not."

Seth moved his hands. "I'm sorry, who's Foster?"

"He's the boy I will marry."

"But Miriam, your sixteen. How can you possibly be even entertaining the idea of marriage? Besides, I thought the whole set-your-teenage-daughter-up thing was just for Eve's specific problem."

Miriam cleared her throat and started rocking. "Well, yes, but I guess she isn't the only one with issues."

"Wait are you saying that this is a town of arranged marriages? That Eve lied to me?" But then he remembered that Miriam was upset about not being able to go outside. Like everyone else. "So, you have some special circumstance too? What is it?"

Miriam eyed him. "I'll tell you my secret if you tell me yours."

That shut him up. He didn't know what to say. Which secret could she be talking about? "Got too many? Trying to decide which I'm talking about?" She smiled as she said this, her voice playful. "Well we all have issues and secrets. Speaking of which, I thought you were going to pay up."

"Pay up?" He turned his head in question

"Yes, and by the way I wasn't done looking at that phone. You wouldn't happen to have it on you?"

Instantly Seth was wary, and without even considering the consequences he shook his head. "Nope, sorry, not today."

"So, are you almost done with your business?"

He moved his head back and forth and raised his shoulders. "Some progress has been made, but not as much as I would have hoped."

"Anything I can help with?"

He considered her. How could he ask her questions in this context and not get discovered? There wasn't a way. He could display a tiny bit of faith and turn his questions toward Lillian's issues. She actually might help him if he were to tell her.

He considered it. He thought maybe he could. He thought she could be trusted. She hadn't sent the army of super-freaks to steal his phone away, though she could have. He wanted to tell her. He opened his mouth. He formed the words in his mind. *My sister will die if I don't save her. Unless this place can help like my parents claim it can.* But then he thought of his father the promise he'd made to keep his mouth shut, and the ugly anger of betrayal crept into his heart. He would not be like his father. He heard himself say, "I wish," instead.

The moment died with the darkness of pride and resentment, and he felt himself getting sucked down. He didn't want that. He knew he only had ten more minutes with Miriam, and he wanted to take advantage of them.

He smiled and said, "You have kept my secret, so what do you wanna know?"

Her eyes lit up. "Everything."

Seth laughed. "Well let's start you off easy. There's this little thing called soccer. And it is the true love of my life."

MIRIAM

Miriam's hands would not stop shaking. How had she been so brave? Had she ever spoken like that to any boy in her life? Furthermore, not even Foster, whom she'd grown up with and whom she was sure to be betrothed too within a few weeks, had ever looked at her, really looked, not the way Seth had. It was like he could see all the things she wanted other people to see. It made her stomach twist and her head light and her cheeks flush.

And then there was that one moment when he was looking at her mouth...

"Miriam," a familiar voice called from behind her. She turned and saw Peter walking her way, and her fantasies melted away.

He pulled her to the side of the hall.

"How did it go?" She asked quickly, hoping he would go on long enough that she wouldn't do any reporting of her own.

Animatedly putting his hands out in front of him he turned to her. "I'm trying to make lemons into lemonade here. I did it." The beam in his eyes made her smile. He loved this. She couldn't help the warmth in her heart. "Easy as pie, my Nature was obedient as a sweet little puppy. Unfortunately, no one was home, so I didn't even need to be concealed. And, I didn't find the phone." He whispered the last part with a slight worried tilt to his mouth.

Miriam sighed. "That's because he had it on him, I'm pretty sure." She shouldn't have said that. "I think I can sort of tell when he's lying. He does this thing..."

"Never mind I don't want to hear all of your love-sick observations." His impatient look turned to his evil smile. "And..." his eyebrows lifted, "did you get it from him."

Again, a sigh escaped her mouth. "No."

"Okay, go on."

"He lied to me. What was I supposed to do? Call him out. 'Oh, you don't have it, well what's that large lump in your pocket?' I couldn't do it, I failed."

"Why didn't you use your Nature to mesmerize him." He wiggled his fingers out in front of him, like he was doing a magic spell. "Come on Miri we're Guardians, this is what we do. That was literally the perfect time for you to use all your Master-given skills. To save the garden. That is what we are doing here, right?"

Blood rushed to her cheeks, and she pushed past Peter to start down the hall to her class. Using her Nature on him would have made short work of this problem, but she had not even thought of it.

She had not even thought of it!

She was so angry with herself and ashamed. She was the worst Guardian ever in the whole history of Edenia. She was horrible. Why, she wondered, couldn't she do what was best, the thing she was made to do? She almost did it. The first lunch they'd shared. She pulled it to her. But once her irises moved, she saw Seth's eyebrows crinkle. His stare changed, for a moment...And then the bell.

Recalling Seth's long, sinuous black hair, his straight, white teeth, or his thick black eyelashes didn't help her now, and it was definitely a distraction then. It also didn't help how the cold, hard, contraband object had felt in her hand and how her curiosity got the better of her.

Then today Seth kept talking about their relationship and he kept touching her. How was a girl to deal with methods of torture such as those?

Peter let her pass and didn't chase her down. Just as well, she was done talking to him. They could figure out a new plan later. For now, she sat down in her biology class and put her head down on her desk, tears on the verge of falling.

Her heart was at war. Edenia had her in what felt like a vise-grip. She was needed here, even important here. She felt good having a mission that didn't include using her Nature. And since that night outside of Edenia, on the hilltop, she knew that Guardianship had her loyalty in a way she could not deny.

But...

She felt tears gathering in her eyes, but she also felt something else gathering in her belly. Anger. And she found the source of that new inner trouble; Seth. Her heart and her body felt things when he was around.

Just now, in the twenty minutes they'd spoken, Seth treated her more normally than anyone had in years. Yes, he'd lied to her, but she knew he had to protect his secret. She understood that. But in the other things he said, he was sincere. If she couldn't have the outside, at least she could have Seth and Seth told her things that made her feel like she had both. And to her shock and dismay the fact that she was not the girl with the violet eyes to him, the girl who took memories, was more important than any or all of that.

She squirmed in her seat. The thought of Seth truly swirled her stomach. She was getting the inkling that things were getting serious. At least inside of her. So, how would this proceed? She had to consider all the different avenues.

Best case scenario: now that Peter was on the job, the phone would get taken, and communication would be severed. Thus, in a few days Seth would be here for good. She knew what he was and why he was here, but that wouldn't matter at that point. Then he would be one of them.

Then, how would things progress? All the options were open. She could stall her parents when it came to Foster. Then she would just see where things went.

Miriam got very still. Even her breathing stopped. The prospect was fraught with possibilities. Without the baggage of history. Without preconceived notions and prejudice. It almost felt like happiness was within her grasp.

Another possibility: Peter would get the phone, making Seth upset. Miriam had already destroyed the Joneses' little box in the shed by throwing it in the river. That would surely be an exacerbating issue. Seth might, in his desperate state, make desperate choices. Who knows what chaos that would bring?

Or: They would fail, and Seth would keep the phone and would give the Joneses everything they wanted, making her and her family upset. And...and bring an end-of-world scenario to Edenia.

The next few days were a minefield of possibilities.

And now, because of Seth's stupid way of pulling her in, her heart was also at risk.

CHAPTER 34

It was his day to work in the stables. Of course. Where else would he work today, when Edenia needed saving? Well, at least the monotony of shoveling gave him time to think. And if he were honest with himself, he was grateful for the job. Manure had been good to him.

On the other hand, did horses really need to defecate quite so much?

He tapped Twilight out of his way, and the mare's shiny black mane made him think of Lilly...and Abby. The jury was still out on how school went today, once he showed up. At lunch, the girls pelted him with question after question of Edenia, sticking mostly to how the place was run and how they lived. They asked about Eve's betrothal and Peter told them that Miriam would be betrothed soon too. They laughed at how strange that would be and how anyone could want to marry someone so scary. Though Peter laughed with them, he felt himself cringe a bit at the act. In a few short days his sister had gotten to him. He was one hundred percent on her side, in her corner, had her six; and all of a sudden it felt like a betrayal to laugh at her.

He knew how uncharacteristic that was.

After that, the girls stayed on the topic of Miriam; they wanted to know what her Nature was. Feeling protective Peter had to fight to keep his Nature in check when he was with the girls since they set off his instincts like crazy now.

He shoved a huge pile of dung into his wheelbarrow and shook his head. He was in big trouble. The Johnson twins had him in their clutches.

A familiar whinny distracted him. He smiled as he spied Old Bull. Hoof-shaped bruises and broken toes were a thing of the past. Finally, Peter's Nature worked fully, and the great menace would get his comeuppance.

He closed his eyes and called his Nature. Calling it was more difficult than when his instincts caused it to take him. But soon enough the happy sensation began in his toes. When he completely blended into the barn boards, he stepped in the mature stud's stall. Bull sniffed at the air and swung his head back and forth searching for his prey.

Peter smiled bigger and started mucking out the stall. The big bully didn't seem to mind the poo Peter flung all over the stall with his shovel. So, Peter smacked the animal on the rump to move him out of his way. He was gentle-ish, but Old Bull's eyes rolled, and he snorted and whinnied. He even kicked out a few times, but Peter was not alarmed. He knew those with earth Nature could take an extreme amount of abuse with no effect.

Finally, just before lifting the rope to exit the stall, he let his Nature go and yelled, "Boo!" at the horse who, seeing his enemy, reared up and kicked his legs wildly. Peter laughed and called his Nature back, then moved to another corner of the stall and repeated the scare tactic. It worked even better that time. Once more he did it and laughed to himself as he ducked the rope.

Letting go of his Nature Peter turned and froze. Standing between Old Bulls stall and Twilights, was Seth Johnson; his shovel in hand, his mouth wide open, and his nose sort of twisted in disgust.

"That is just so..." He paused, his eyes never leaving Peter's, his body as still as a statue, "...I don't have words for what that is." He finally finished.

Once again Peter had done the one thing he was absolutely forbidden to do. How could he be so stupid?

Somehow, Seth knew what was going through Peter's mind because he said, "Unless you have someone who can suck that back out of my head—which please tell me you do, because I do not want the image of that forever stuck in my brain—it's too late, dude. I saw it, and man that is so..."

"Amazingly awesome." Peter supplied with a charming smile.

"No, I was thinking more along the lines of creepy." He shivered.

"Wrong, it is the best..."

Peter started but then Seth's eyes grew alarmed. "Watch out!" he yelled.

Peter felt a horrible force slam into his back. He flew a few feet, hit the stall across the way, and landed face first on the hard-packed dirt. Before Peter could catch his breath or even comprehend what happened to him Seth was there, yelling into his face.

"...all right...Peter, Peter..." Seth pushed something off of Peter's face and put his own face to the ground. "Peter, can you hear me?" Lifting his head, Seth yelled, "Help!" Sitting up, his hand dipped into his pocket and pulled out a small metallic box. He flipped part of it open, and, even through the pain, Peter knew this foreign object was the cell phone he'd been after today. Seth pushed several buttons and then must have remembered where he was because he swore.

Life rushed through Peter's body and finally he could breathe, but it came out as a gurgling wheeze.

At that precise moment, Bull whinnied loudly, and out of the corner of Peter's eye he saw the horse take a few trotting steps toward the rope. He was going to jump it.

Seth must have come to the same conclusion because he grabbed Peter by the arms and pulled him as he did a sort of backwards crawl/fall.

Peter landed halfway on top of Seth as he watched Old Bull land right where he had been a moment ago. Seth shoved Peter off him, and pain like Peter could not believe crippled his will to stay conscious. He was sure he would have lost it if his eyes, rolling upward, hadn't noticed the metallic phone.

Seth hadn't put it back in his pocket.

Without knowing where the strength came from, he moved his hand the needed five inches and covered the phone. As quickly and carefully as he could he slipped it into his shirt cuff.

Seth swore again. "That crazy horse! He took off. I couldn't catch him." Then Seth was next to him. "Peter," softly he slapped Peter's face. "Pete?"

Peter opened his eyes and tried to take a breath but there was none for speaking. He closed his eyes and tried again, but only more shallow gurgling sounds came. But his lips moved.

"What? Peter, you're hurt really bad." He actually looked concerned. "Help!" Seth yelled again.

But yelling was no good, Peter's father assigned him to work this shift alone; people were tired of having manure dropped on them.

He tried to reach for Seth, but it hurt too much to move this arm. Thankfully, the other side, the side with the phone, didn't hurt quite as much. His cousin looked at him. "Okay, Pete, either I need to move you or leave you here and get help, because no one is coming."

Peter mouthed, "Eve."

"The doctor? I don't know who he is."

"Eve?" Peter mouthed again.

"Peter, I don't know where you live." He looked panicked.

Peter moved his finger the tiniest bit but then a surge of pain overtook him and he passed out.

SETH

Seth ran. After finding the first person he could, which happened to be Gregory, Eve's boyfriend, Seth went back to sit with Peter while Greg ran to get help. His cousin's breathing sounded labored and strange, and though he was passed out his eyes rolled in what Seth could only assume was pain.

Carefully, Seth lifted up Peters shirt where that brute of a horse kicked him. Black and red bruises covered the entire middle of his back. Seth could see the indent of the horse's hooves, like crescent moons of purple. Helpless, he replaced the shirt.

His cousin could die, and though he did not know the kid well, he would not wish that on anyone. If only he was a doctor or had a magic wand or a superpower. This thought startled him. Two seconds ago, he was creeped out by the thought of superpowers, though he suddenly didn't feel creeped out now.

That made him return to the situation. Someone was coming to help. A healer perhaps. A touch of guilt entered his mind as he looked down at his cousin, and gratitude entered his heart. *Bless that stupid horse, I might get some answers.* That thought brought on instant guilt.

He felt of two minds about the subject of Edenia. One thing was certain, he knew this was a good place, with good people, and the idea of using them sat wrong in his gut. The other side of the coin was that his sister could die, and what wouldn't a brother do for a sister?

He heard running feet, and several members of the Miller family rushed into the barn. To Seth's surprise, Eve, who usually had nothing but an airy smile on her face, was stoic as she knelt by Peter's side.

Their father Hirum, asked, "What happened Seth?"

"That crazy horse kicked him in the back." His hand rose to point at the missing animal. "Then he jumped the rope and ran for it."

"Father," Eve's voice came in interrupting his shock. She sounded a bit panicked, "We need someone else. I think his rib has punctured his lung. He is bleeding inside of himself, and he can barely breathe."

Hirum, his uncle, knelt at Peters head, placing a hand on Eve's knee. "Eve, do your best, the Doc is on his way. Peter can't wait."

"Okay, okay." She said with a touch of hysteria but then she took a deep breath and looked up into her father's eyes. Her trembling hands stilled, and her face calmed. Even as Seth watched, her blue-green irises moved and swirled. It was as if the most beautiful, cerulean ocean formed a whirlpool. Her dark pupils became the bottom of endless water. Spinning, spinning, turning...Seth blinked rapidly, feeling hypnotized, like he entered the old-school Willy Wonka movie.

The boat ride...yeah just like that.

"Mint will revive him and birch will ease the pain." With that, Eve scooped up a handful of dirt, which was impossible. The floor of the barn was packed so hard it even sounded like wood. But her hand went right into the earth as if it were loose potting soil. She pressed the handful of dirt, and when she opened it up there was no dirt to be found, but a bit of what looked like bark.

"Good, Eve," his uncle said, and Seth's attention went to him and his crystal blue...swirling irises. Hirum Miller, his uncle, turned his head to the side and Seth felt a slight breeze touch his face as Hirum spoke softly, "Garren hurry, the Doc is needed now!" to no one in particular. He turned his pulsating orbs back to his daughter and nodded.

His eyes went back to Eve. After she scooped some more dirt and pressed it, she handed Greg several handfuls of 'not-dirt'. "I need this mashed to mulch."

Seth watched Gregory take the stuff from Eve. He ripped it apart like paper and mashed it in his hands like dough. Then he pulverized it into an almost liquid state between his fist and palm, which, as they connected, sounded like two rocks hitting one another.

As he watched Gregory's efficiency at the task, he realized Eve asked Gregory to do this not because she wanted to ask him. He was neither close at hand nor as seemingly capable as someone like her father who sat at her elbow. Seth wondered what his superpower was. His eyes were hazel though and his irises were swirling.

Next, he saw Eve stab two fingers into the hard dirt and pull them out again. Something green and plant-like came with them. The green stems seemed connected to her fingers, yet they moved and wriggled out of the floor. It almost looked like green silly string was being squirted out of the hole her fingers made. But then buds appeared and developed into leaves before his eyes. Like some strange, hyper speed version of the life cycle of a plant.

At that moment, he really did have a superhero experience. Something whizzed into the barn. Seth only saw it from the corner of his eye, but it was distinctly a human-like blur, and the next thing he knew, an older man with stark white hair had taken Hirum's place. He had a hard doctor-like bag which sat open between him and Eve.

Eve said, "We stuck it under his tongue and on the bruises."

"Well done, Eve. Garren," the old doctor said, looking at a tall blonde guy Seth sort of recognized, "a bowl with water from the river, quickly." The young man blurred through a door. And Seth realized how the doctor got there so quickly. Seth counted to five, and with a gush of air—that Hirum settled with a wave of his hand—a bowl appeared at the doctor's side, full of water. That guy was the blur. HE was the blur, like the Flash blur. *What the actual crap!*

This afternoon he'd seen a lot of craziness but this, for some reason, beat all. Faster than a speeding bullet and everything.

Eve didn't wait. She pressed the water to Peters lips and then poured it on his wounds. It did not spill on to the dirt, not one drop. It seemed to absorb into Peter, like a sponge.

The doc yelled, "Garren, regular water, now."

Garren waved his hand around in the air super-fast. Moving slightly around the barn as he did, holding the bowl at his elbow. However, when he stopped his strange dance and tipped the bowl toward the doctor, he asked, "Is this enough? I can pull some from..."

"No that is perfect," the doctor said, and took the bowl, handing it to Eve. Then he did something that absolutely made Seth ill. The same way Eve had stuck her fingers into the hard ground, Seth saw the Doc stick his fingers into Peters back. He pressed them through the skin and muscle as easily as one would press through butter.

"Yes, yes." The Doc said. "Two ribs broken and into his lung." He maneuvered a moment. "But they can be set to right. Hirum, hold him down, I'm going to have to back them up and pull them out of the lung tissue."

Seth felt ill.

As Hirum set to bracing his son, the doctor glanced up at Seth for the briefest of moments, revealing his face. Seth could see his eyes clearly. They were a bright blue-green. They were the exact same color as...

Seth looked at Eve. Yes, her large eyes were that same bright blue-green, a perfect teal, the exact mixture of the two colors. They called him Doc. And they counted on Eve to take his place until this man got there. Could teal be the color of the superpower that could save Lillian?

A warmth flooded him. He knew in that moment that these people could save Lillian. They could, that was why his father brought them here. He knew down to his toes that he didn't need to rely on the Joneses. He just had to trust his father.

He looked at the faces surrounding him and his heart burst with love and excitement and hope. They could save her. They could. And that meant that he didn't have to betray them. He could just stay here. He could be with Miriam, he could love her and stay with her.

He thought of his father and mother in this moment of clarity and wisdom and what a terrible jerk he'd been. He felt guilt but also understanding that all could and would be forgiven. He remembered all the moments of love they'd given him and all their years of integrity toward him. He wanted to rush home and tell them he was sorry. Tell them that he knew now. Tell them that he would stay here, even if it meant becoming a freaky superhero, because this was the place that saved his sister.

He rose, needing to do just that. He raced out the door just as Miriam entered the barnyard. He stopped, but she kept running past him into the barn. He saw her pause, assess what had happened, then look back at him. Miriam took two more steps into the barn and Seth saw her father, Hirum, approach her. He spoke to her and pointed to Seth. She shook her head, once, then again but fiercely this time, as her father continued talking. Hirum took Miriam by the shoulders and she bowed her head as he conveyed something of seeming import to her. Then it was over, her father went back into the barn.

The whole conversation confused Seth, especially because Hirum kept gesturing toward him.

A few seconds later Miriam turned toward him. She came toward him, pale and uncertain.

Miriam was so fiercely beautiful, but that was not all. She was so calm and confident. She stood before him, her incredible violet eyes still as a stone, not spinning, not even pulsating. Again, he wondered if she had a power.

His hand ached to reach out and smooth her white-blonde hair down, for it was stirring in the breeze that had suddenly arisen. Miriam grabbed his hand as if she knew his thoughts and wanted to stop him from acting. He looked down at her tiny hand in his, then up to her eyes. They seemed to plead with him for some reason.

He did not understand where the depth and breadth of his awe for this girl came from. She was a treacherous slope, and he tottered at the edge. He opened his mouth to tell her everything, that he loved her more than he thought was possible. That he would stay here to be with her forever. That he could never thank them enough for saving Lillian. That he would do anything, live under any strange customs they wanted him to, in exchange for that gift.

As he realized what he was promising to himself, and silently to Miriam, he felt the blood drain from his face. He felt the recoil of doubt…insecurity, no, vulnerability, slither into his soul—like a snake into a warm sleeping bag. He shivered.

And the vulnerability he'd seen in her gem-like eyes changed, instantly. She whispered, "This," She thumbed to the inside of the barn, "it's too much. Isn't it? It's too creepy. We are too creepy, right?" She narrowed her eyes assessing again. "You are not ready to except this. My father says you are not ready, and I think I agree with him. You look like you're totally going to freak out."

Surprised by her comment, he blinked. That was his old self. But in the last ten minutes he had been irrevocably changed. There was no other way to describe it. It was irrevocable.

He looked down at his feet wondering how to explain it all, because he knew he'd have to tell her everything. About the Joneses, about the cancer, about his deal. He took a deep breath, determined to be vulnerable, to be brave, but Miriam grabbed his head in her hands, her violet irises swirling.

CHAPTER 35

Miriam had no idea how her father knew of her feelings for Seth, but he'd used them brutally against her just now. *"Seth is not ready Miriam. He will leave us. Do you want him to leave? Protect him from this. He cares for you. Your mother and I are willing to consider him as a suitor if he accepts Guardianship. Don't let this accident ruin that."*

He had struck every nerve perfectly.

She did not want Seth to leave. She did not want him to freak out. She wanted things to move forward. Thus, she had to make the last ten minutes not exist. Her father, her leader told her to do it. She could do it. She could make it all go away. It would be easy. Her vow to never use her Nature was predicated on that Nature not being needed. Her father told her this *was* needed, now. He asked her to do her duty. He reminded her how important this was. And as she looked at Seth, she knew that for her heart, this was life or death. So, she moved around her promise to herself. She justified it. She discarded it as easily as she discarded a rotten apple.

Seth stood there, head bent to the ground as if he were giving her permission for what must be done. She could not stand the uncertainty she'd seen in his eyes a moment before; it made her braver than she'd ever been in her life.

Her hands rose.

She pushed down the throw-up sensation and pulled strength to her. She would ignore the budding force inside her heart that thumped and moaned *don't do this*. She had to ignore her own passions, her lust at the strength of Seth's jaw, the strands of his lovely black hair, or the depth, the very nearly never-ending chasms that were his eyes.

Truly, none of that mattered anyhow. Right now, he was disgusted by who she was, who they all were. She saw it in his eye so many times, and even just now.

Pulling bravery to her and with her Nature swirling in her eyes, she took his head in her hands with the intention of taking the whole barn situation away from him. She would make it not exist.

But before she pulled, Seth's eyes met hers and his face filled with shock. He said, surprised, "I thought you were different."

She was humiliated by his words, for reasons she could not understand. Yet his words drove her.

She pulled.

Immediately his face went blank. She willed time to move backward.

But something was wrong.

This pulling was nothing like what she'd done to the many Joneses. This was like a five sensory experience. She was completely inside Seth's memory the way she had been inside Josie's.

The first sensation that hit her was Seth's passion for her. His need to tell her everything about his sins, because his heart had been changed. He wanted to be honest.

As the moments ticked by, Miriam saw how she'd been completely wrong in her analysis of his reactions. She'd forced her own fear and judgment onto him and so had her father.

Shaken and distraught that she had made a terrible mistake, she tried to cut off the connection. She strained to pull her hands away. She attempted to shut down the vision, but she could not. She watched through his eyes as he saw her and tried to capture her crazy hair. He thought she was amazingly lovely. He thought she was his person.

The betrayal of seeing his thoughts, feelings, and actions, and understanding them completely was so vast, so all-encompassing Miriam wanted to hide under a rock in shame.

Needing to do something to make it stop, she mentally pulled hard on the connection between them. All that did was pull time faster. In fact, she saw, felt, heard, everything in a blurry jumble. Nothing distinguishable.

But then, all of a sudden, she was in the barn, Seth yelling at Gregory to find someone to help him. She watched Peter get kicked, she watched as Seth watched Peter toy with Bull. And then, when she thought the agony would never end, it stopped. She did not cut it the way she normally did. But she did feel the loss, physical and visceral. Shame for what she had done surfaced out of the slopping lava of guilt inside her, and memories faded into her as she faded into them. Then her mind emptied, and darkness filled her vision.

CHAPTER 36

Seth

Uncertain exactly how he came to be sitting in the middle of the road, Seth looked around, and was surprised to see Miriam, lying on her side, next to him. Or he thought it was Miriam, her massive amounts of hair covered her face. Without considering, he carefully swept the silky strands to the side. Why was Miriam unconscious in the road? And how was it possible for someone to look so hot while lying in dirt?

He shook his head to clear that train of thought, and it occurred to him that she might be hurt. This thought amped him up. Quickly, he knelt, and touched her face, "Miriam?" Wow, her skin was soft. His hands cradled her face, and he turned her head out of the road dust. "Miriam." There was dirt on her mouth, so naturally he needed to wipe it clean. But the moment his fingers brushed the perfectly pink, amazingly silken flesh, he wished he could take it back. How could he think of anything but those lips now?

He bit the inside of his cheek, his hormones all but raging out of control. What was wrong with him? He felt groggy, and all his squelched teenage male baseness seemed out of control. Squeezing his eyes shut, he forced himself to pull it together.

"Seth." Seth turned. His dad was leaning out the front door of some random house yelling to him. "What in the world is going on?"

Seth looked back at Miriam before answering, "I don't know. I just found her here. She won't wake up."

In what felt like a moment, a moment Seth spent staring at Miriam's face, his dad appeared at his side. "Is she hurt?"

"I don't think so."

His father leaned down and straighten her skirt. Seth hadn't even noticed the hem was around her knees, then he looked her over. "Is she just unconscious?"

"Dad, I don't know! I know less than you do, I just found her here. I mean, I was just here and there she was."

His dad looked at him, "What do you mean you were just here?"

Seth shook his head, "Five minutes ago I was walking toward the barn...and the next thing I know, I'm looking around, and here I am with Miriam next to me. But she won't wake up."

His father's brow crinkled up for a moment, and then he stood. "Well, let's get her home." His father scooped Miriam up as if she were a sleeping two-year-old and started down the street. Not wanting to leave Miriam, Seth followed.

The Miller home was almost identical to his, though it was bigger and had a fresh coat of paint and a ton of flowers in window pots. For some reason, his father stopped in front of the home and took several deep breaths before approaching the door. A red cheeked, blonde-haired, beautiful woman—like celebrity beautiful—pushed the screen door wide before they knocked.

Sparkling eyes the color of amber agates flashed first to Miriam, then to his father in such rapid succession it made his foggy mind dizzy. Finally, she stepped out. The screen door slammed with a loud thwap as her hands touched Miriam's face, shrewd, unemotional eyes assessing. "What happened?"

His father spoke as he shrugged, "My son found her in the road."

After a moment her hot gaze fell on him, "Well, Seth Johnson, today is just not your day." He had no idea what she meant. She looked at Miriam and then back at Seth. It looked like her mind was working a million miles an hour. "You found her?" She repeated squinting at him.

Seth nodded a bit thunderstruck by the woman's face and glance.

His dad said, "He was confused, he said he was just *there* and so was she."

Quickly, she turned to hold open the door, "Please come in, set her down on the couch. It is to your left."

Seth's father strode in and set Miriam carefully down. Without knowing why, Seth pulled a chair from the corner and sat next to her, his attention on her unconscious face.

"Seth?" The woman asked. He looked up and noticed her raised eyebrow as she eyed the proximity of his chair to the couch.

All of a sudden, he felt very self-conscious. Sitting up straight, he shook his head again and said, "Yes ma'am."

His father stepped in, "Is she going to be alright Lu?"

The woman turned to his father, "Luanne, if you please. Only my husband has permission to use that kind of familiarity." Her voice was not angry, but it was pointed, and Seth did not understand why. "And yes, she is fine, thank you. She just passed out. It happens every now and again. She will be right as rain in a few minutes."

A sigh of relief escaped Seth's lips, and both his hand and glance went to Miriam. Looking down, he saw that he touched her hand and pulled it back. What was wrong with him? When he looked back to the adults, they both were staring at him. He stood, smiled at them, and walked to the window.

"What were you saying before? About Seth and this being a bad day...or something?" His father asked.

Now that he was away from his cousin and looking at the flowers, his mind seemed to clear. His aunt, Miriam's mother, Luanne Miller cleared her throat. "Oh, did I say that? What I should have said was this is the second incident we have had today."

"Oh, that's what you should have said, huh?" Seth knew that tone. He looked over, and sure enough, his father had crossed his majorly muscular arms, his jaw set to pounce. He smiled to himself, his aunt had no idea what she was getting herself into.

Surprisingly, she met his stare and raised him one. "That is what I said, is it not? If there was a need for me to say something different, then that is what I would have said. I might make a mistake on the first time around, but I never make the same mistake twice."

"Mistake?" His father was upset now. His voice had that high-pitched thing going on.

She huffed, "Must I repeat myself?" Then she turned. "Now if you do not mind, I have a truly sick child to care for. I thank you for bringing Miriam here." She held her hand out toward the door, but his father stood his ground, and Seth walked back to Miriam's side, with no intention of leaving until she woke up and he knew she was all right. Hoping he wouldn't have to confront Miriam's mother—he could see where Miriam got her formality, and her beauty, and her moxie—he attempted to blend into the furniture.

"Lu...anne I would like to talk with you."

Seth watched from the corner of his eye. His aunt's arm dropped to her side, and she studied his father's face. Once she met his eyes, she did not look away. Then something unspoken and strange occurred between the two adults. They stayed equally locked in each other's gaze a very awkward length of time. An uncomfortable heat filled the room. Seth pulled at his collar.

Thankfully his aunt ended the contest; not by looking away, but by cheating. He had to hand it to her, she broke the spell all the same.

She called, "Esther, Gabrielle, Simon, come please."

Footsteps from throughout the house thundered, as the children came to obey their mother. When blonde heads arrived, the mother said—still without breaking eye contact with his father.

"Be polite now and say hello to your uncle." Then she smiled, wickedly, and holy cow did that turn her face from beautiful to breathtaking.

Seth's father smiled, too, in a playfully defeated way, and he shook his head. Then something he had never before seen, happened. Ezekiel Johnson blinked—or looked away, same thing.

He. Lost. A staring contest.

His father looked to Esther who gave her uncle a small hug. "Good to see you uncle." And the other two children followed suit.

Esther came over to Seth and with a sheepish look on her face asked, "How are you doing with all this?"

Confused Seth asked, "All what?" Then he thought she probably meant living here in Edenia. Man, his brain was foggy.

However, before he could answer, his aunt jumped in. "Esther dear, as you can see, Miriam is sleeping. Seth found her and made sure she got home alright." She put emphasis on several words, as her brows furrowed forward and she looked expectantly between Seth and Miriam. Then Esther's bright green eyes followed her mother's pattern and Seth watched as some kind of lightning struck her mind.

"Oh. Yes, mother." She said slowly. "I see. You probably would like me to get her a blanket."

"Yes, indeed I would, thank you so much."

Esther left the room, and that was when he noticed Gabrielle looking a bit shocked, but before Gabrielle could say anything, his mother said, "I am sure Eve would like some help with Peter." She took Gabrielle's arm. "After you have done that, I think your father should come home," she said carefully. He nodded.

"Simeon," she continued, "I need to speak with your uncle in private. That means you are in charge of Joseph and Dorothea. Understand?" The boy nodded. "So, take them into the backyard and play until I come get you."

"Yes, mama." Simeon said and ran off to obey.

"Wow, Luanne," Seth's father said. "Was that production for us? Thank you very much. Should I clap?" He pointedly folded his arms again as Esther reentered the room with a quilt she placed gently on Miriam.

"Thank you, Esther," her mother said. She completely ignored his father. She gave Esther a shooing nod toward the door.

Picking up on whatever her mother was trying to tell her, Esther left the house.

His dad had obviously now had enough. "What in the name of all that is good and holy is going on here?"

Seth had a question of his own, but at that moment Seth felt a hand touch his. He turned and saw that Miriam's eyes were open looking at him.

She squeezed his hand and whispered something. In a second he was out of his chair. His face as close to hers as he could manage. "What?" He whispered back.

"I'm sorry." She said and closed her eyes again.

Confused, he sat back in his chair, but he kept her hand in his.

Ten minutes later his father and Miriam's mother stood together talking in an uncomfortably familiar way. Seth pushed the blanket down so he could see Miriam's face better. After a few moments of unabashed staring he glanced yet again across the hall to the shut glass doors of the Miller's office. What they could possibly say bothered him, but not as much as seeing Miriam crumpled on the couch. This girl, with her kindness, and quiet strength, her discerning advice and wild desires for freedom, captivated him.

He smiled at her and felt his heartbeat accelerate. He shook his head, overwhelmed a bit.

There was some kind of undeniable force at work here. As he pulled at a golden strand of hair caught between her pink lips, he felt an attraction inside him that was so strong it bordered on violent. A part of him registered that it was much stronger now than it had been at noon. Then, his emotions were at an understandable 'date three' kind of 'super intense like', now he was at more a 'date fifteen' almost 'obsession slash love'. Like his insides were riddled and writhing with...anticipation?

He rose abruptly and walked away from her. What had changed? He closed his eyes, and when he did, he could feel her behind him. He knew exactly where she was, he knew he was five feet away from her.

What was this?

He looked out the window at the nice neat houses, green lawns and flowerpots and saw them as they really were; little patches of heaven. He watched the kind and gentle men and women walking down the street. This led his mind to race over all the times in the last few days the people of Edenia had spent their goodness, their kindness, their absolute wonderful nature on him. From people bringing them dinner, to his teacher's kind words, to everyone in town offering certain household items they didn't exactly need. Kids at school genuinely attempting to include him and get to know him. Such a far cry from the bullies and gangs at the other schools he'd attended.

He'd forced these kindnesses out of his mind the last few days. Trying to focus on the freaky, alien nature of them all. But now, it was like a switch was flipped. He felt solidarity of all things with these people, because they were part of Miriam. This place and these people had made her. And anything that made her couldn't be bad. His heart swelled as he turned and looked at her.

The sane part of him recognized his passion had just bled into his attitude toward Edenia. That bothered him. He had to not attach to this place. He had to remember he was going to sell out all their secrets to his cousin, Jeremiah.

Huffing, he turned and focused, *Lillian*. This was life or death! He thought of his sister. Her condition was so strange. On top of the monster headaches, this morning, Lilly fell down a few steps. Thankfully he'd been there to catch her. He had to carry her afterwards. She could not make her legs work nor would the left side of her face cooperate; it drooped in a sickly animated way.

Moments later, she roused and almost became her normal self; teasing him and trying

to hurry him out of the bathroom.

Out of the corner of his eye, he noticed Miriam's blonde-haired siblings, his little cousins, playing in the yard. Cousins. Cousins. Miriam could only ever be his friend; she was his cousin.

Miriam's friendship would only last as long as it took him to get the info he needed anyhow, because when she found out how he'd betrayed her and everyone she loved, she would never smile at him again.

There was only one thing to do. Harden his heart. Clenching his fists, he paced the room. He knew exactly what needed to be done he just had to do it. He pounded his fist into his palm and growled deep in his throat.

Almost as if in response, a moan came from the couch. When he looked over, Miriam attempted to sit up.

And like a man with two faces, Seth flipped.

All his anger melted away, and he moved to her side, "Whoa there, Tiger. Let me help."

Finally, she was awake. His heart raced to see her lovely violet eyes blinking up at him. He placed a hand at her back and another in her hand. This sent a shiver up his spine like he was an idiot eleven-year-old who'd never touched a girl before.

Exhaling and bracing her with his own body, he slowly pulled her to stand conveniently in his arms. Their bodies, not uncomfortably, pressed together. Seth's stomach swirled and lurched, and if it wasn't so pleasant to hold Miriam so close, he might wonder if he was sick.

After a minute or so of her breathing, head hovering on his shoulder, eyes cast to the floor, electricity sizzling around them; she looked up at him and he worried what his face was telling her. He stiffened his features, not ready yet for her to know all his innermost thoughts. But her radiant face shone. How could he not expose his feelings, his attraction, his awe? His mind basked in the chemistry crackling between them; she was an angel.

Maybe she could be his angel of mercy, if only he would tell her his issues.

Though he didn't want to hope she cared for him, her eyes and lips betrayed her. Her breaths betrayed her. In that one moment, he had no doubts that she too felt whatever was happening between them and she knew it just as strongly as he did.

CHAPTER 37

Miriam

Obviously, he didn't remember a thing, as she knew it would be. His eyes were back to looking at her like she was any other person and not some 'freak'. Her bravery, her strength paid off. For the most part.

Something else was obvious. His feelings for her. At least it was obvious now that she knew. She knew that he wasn't trying to deceive her with forced or false attraction. She knew that he wanted to be honest with her. To tell her everything. At least she was certain that was what she had learned. When she pulled hard on his soul and memories, they had sped before her and she didn't get to experience them, thus she could not remember them.

Something else fluttered in her brain as she stood dizzily in his arms. She pulled at the remnants of the pulling from her own memory because she could not review Seth's. She found hope there. And the seed of faith. He had seen something that gave him hope. That made him believe. Not only had he been changed by what he saw, he'd been relieved, grateful, confident. And she'd taken that all away.

She also felt the remnant of his sister, Lillian, tangled with that relief. But the reason why was not clear, not in her memory.

Still, Seth's face hurt her now. She saw something in his eyes that just looked like beautiful agony to her. She had betrayed him. She had invaded him. The tables had turned in an excruciatingly tragic way. She thought of the hated piece of his soul she'd sliced away as it twirled at the bottom of her gut. And she wondered how she could have misunderstood that little piece of him, and what his soul told her.

She thought back to the look of disgust on his face right before she'd done it. And again, how his nostrils flared as he looked around at all the Guardians his first day of school. How he did not want to sit next to them, ever. How he glared in class. How he pushed everyone away. How he had spoken about Edenia to the Joneses.

He hated Edenia, and he hated their Natures.

But he loved her?

Right now, in this moment, his face told her that he wasn't grossed out by her any longer. But a few moments ago, while he paced the floor, she felt like all his feelings of *right now* didn't matter. The set of his jaw and tension in his shoulders told her that he was determined. He looked like he'd rallied himself.

However, *right now*, with his dark eyes completely unwavering, he stood totally steady and mesmerized, his face soft and relaxed with tenderness. His lips were slightly upturned with happiness. It felt like all bets were off, and unfortunately, she understood the sentiment because her emotions were also duplicitous when it came to him.

"So, how are you?" he asked into the magic that surrounded them.

What was she to do? How was she to answer him? She was not well. She was muddled by him, her focus wrong. She had a task, and all she could think about was what his lips would feel like. It was time for her to steel herself. She had to make him into the villain he was if she ever planned to fulfill her mission.

In reality, he had nothing. She'd taken it. She wasn't going to give him anything more. He had two-and-a-half days before he changed. She could hold him off for that long. She was just going to distract him, and she had to do a good job. She'd succeeded today, and though putting a piece of his soul inside her had also deepened her feelings for him, her understanding of him, her connection to him, it also deepened her commitment to the garden.

She just had to do as Peter and make lemonade out of lemons.

Because of her Nature, he would go through the steps like a normal newcomer. He would change in the way he should. Things would go on as they had before. She would get the phone from him, as her plan dictated and then...nothing.

Her dedication to the Garden battling with her lust for Seth made stepping back out of his arms and sitting on the couch an intensely complex action.

Once she'd done it, she finally answered his question.

"I'm feeling much better. Thank you."

He sat, too. They were as close as they could be without touching, "Does this happen often?"

"Oh, no, not at all." She stumbled.

His brow wrinkled. She knew he was concerned, but what he said was playful. "Well, we can't have you overexerting yourself, now can we? You need to be all rested up for our date."

Blood rushed from everywhere at once and landed in Miriam's cheeks, which warmed. She smiled. "What date?"

He smiled back, "The one I'm going to take you on, tomorrow, right after school."

"But you can't. I told you..."

"I know. But Miriam, I don't care what other people assume. What I am proposing is perfectly harmless. It involves a lot of talking, of getting to know one another better, eating a meal together, playing around, racing around town listening to loud music with the windows down. Or whatever the Edenian version of that is." He clasped and unclasped his hand and glanced away from her for a moment. When he looked back, he shyly avoided her eyes. His voice had softened, and he spoke imploringly. "Miriam, I have a swirl of something inside me, a jumble of feelings. It is distracting me big time and...and it has your name all over it. I'm certain the only way to sort it out is to be with you." Finally, his eyes found hers. "You say that this is normal, people feeling things for people they are related to, but I don't feel normal and I don't feel this for any of the other people here." He motioned out of doors where the little kids were screaming in play. "Besides, you may literally be the only person that can help me because you see what's inside me so much more clearly than I do. I've known you for three days and you have basically done a years' worth of therapy work on me. So, will you? Help me understand what is happening inside here?" He pointed to his heart.

Her mind was an echo-room of his words. "*Jumble of feelings; only person; date; distraction to me; be with you; date; date; date.*" Not trusting herself to speak, she only nodded, scared/excited—how could she not after a speech such as that—but also aware that spending time with him fulfilled so many wishes at once.

"But don't think I'm the only one who's going to benefit." Putting his hand up to the side of his mouth, he whispered. "You see, I've been thinking about our little deal too, and I think the only way you're gonna know what it's like out there, is to let me show you. Like a major imagination exercise, but I think it will be fun." He smiled even wider and so did she, "So...is that a yes?"

"I suppose I don't have a choice. You've tempted me beyond my ability to deny you. But Seth, I must think of Foster. We cannot let anyone see us. I was not exaggerating. We do not go on 'dates' here unless we are serious. And my parents are serious about Foster."

He took her hand. "Miriam, I'm as serious as a brain tumor."

Her face screwed up, "Don't you mean a heart attack? As serious as a heart attack. That's the saying, right?"

"Yes, I guess it is." He nodded somberly.

CHAPTER 38

Seth

Wow. If there was one appliance that was necessary to happiness it was a dishwasher. How did people live before dishwashers? There must have been some pretty epic arguments over who would wash and who would rinse and who got to rest.

Once again, he plunged his hands into the steamy, soapy water and felt around for the rag. "Seth," the word hissed from Abby's teeth, "you're taking forever!"

She was rinsing and drying and keeping the kettle on the stove for the constant stream of hot water required during dish washing. He looked at her flatly. "How about we switch if you're in such a hurry."

Rolling her eyes, she tapped her foot while Seth slowly wiped a dinner plate with the sudsy rag. "I just want to go sit with Lilly. She looks so awful, Seth I'm afraid for her." Her tapping stopped and her face crumpled. In the space of two seconds gigantic tears streamed down her cheeks. "I can't..." she sniffed, "I just can't live without her. She's my best friend."

Seth was used to this emotional whiplash from the women in his life. He immediately stopped washing and whispered, "I know." He set the plate carefully in her side of the sink. "I can't believe how quickly it's getting bad." Turning to her he went on. "I can't believe she's still walking around. How does she do at school?"

Abby sniffed again and looked up at him. "That is one thing that's strange. At school she seems almost like her old self. She's tired, but she's there, ya know." She pointed to her head with a wet hand. "I don't want to wear her out, but I don't complain about mom forcing her, because I get to be with the real Lilly while we're there." Abby's teary eyes rolled up as she said this last bit.

"Don't worry, I haven't given up on my plan. In fact, I have definitely made some progress. The whole 'water maybe giving them their powers' thing, I'm sure will be very useful information." Miriam was the only stumbling block. Though at this exact moment, now that they were apart, he felt free of her influence, of his over-the-top love for all things Miriam. Although he still had the strangest sensation that, if he needed to, he could point to her exact location.

Seth thought of his premonition of today. He couldn't care about Miriam anymore. She would want to murder him after all was said and done. There was no helping it, his sister was dying. All he could do was try to get as much information as possible. Because one way or another he was out of Edenia before the clock struck twelve. No way was he turning into an Edenian.

He just wished his brain didn't turn to mush when Miriam was around, and he wished he didn't have the need to be with her.

"Oh, yeah, speaking of that." She turned on the water and spoke quietly. "I overheard something today that was...concerning. Something that your friends might be interested in."

Seth looked behind them and all around the kitchen. "What?"

"Well, first, you tell me what happened inside the barn, after you were all heroic and stuff."

Seth's eyebrow's knotted, "What are you talking about?"

Abby didn't look up from her dish, only elbowed him playfully, and said, "Get over yourself. Tell me what happened."

Seth stopped washing and turned to her, "No, Abby, what are you talking about?"

She looked at him. "What am I talking about? I'm talking about when you saved Peter from getting trampled to death by that crazy horse. Did that not happen? Because as soon as Bertha, ya know, that real pudgy lady, I can't remember her name so that's what I call her," she started rinsing again. Seth refrained from asking questions while trying not to feel alarmed as Abby went on. "Anyway, when Bertha saw that huge horse run out of the barn and then you a few seconds behind, she told me to stay and keep picking the apples and she ran to see what was happening. FYI when I say 'ran' I really mean..."

"Abby!" Seth interrupted, "Focus please. This is important."

She looked at him and rolled her puffy eyes. It was hard to believe that five seconds ago she was crying. "Geez, Seth. Touchy." After a few seconds of huffing, she went on. "Fine, I'll tell it from our side, but I want details from you. K?"

Seth nodded. Anything to keep her going.

"So, Bertha didn't come back for a while, but when she did, all the girls were talking about how you saved Peter or something. Like the horse charged him and you pulled him out of the way. All the girls know he works in there alone. They, like, keep track of him or something, I'm not sure." Abby didn't give him a chance to admit that he wasn't even in the barn today before she was speed-boating-it away. "But later, and this is the weird part," she quieted her voice again, "we were all kinda standing around and watching the barn 'cause Hirum and his whole family were in there. Then, Miriam was there and ew, it looked like you were like kissing her for a second, and all the girls started talking about that and I was so embarrassed because you should hear what they say about you. GROSS! Even worse is what they say about Miriam. Stuff like 'she so plain she's not worth remembering' and 'no one can get a memorable word in when she's around' stupid stuff—nice-girl insults—ya know. Anyhow, I started picking apples again, because I was bored and disgusted with you, and that's when I heard someone say, 'he saw it, that's not good.' Then another girl said, 'like it matters, the freak will clean up the mess.' That girl is really annoying. I can't stand her. So, then all the girls like gasped or something all-at-once—like you know what happens when a crowd of people all see something cool at the same time and they react. So, I walked back over and they all turned on me, and made like a human wall." She took a deep breath. "When I finally got past them, you were hovering over Miriam, and she was lying on the ground. But it got me thinking, right?" Another deep breath and she looked expectantly at Seth. "So, obviously you see where I'm going with this story, I know it's just a theory, but it might be worth checking into. So, before we get to the *you laughing at my idea* bit, I have to ask..." She turned and eyed him, "Were you?"

Still trying to unravel the monologue, Seth was too stunned to even acknowledge the question. "Huh?"

"Where you really kissing Miriam?"

He had zero memories of her story, but one thing he did know, if he had kissed Miriam, nothing in this world could make him forget it. "Uh, no, I don't think so."

"Seth. What. The. Crap! You either kissed the creepy alien girl or you didn't. Which is it?"

Seth just couldn't handle this right now. How could he talk about doing things he knew he'd never done with an eyewitness of him doing the thing he'd never done?

Something she'd said did make sense, and he latched on to it. "Forget about that."

"Not likely, it scarred me. Like, for forever."

"Just tell me what you think I should understand about your story again?"

"Miriam, stupid. I'm pretty sure she's your dangerous memory girl. The one Jeremiah wants you to find. And no wonder, I knew she was a freak." Abby stopped drying her hands, a look of understanding suddenly in her face. She walked up to him and looked into his eyes, "Holy crap. You really have no clue what I just told you, do you? Do you even remember what you did after school today?" She looked at his stunned face and went on. "You don't remember any of this, do you?" Numbly Seth shook his head. "Oh my heck!" She squealed, "I did it! I got what we need, didn't I? And you're the proof. Now all we have to do is call your little friends, and Lilly is saved." Her hands went to her cheeks. "I can't believe it." She hugged him and said, "I'm going to tell Lilly!" And off she went, leaving Seth fumbling and spluttering to himself.

Saying that he was in a daze was putting it lightly. First of all, he couldn't believe that someone could tamper with someone else's memories. For legitimately real. Of course, Mr. Jones said it was possible, but Seth realized he never believed it. Second, he couldn't believe that his memories were the ones tampered with, and third, he couldn't believe that Miriam had done it to him. Miriam.

How his body could mix sorrow and indignation to a blended cocktail of emotions that raised the hairs off his neck, pumped extra blood to every cell, and made him want to cry out in pain, he would never know. But that was what his insides felt like right now.

He gripped the side of the sink and thought back. He could remember school and the nice, cool walk to the barn. He remembered the barn, but the next moment, if he concentrated hard, he was on the street, Miriam lying next to him. There was nothing in-between. If Abby hadn't told him there should be an in-between, he never in a million years would have known he didn't just walk home after school, passing the barn on his way. His mind bridged the two events with no spaces or gaps. It all felt perfectly normal and logical.

What a flawless trick. There was no way for her victims to be the wiser. How could she stomach it? How did she do it? He was going to barf. Miriam, his Miriam, wasn't normal like him. She was the freakiest freak of them all. And her freakiness just infected him.

No more was this some third-party weirdness he witnessed, reported on, and would soon be free of. He had feelings involved here, he had memories, and he had physical actions. He could no longer ignore the dangers of this place, excuse them like he was briefly in the twilight zone and would soon leave, unscathed. He was scathed, badly. He cared deeply for Miriam. He knew he did against all reason and explanation. It was against his will, against his plans. But it was real.

Had he kissed her?

Anger, no, rage barreled through him with fiery heat, and he didn't know if he could contain it. He would never know if he'd kissed her. Fingers involuntarily went to his lips. That potentially amazing piece of himself had been stolen.

Then a thought snuck in on him. He knew Miriam knew that things, emotions, feelings were happening between them, dang her. A girl who—unflattering though it may be—was practically a pariah in her own town would not thoughtlessly endanger a budding relationship, would she? She had to have a reason for doing what she did, and she'd said sorry to him.

When she woke up, she'd grabbed his hand, the only time she'd reached out and touched him, and the only words she had were sorry. So, he knew she wouldn't just fiddle around in someone's brain, his brain, without cause. Leaving the question, what happened? What changed? What had he seen? What circumstance would be so crazy, she couldn't let him remember it?

Anger burst in him anew. He probably learned exactly what he needed to save Lilly and get the hell out of here. Now, the only info he had was on her, Miriam, the memory girl, and time was running out.

He recalled the urgency in Willis's voice as he spoke of Miriam. *'Yes, they take thoughts, or memories, we think. Of course, you can see it is precarious to know exactly what is happening. It only started a few years back, but it has complicated our objective exponentially...We don't know if it is one individual or a new ability. So, we assume the person is your age. Regardless, we are extremely interested in this. We must figure a way to put a stop to it because every effort is thwarted so decidedly, we cannot progress.'*

This caused Seth to wonder if Miriam might be what they needed to conclude their deal. He might not know exactly where the tree was, but what if telling them about the dangerous memory girl was all it would take?

In his mind he went over and over the conversation and Mr. Jones' inflection. It just might be that important to him. It might be enough. That, and confirmation that the eyes meant something and that the tree was there, hidden behind some kind of illusion, and that the water gave these people their power. He sighed, maybe he could bring this around. He would save Lillian at any cost, he told himself.

The moment this thought settled inside him, his heart revolted in spite of all that had happened with Miriam messing in his head and the anger he felt. His brain told him, his feelings were petty, shallow, fake, nothing compared to the deepness, realness of a sister. But then his heart pushed those words out of his mind with an accelerated rhythm of blood that vibrated his body and sounded like Mir-i-am, Mir-i-am.

Pulling out a kitchen chair, he sat and put his head between his knees. He was between the harshest rock and hard place he could imagine.

He put his hands in his hair and tangled them all together in frustration. Willing his body to not tremble.

"Seth, are you alright?" Abby's voice sliced into his torment. He looked up, and she hurried over to him. "Oh my heck, I didn't realize how much this got to you." Kneeling at his feet, she touched his leg and looked up at him.

Confused by what she was referring to, he just sniffed and blinked and wiped at his face.

"You are really truly freaked out by these people, aren't you? I mean, I can see it. You're grabbing your head like...like you want to rip it off and..." She trailed off and looked away. In a matter of moments her face was red. "It's that stupid witch Miriam. She...she, defiled you. She used her freaky little power on you and messed around in your head and now you are absolutely wigging out." Abby stood and paced. "Oh, if I ever get my hands on her."

It took that long for Seth to wrap his head around what Abby was talking about. But as he listened, his hackles rose unbidden, and he began to squirm. She was so right. It was so creepy thinking about some supernatural something wiggling around in there. He pulled that discomfort to him like a life line. It anchored his direction. A direction that favored his sister.

He stood and took several deep breaths. He had been violated. He had been tricked.

Attempting to clear his head, he paced the living room for a few minutes. Abby watched him and finally he looked over at her, loving her but wanting her to leave. He said, "Thanks Abby. I was having a bit of a moment there. You snapped me out of it. I'm good now." Abby nodded to him but continued watching. After a few more moments he turned to her and said, "Hey, um, I need some time, alone. Will you ah..." he nodded toward the bedrooms.

She was surprised by his rejection but agreed. "Sure, I'll go check on Lilly." But as she walked away, he heard her muttering about how everyone was cracking up around her. He smiled a real smile. Abby was a rock.

Taking a few more deep breaths he paused in his pacing, a vengeful idea coming into his head.

One simple phone call and the Joneses would know everything. He would tell them every secret, every oddity he'd seen. He would tell them that Miriam was their memory eraser. That is exactly what she deserved for messing around in his brain.

His heart thumped.

He ignored it and moved toward the door while he reached in his pants pocket for his phone.

His heart thumped again. This was a betrayal.

His regrets were interrupted when his hand failed to find the familiar lump of his phone. It wasn't there.

He patted himself down. It wasn't on him. He sighed. It was probably in his backpack. Walking across the living room, he felt a knot of fear form in his gut. Ripping through his bag, he came up empty-handed. Maybe he left it in his room.

It wasn't there either.

Pulling at the collar of his stupid country-bumpkin shirt, he realized he couldn't breathe. He'd lost his phone. He was sweating and gasping. He'd lost his phone. He made it down the hall to the bathroom where he splashed ice-cold water on his face. Miriam knew about it. What if she took it from him? Bracing himself against the rim of the sink, he tried to remain upright and not vomit.

She had taken it. She had. He knew she had. She was the only one that knew about it, and she was the only one that had the opportunity. His throat tightened in panic, his gut in despair. Why had she done it?

What was he going to do now?

How could he help Lilly now?

Just then, Lillian shuffled out of her room and into the bathroom. She looked pale and miserable. Not paying attention to him, she riffled through the bottles of medication lined up on the bathroom shelf.

He watched her down a handful and mutter, "My head hurts so bad I swear it'll explode."

Without thinking about it he grabbed her and hugged her fiercely.

"Ouch, ouch, ouch, Seth. Have mercy."

He let her go and looked into her eyes. She smiled a small smile. "I heard the good news. Thank you. Thank you so, so much for trying so hard to take care of me." She pulled his cheek down and kissed it. "I love you, you big butt cheese."

"I love you too."

She walked out into the hall. "Who would have guessed it was Miriam? She's like one of those creepy deep-sea things. The ones that are invisible until they eat you."

Abby's voice came from down the hall. "An anglerfish."

"Yes, that's it." Lillian said. She shook her head in disgust and dismay as she shuffled back toward her room.

Lillian tripped. The banging sound sent Seth leaping for the door. But his dad was already there, picking her up in his arms and taking her to her bedroom. "I gotcha, baby girl." He crooned and kissed her forehead.

Seth glared at his dad's back. This was his fault.

Seth had to get Lillian out of here. But how? He had no phone. And even if he did, it wasn't like he could call an ambulance.

He moved back into the bathroom and stared at his reflection. His dark eyes were tight with stress and anger and betrayal and fear. What would saving Lillian even look like anymore? Was this it? Was he finished? Was he throwing in the towel?

He considered carefully.

Jeremiah wanted information he had. He just had to get it to him, and the deal was still on. They said if he needed any help, to ask. So, he had to get to Jeremiah.

He could walk there. He could walk there tonight. It was only a few miles. He could run that distance in fifteen minutes if he put his heart into it.

As if by magic, a plan skittered to life. His mind started turning.

Seth used the wall of the bathroom to slide his way down to the floor as he asked, "Can I do this? Can I actually betray Miriam? Kidnap my sister? Take her to another state? Watch her go through chemo and radiation and surgery, without my parents?" His whispered words seemed to ricochet off the small bathroom's white walls and white sink and white toilet and white bathtub and garble in his ears like dead, flat discord.

He grabbed his head and squeezed. He couldn't do this anymore. He had to choose.

Just when he was about to be pulled under by the sea of thoughts and doubts, he grabbed onto the first emotional lifebuoy he felt. A lifebuoy of anger.

Anger toward his father, anger toward Miriam. She'd taken his memories, she'd taken his phone, and she'd taken his heart and she'd tempted him to ignore the facts before him. Getting Lillian to the hospital was the only way to save her.

Falling back on old habits, Seth let the feeling rush over him like a siren's call to act.

He stood.

He opened the bathroom door.

He walked through the house to the front door.

He pulled it open, slid over the porch and down the steps.

When he was in the middle of the street, he turned toward that invisible tether he felt for Miriam. He allowed himself one moment of grief.

Then he turned south toward the Edenia road, toward the Joneses. As the sun went behind the trees, Seth Johnson started walking.

CHAPTER 39

Miriam

After Seth left, Miriam watched the sun set from her back porch. This day was done. Tomorrow would be the seventh day since the Johnson family moved to Edenia. Miriam smiled, confidently, but then sighed so loudly Garin glanced at her with bunched eyebrows as he passed her to move into the house.

The Joneses had attacked the orchard side of Edenia and Guardians were coming and going and distracting her from pondering all that had happened that day. She was glad that none of the Guardians were asking her to come fix their messes. Still, she wished for peace.

She left the porch and made her way into Peter's bedroom. It seemed the quietest place in the house now.

Miriam moved silently and sat across from Eve who snoozed in a chair. Miriam had no idea how she could sleep with so much noise. She supposed Eve was tired. She had done a lot today. Though she looked haggard around her eyes, her face was perfect, and with her hair piled on her head and that cute little apron she had on, she looked like a nurse out of a storybook. Beautiful and serene. Miriam wondered what her life would be like if she looked like Eve.

But Seth hadn't liked Eve. Seth liked her.

She felt a familiar swirl in her stomach. The Seth swirl. She smiled a secret smile.

As she fretted/basked in the swirl, Eve patted the pocket of her apron in her sleep.

Miriam noticed a lump there.

After the fourth of fifth time of Eve repeating this behavior, Miriam stopped thinking about what she'd learned from taking Seth's memories, and paid attention to Eve. Once she patted her pocket again, Miriam couldn't help her curiosity. She rose from her seat quietly and went to her sister on tip toes. Inching behind her chair and crouching just so, she slipped a finger over her sister's arm and pulled the pocket open just enough to see a gray box, metallic and...

She recognized it. It was Seth's cellular phone.

Why did Eve have Seth's...

Then it all made sense. Peter had gotten Seth's phone. He had sacrificed himself somehow and got Seth's phone. Excitement fluttered in her stomach. She rose quickly. He'd done it! Her hands went to her mouth to stifle her joy.

Seth couldn't tell the Joneses anything. Not ever.

This was all over. The Guardians had once again won. Eden was safe. Edenia was safe. All would be as it was before.

Except for Seth.

Miriam felt her cheeks burn with a smile so big it felt as if it could fill the whole room.

This changed everything between them.

Relief and happiness shook through her as she attempted to quietly return to her chair. Her mind buzzed. It did not matter that she took his memories. It didn't matter that Seth was a spy. None of it mattered now.

Her heart reminded her how Seth felt about her and how she felt about him. They could start over. They could begin again. No issues between them, and the pleasure and anticipation this thought planted in her heart overwhelmed her.

The image of her beautiful aqua dress, her betrothal dress, came to her mind, but this time instead of seeing Foster before her, she saw Seth. She felt tingles down to her toes. Some way, some day, that fantasy would be real. How could it not? Seth loved her and she loved him. No one could make it otherwise, not even her parents. She would wear that dress for Seth.

If she had to marry, she would marry him.

And with this inner declaration, the lingering doubts about her not using her Nature in the way she had done before, her angst about staying in Edeniaj forever, her anger at being married off and not experiencing the world, all of it made sense.

Seth would ease all those issues. The Master had brought Seth here for her. Seth would tell her stories of the outside and she would smile and kiss him. They would work together as Guardians and the work would suddenly be sweet. He would help her figure out her Nature. He was smart like that. They would be happy here in Edenia, as Guardians, until the end of days. She smiled and wiped tears of happiness and gratitude from her cheeks as she sat back down in her chair. She was so glad she hadn't run away. That she had faced her trials head on, that she'd had faith. She would never have found this joy without the trial.

Her mind flitted back and forth. Images of bliss circling and becoming more and more solid in her imagination.

After a while, once the excited thrill of her imaginings quieted, she found she couldn't ignore the swirling of her gut, nor the trepidation in her mind that things might not turn out exactly as she hoped.

Hugging herself, she whispered as if to heaven. "I know that after the trial comes the joy. For Seth's sake and mine own, I accept the price."

EPILOGUE

It didn't take long for Seth to get to the edge of town. Once there, he started to jog down the dirt road. About the time the dirt turned into blacktop, Seth found his pace and settled into the run.

Though his mind was a jumble of worries when he started out, the jog had cleared his thoughts. Now his inner dialogue repeated, 'I've made my choice. I've made my choice.'

About the time his feet noticed he wasn't wearing tennis shoes but Edenian-made leather shoes, he heard the sound of an engine. It whined and revved in the distance but before long, it drove toward him.

Seth slowed down, moved over to the side of the road, and watched the pine green Land Rover as it slowed, then pull up beside him.

"Well, looky what we got here." A man with rat-like protruding eyes crooned.

"An Edenian runaway." The passenger with a huge gap between his front teeth and bright red hair said.

With that, Seth knew he must be talking to part of the Jones clan. Who else would know about Edenia? Seth stopped, and the SUV moved past him but quickly put on the breaks. The bright brake lights reminded Seth that it was almost dark out.

The men jumped out of the car, chests puffed out, noses high, sneers in place. He wanted to tell them who he was before this got out of hand.

Seth breathed heavy, but not too hard. He said between breaths, "I'm Seth, Seth Johnson. I'm helping Jeremiah. I have information that Willis wants. Can you take me to him?"

They stopped in their advance and looked at one another. Then back at him with narrowed eyes. "You're Willis' nephew?"

"He does look like them." The gap-toothed man said.

"He does, indeed." The other replied.

The first nodded and moved back toward the driver's seat. "Sure kid, get in."

The men took the front seats, and he slid in the back. They started off in silence. But once they reached the speed limit, rat-face asked, "So, what can you tell us about Edenia, Seth?"

Surprised by the question Seth countered with one of his own. "That's a big topic. How about you tell me what you know and I'll tell you what I know that you don't know."

The man thought about that for a minute before he laughed. "He's as slippery as an eel, right Boaz?"

Boaz eyed Seth in the rear view. He seemed tense. After a scary few moments of eye contact with Seth instead of eye contact with the road, Boaz lifted his chin and glared out the windshield. "I only want to know one thing." His voice was quiet but deadly. "Why, do I always know what direction Edenia is?"

He glanced back up at Seth, as if he were watching for Seth to prepare a lie, but Seth had no idea what he was going on about.

His response was furrowed eyebrows and a shake of the head.

Boaz continued, "I can be in Washington DC in the middle of the capital building in a room with no windows and I can point out the exact location of Edenia." He paused and eyed Seth who gave him nothing. He went on. "I can be underground in a Montana mine and still know which way is southeast. Can you tell me why that is?"

Seth was impressed, but he didn't know what could help the man. "I'm sorry. That I don't know."

The man's disappointment was palpable.

He thought about it and it did tickle the back of his mind. He felt that way about Miriam in a way, like he could point right at her if he needed to. He thought that was just because he was drawn to her, that they were connected. But maybe it was something else entirely.

Boaz's friend gave him a brotherly pat on the bicep. "We'll get them. Don't you worry, brother. Willis is planning something big. And we will get them."

Seth's mind was instantly relieved of the puzzle as he wondered, "Get who?"

"I'm sorry. That's for The Phantom Hunters to know..."

"...and for you to feel." Rat-face added and laughed.

The men pounded their fists together. The comradery thick.

The car was silent once more. As Seth worried his palm with his nails. Were the Edenians in danger from Willis? What exactly was the relationship between the Edenians and the Joneses? Were they at odds? Real odds? 'We are gonna get you' odds? What did all this mean for his family now that they were committed to staying in Edenia? Had his father picked a side?

Seth's stomach twisted and turned with the bends in the road as he considered that, in his betrayal of Edenia, there was possibly a huge backstory with many delicate matters he didn't know and hadn't considered.

It only took three minutes of driving before they passed a huge sign that stated they had arrived at The Josiah G. Jones Compound and Airfield but that was plenty of time for him to get very nervous that he was about to do something irrevocable.

One hundred feet passed the sign, Boaz took a right onto a tree-lined drive that ended in a massive well-defended gate. A camera rotated his way, and a voice came over a speaker.

"Who's the tourist?" The speaker's voice was deep and gruff and militant.

Intense. He thought.

"Seth Johnson."

There was a pause.

"Who?"

"He says he's working with Jeremiah. He has information about Ghost Town."

There was a bit of a longer pause but soon enough the metallic sound of the gate opening signaled they were welcome. The car pulled forward.

Seth's palms were sweating. He was here. He couldn't go back now. He couldn't change his mind. He had to follow through with this. He had to. He went over for the thousandth time what he would tell Willis and Jeremiah. How he would phrase things carefully so that they would know he was serious and that he needed help. How he would emphasize their kinship to Lillian and himself, and how she needed their help. And how he would tell them about Miriam, the water, and the food, and that his arm had gone inside the Garden of Eden.

The main building looked like a mashup of a military compound, an office building, and a modern home. Parts of it looked new and fresh others looked old but well maintained. Jeremiah stood on the front porch.

He leapt down the steps and put a hand out to Seth as soon as he was out of the car. Seth took the hand and shook it once. "Hey there Jeremiah."

"Hey there pal. Have I got a surprise for you. Your grandfather is here."

Seth stopped. "My, what?"

"Talbert Jones. Your father's father, your grandfather."

"Talbert?"

"Yeah, keep the teasing to yourself if you like your skin on your body." His voice was serious but sort of playful. It confused Seth. "To be safe, we all call him Tally. You can meet him tonight if you want. But first, what do you have for me. I'm assuming that things are not going well or else you wouldn't be here."

"Yeah, I broke my phone. Got stepped on by a horse," Seth lied. "But I know who the dangerous memory person is. It's a girl. She's my age, just as you predicted. Her name is Miriam. Miriam Miller."

ACKNOWLEDGMENTS

Esther P., Sarah C., Eden J., Brett C., Dorothy O., thank you for reading this story before it was completely developed and for supporting me with your constructive comments. Holli, John, Ashley, Beth, Staci, and Rachel and all the team over at Immortal Works, thank you for loving my story and helping me make it the best it can be.

I have spoken to so many people about my work as an author and am so grateful for the people who keep the ideas I share with them in their hearts and wait for me to get them out on paper. To those of you who have supported me, I acknowledge you and I love you. The comments you send me, the time you give by reading and rating and sharing my work, the joy you feel at my stories, brings meaning to this obsession of mine. You are the heart and soul of my work.

And to my Father, all these ideas come from You. I feel You guiding my mind and hands. Thank you. I hope it is all it should be.

ABOUT THE AUTHOR

Theresa has been writing for fifteen years and has more story ideas than she could possibly write and still have a life. She is an avid audible 'reader', boardgame lover, Zelda player, book collector, adventure chaser, and history 'studier', besides being a mother of three, a musician and a homeschooler. Also in her life are, a white schmorkie named Percy Jackson, a hot husband named Andy and many many supportive and amazing friends. She lives on the Olympic Peninsula but is an Idaho girl at heart.

This has been an
Immortal Production